THE SAFEST PLACE

Suzanne Bugler lives in south-west London with her husband and two sons. She is the author of *This Perfect World* and *The Child Inside*. She has also written two novels for young adults: *Staring Up at the Sun* and *Meet Me at the Boathouse*.

By the same author

THIS PERFECT WORLD

THE CHILD INSIDE

THE SAFEST PLACE

SUZANNE BUGLER

PAN BOOKS

First published in Great Britain 2013 by Pan Books
an imprint of Pan Macmillan, a division of Macmillan Publishers Limited
Pan Macmillan, 20 New Wharf Road, London N1 9RR
Basingstoke and Oxford
Associated companies throughout the world
www.panmacmillan.com

ISBN 978-0-330-54496-2

Visit **www.panmacmillan.com** to read more about all our books
and to buy them. You will also find features, author interviews and
news of any author events, and you can sign up for e-newsletters
so that you're always first to hear about our new releases.

Acknowledgements

With thanks to Jenny Geras and the staff at Macmillan, and to my agent Sara Menguc. Thanks to my family and friends for their support, and especially to Nick for his encouragement and love.

ONE

When I imagined us moving to the country I pictured a low, stone house with a garden filled with wild flowers and an apple tree, and beyond that, for as far as the eye could see, fields in which the children could roam at will. I dreamed of space, in which they would develop and grow, away from the constraints of city life. I pictured rosy cheeks and muddy knees, and more of the things that really mattered to us instead of the constant pressures of the south-west London parent trap. No more obsessing about schools and music lessons and property prices; I pictured us simply packing up our stuff and moving away to a better life. I saw the smiles, spreading across our faces. I felt the freedom, lightening up our hearts. It would be an adventure. For David it would be a bolt-hole, a Friday-night escape from the stresses of work. Our weekends would be like holidays, our time together precious.

That's how I imagined it would be. And that's how it was, at first.

We used to come here for short holidays, and stay in the hotel in the village. Quite often, when there were just the two of us; less so after the children were born. But still we came when we could, snatching the occasional, precious weekend away on our own, when my parents could come down to London and look after the children.

It was our favourite place in the world.

We'd walk for miles. Across gentle hills and fields so soft and untrammelled it was as if no man since God had ever walked the earth. We'd walk and see sheep, and rabbits and squirrels and deer – but no people, for miles and miles no people. And then in the distance, suddenly, through the trees, the grey stone of a village, the smell of wood smoke in the air.

The walk we loved the most took us from one sleepy village to another alongside a fast, gurgling stream, over a bridge and up a hill, rising steeply above the allotments of the village below laid out in glorious, celebratory rows of pumpkins, and sunflowers, and jack-and-the-beanstalk beans running green and red up their sticks – past all of this into fields of corn, where we would stop, and look back and down across the rooftops nestling below.

And we talked, and we dreamed.

'What would it be like to live here?' we wondered.

'I would make jam,' I said. 'I would pick fruit from my garden and make jam.'

And David said, 'I wonder how far it is to the station? I wonder how long it takes to get into town?'

And at night, back at the hotel, drowsy in front of the log fire, our faces glowing from the fresh air and good food, and good wine, we'd dream again.

'What if?' we said. 'What if?'

And it was that dream that sustained me through those tough, early years of small children. It played through my head on a constant, background reel, fantasy-like, as I manoeuvred my way around the pushchair blocking the hall, the highchair squeezed into our minuscule kitchen, the stair-gates, and the endless, endless washing, heaped up all over the place, taking forever to get dry. We lived in a desirable corner of south-west London, in a two-up, two-down-plus-bathroom Victorian terraced house that we'd paid a fortune for, before the children were born. We'd liked living there when there were just the two of us, in our quaint little street full of quaint and over-priced homes. We liked the look of the window boxes bursting with colour beneath sash windows, the deli on the corner, and the other young, professional and trendy-looking couples hurrying for the train in the morning.

But then Sam came along, and I started liking it a little bit less. I had nightmares about dropping him down the ridiculously steep stairs and smashing his head on the unforgiving slate tiles of the floor. I noticed the damp, made worse by the constant washing draped over the clothes drier that we had to keep in the living room because there was no room for it anywhere else. The cranky heating system was no longer endearing, the downstairs bathroom a total pain. And I longed for a garden, a proper garden with a patch of grass on which Sam could play, instead of our poor excuse for a patio, poorly laid with ill-fitting stones, no good for anything other than a learning-to-walk toddler to trip himself up on.

When Sam was six months old I went back to work for three days a week, but most of the money I earned was used up just paying for his nursery fees. I worked for a magazine company in Soho, as a designer in the advertising department of an upmarket glossy. It was my job to create the small, house-style adverts for those old-fashioned clients who preferred not to use agencies – the specialist perfumers and family-run jewellers – and to style the layout for the property classified pages and the twice-a-year interiors spread. I loved my job but it hadn't paid very much before and paid even less part-time.

David worked for the same company, as a marketing executive on a different magazine. That's how we met. How trendy we thought ourselves back then; how smug, in our arty, media way, living our arty, media lives. And what a bolt through it all to find our income and our aspirations so slashed by the arrival of Sam. I used to wheel him down the high street in his pushchair on my days off, and look in all the estate agents' windows. How would we ever afford a bigger house around here? We couldn't even afford to get the boiler replaced.

But still, I had my dream. I pictured the magazine coverage, the spread in a Sunday supplement:

JANE BERRY MOVES TO THE COUNTRY.

AT HOME WITH JANE BERRY IN HER IDYLLIC COUNTRY RETREAT.

JANE BERRY LEARNS THE TRADITIONAL ART OF JAM-MAKING.

I saw it all.

On the rush back from work to pick up Sam from his nursery, squashed onto the train with a million other people, hot and anxious. On rainy days at home, trapped in our living room building endless towers out of Duplo, while condensation clouded up the windows. And when I got dog shit from the street all over the wheels of the pushchair and didn't realize until I'd wheeled it indoors and found Sam drawing his fingers along the tram lines on the floor.

I dreamed my dream; the roses around the door, the space, the better life.

And sometimes, late, on summer evenings after Sam was asleep, David and I would sit on the tiny metal bench in our tiny patio garden, and drink wine, and dream together. 'What if?' we said again. 'What if?'

But before Sam was even three I fell pregnant again, and when Ella was born the following January there was no more time to dream. The reality of daily life bore down on me; the sheer weight of it an unremitting burden. Sam was an easy baby and an easy toddler too; sweet-natured and passive. But then one child really is easy; two is a completely different story. And Ella was impatient and inquisitive; at six months she was crawling, at nine she could walk, lifting herself up from the floor by pulling down everything within grabbing height; the clothes dryer, the kettle, the CD collection – which she took to hurling around the room like a selection of frisbees.

I didn't go back to work after Ella was born. It just didn't seem viable. All the money I earned would be spent on paying someone else to look after my children, and I didn't want someone else looking after my children. I wanted to be the one painting pictures with them, taking them to the park, picking them up from school. So I hatched a plan. Money was short and would be shorter still without me working but I would do my own thing, put my creative skills to real, artistic use. I'd make cards; birthday cards, Christmas cards, unique one-off, hand-made cards, and sell them to the local gift shops. I bought the stuff I'd need, the card, the miniature brushes, the little pots of paint and glitter. I imagined sitting at the table with Ella when Sam was at school, the two of us painting and sticking together. What could be more idyllic?

But Ella scribbled all over my cards. She threw my glitter up in the air, and watched it fall, and screamed hysterically when flecks of it landed in her eyes. She stuck her fingers in my paint pots, and daubed paint on the walls.

I used to have long hair, so long that I could sit on it if I tipped my head back far enough. I wore it centre-parted, hanging straight down my back. It was statement hair, and being short as I am, I needed a statement, something to get me noticed. I didn't bother much with clothes or make-up; I didn't need to, I had my hair. It was the first thing that David noticed about me. He loved it. He was always stroking it, without even knowing that he was, and twisting it around his fingers. The children loved it too, tugging at it with their little fists, rubbing it across their faces. But one day, when I was sitting at the table with Ella, trying to make my cards, she picked up my scissors, opened them, stuck them at an angle into the length of my hair, and cut. It happened so quickly, the grating of the blade, the pull against my scalp. I dared not move, not at first. I did not want to believe it had happened.

When I did turn, slowly, carefully, as if I had eggs balanced on top of my head, Ella was holding up a great fistful of my hair, clutched in her chubby hand like a horse's tail. She held it out to me, like a prize. Here you are, Mummy. This is what you get. Her blue eyes looked at her offering, then they looked at me, innocent, uncomprehending. She giggled. She opened her fingers and then there was hair everywhere, wafting about the place like the legs of so many spiders, over-sized, grotesque. Hair on the head is beautiful; off the head it is as repellent as flies. I raised my hand to the gap and felt the shorn tufts, so close to my head. They bristled under my fingers, like rabbit's fur, stroked the wrong way.

I started crying, teeth-chattering, shocked crying. Then Ella started crying too; I remember her soft face crumpling with fear. She started crawling about on the floor gathering up strands of hair, and tried to push them back onto my head.

'Put them back, Mummy. Put them back,' she wailed.

I slapped her hands away. I screamed at her to get off me. And I ran to the bathroom and shut myself in and howled in front of the mirror at the damage, while Ella whimpered and scraped at the door like a puppy.

I'd no choice but to cut the rest off, and cut it off I did, hacking away at it over the sink, staring at myself in the mirror as I did so, watching myself disappear. Long, my hair was honey-coloured. Now it was short, it was mouse.

I didn't stop crying, and nor did Ella. We arrived late at the school to pick up Sam, and when he saw me he started crying too. And when we got home he wouldn't eat or look at me, he wouldn't even let me touch him. 'I want my old mummy back,' he sobbed, shutting himself in his room.

And David – I remember the look on his face when he came home from work. How could I not remember? He opened the front door, called hi, dropped his briefcase down by the pushchair, took the few steps into the living room and stopped. I was sitting at the table, sideways to him, with my head bowed. Both children were now crying upstairs, the sound pitiful and muffled through their closed door.

'Jane?' David said. He wasn't even sure it was me.

My heart squeezed out it's beats in my chest, clogged with misery.

'Jane?' he said again, still uncertain.

And then I turned, and I saw his face. I saw him recoil.

'What have you done to your hair?' he asked, and to me that was the epitome of all that was wrong: that he could think I had chosen to cut off my hair when to me it seemed that I had no choices, in anything at all. Suddenly it wasn't about the hair; it was about us, about him, about the life we were trapped in.

'No, what have you done to me?' I wailed. 'What have you done to my life?' I slammed my head down on the table, my hands in my hair, clutching at the lack of it. 'I can't live like this. Cooped up like this in this stupid little house!'

'What do you want, Jane?' he said. 'What can I do?'

And I railed at him. I said I want this and I want that. I want a new house, a new life. I want to move, far, far away.

And he said, 'But how can we move away, Jane? My job is in London.'

Ironically, my parents sensed we needed a break. They came to stay, and off we went, David and I, to our favourite hotel in our favourite place. And we walked the hills, and we said, 'What if? What if?' But it was all a game, a fantasy. We talked the dream but the dream rang hollow.

David got a different job, as a new-business manager for the same company but no longer attached to just the one magazine. It meant a lot more hours and a lot more stress for a little more money, though still not enough for us to move, not unless we moved further out into the suburbs or nearer to the airport, and neither of us wanted that. We trawled the estate agents, ever more disillusioned. We could swap like for like in our area, that was all. So we replaced the boiler, did up the kitchen and got our loft converted. Sam, Ella and I spent three weeks one summer at my parents' house in Cambridge while builders turned our tiny attic into another tiny room. And I resigned myself to staying put.

And soon Ella followed Sam off to school, and I had time to make my cards. I even managed to sell some through a couple of local gift shops.

I enrolled Sam in tennis lessons, and Ella took up ballet.

It seemed our lives were caught and bound in London.

Yet in me, at least, the dream never died. It stayed stuck and dormant, just waiting for its time to arise. And that time came around when Sam started at secondary school.

His last year at junior school had been a dog-eat-dog nightmare for him, and for me too. The scramble to try and get a place at a decent comprehensive, the competitiveness, the elbows-out backstabbing in the race to look out for your own. Some people we knew could afford to send their kids private, and lucky them. Others moved house to get themselves into the right catchment areas for the right schools. Neither was an option for us; no matter how we tried to jiggle them the figures just wouldn't add up. But the good state schools in our part of London were all hopelessly oversubscribed, the not-so-good ones frankly terrifying. The battle for places was brutal. I don't think there was a single kid at Sam's junior school who wasn't pumped full of extra tuition of some kind; music lessons, extra maths lessons, verbal reasoning exercises, something, anything to make them shine out from the pack, not just in the hope of a scholarship to a private school but for the Catholic schools too, and even in the slim hope of getting into a better comprehensive further across town. It was pressure, constant pressure. Sam hated it. I hated it. Sam isn't musical. He isn't outstandingly clever. He is average, and there is no place for average in London.

He got a place at a vast comprehensive a four-mile bus ride away. I opened the letter informing me of this, and burst into tears.

But still, we gave it a go. After all, we didn't have any choice.

'He'll be fine,' David said, to try and reassure me. 'If it's good enough for the thousands of other kids that go there, it'll be good enough for Sam too.'

Sam was young in his year; his birthday is in July. He was a gentle boy, small like me, and sensitive. He'd be eaten alive, we both knew that. At the very least we'd lose our sweet Sam, and be sent back a very different-natured boy in his place.

It killed me sending him off every morning. He was too young, too small, to be going off on those buses on his own, out into the world. Every day I fretted until he got home again, and when he did come home the sight of his drawn, anxious face filled me with worry. At parents' evening teachers looked at me blankly when I said I was the mother of Sam Berry. You could see it on their faces: Sam Berry? Who's he? They knew the naughty ones, the difficult ones; the ones who made a lot of noise. They knew the very bright ones too; those fortunate few who were cushioned from the masses in their gifted-and-talented accelerator classes. But who would know Sam, who protected himself by remaining quiet and deliberately unknown? Who retreated into the oblivion of the middle stream, where he quickly disappeared?

I couldn't sleep for worrying about Sam. Something had

to be done, but what? We couldn't afford to send him private; we couldn't afford to move anywhere else, at least not anywhere better, in London. The madness of living where we lived, as we lived, consumed me every moment of every day. And that dream of mine, it curled around the edges of my mind, tormenting me. Oh what a better life we could have, elsewhere.

We stuck it for a year and a half. Just before Christmas, when Sam was in Year 8, some boys from his year lynched him at the bus stop. He wouldn't have told us, as he did not tell us anything if he could help it. We would not have known at all but for the fact they took his bag with all his books in it, and his phone, and even the shoes off his feet, and threw them in the river. He came home sobbing and barefoot, but also angry, that now we would know how awful his life had become.

'Don't tell the school,' he pleaded. 'Don't. You'll make it worse.'

We sat at home, helpless. How had this happened to us, to our child? We did tell the school, of course. We made an appointment to see the headmaster and David took the morning off work. 'We are the parents of Sam Berry,' we said, and we saw it on the headmaster's face: Sam *who*?

I planned our escape.

TWO

I went about my plan with the same precision and determination that other women I knew had set about securing their child a desired-school place. I gave it my all; no chance of failing this time. I trawled the internet, looking up all the estate agents within a ten-mile radius of the village where we so liked to stay. I scrolled down the lists of property for sale, picking over the details, seeing what we might afford. There weren't that many houses to choose from out there, and those that there were varied hugely depending on obvious things such as style and size, and, less obvious to me, location. I didn't know the name of every little hamlet in the area, and struggled to picture them all in my head.

We needed to be near a mainline station, and schools. I readjusted my search, made it a ten-mile radius from the station. And I looked for schools within that scope too, graphing it all out on a little map, showing this village and this village, the one and only secondary school in the area, the two primaries, and the station. I drew these markers on a piece of paper, then I got a bigger piece of paper, and drew them out again. And I added more villages. I scaled out the likely travelling times between each place.

I looked up every piece of information I could find about

the schools; the two primaries and the comprehensive. To me they looked idyllic, and the fact that there was no choice when it came to secondary school struck me as a good thing; there'd be none of that vicious competing, no good-school-versus-bad-school and all the snobbery that that entailed. No lying about where you lived, no stamping on other people to try and squeeze your child a place elsewhere, like you got in London. If there was just the one school it stood to reason that it would be a good school, and that all the local children would go there. That was what I wanted for my children. Even better still, it was a mere fraction of the size of the place Sam was at.

So once I had worked out where the schools were, and the station, I really knew the vicinity in which to search for a house. A *home*. I scrutinized the estate agents' websites. For the value of our little house in London, we could afford so much more. I looked at those little pictures of grey-stoned village houses and wide low cottages, and I fantasized about living there. My dream took on a new fervour. And when I'd finally narrowed down my search, I phoned the estate agents and got them to send me the details.

And then I showed them to David.

I waited till both the kids were in bed. Unusually for me, these days, I'd cooked, not just pasta but a proper meal with chicken and rice and salad. I'd set the table, clearing all the junk and piled-up papers away and sticking them on one of the chairs, out of sight. And I'd changed out of the messy clothes I'd been wearing all day into something clean and pretty.

I waited till he'd eaten, and until he'd drunk a good few glasses of wine. And then I said, 'I've got something to tell you.'

He thought I was pregnant. I saw it in his eyes; that double-take, the uncertainty whether to look pleased or just plain petrified. I knew he'd think that of course, and I knew how much easier it would be then for him to accept the idea of a new house that we could afford rather than a new child that we couldn't.

I could barely contain myself. I said, 'I've found us a house,' and relief and then suspicion eased into his eyes. 'Well, three houses actually.'

It's a good number, three. Manageable. I'd spent a lot of time narrowing it down. I fetched the details and handed them to him, and watched the surprise register on his face as he realized that these were not local houses. He smiled a curious, though somewhat closed, non-committal smile. An indulgent smile, but he kept on looking.

And I talked as he looked. I said 'This one is in a village, this one next to open fields. And this one is this far from the station, this one's this far. It takes two hours, twelve minutes into Paddington.'

I talked in a fast, high-pitched voice, persistent. I could hear myself, as excited as a child.

David took his time looking at the details. How thoroughly he read every word, turning the pages over, and over again. I saw the possibility, however slight, however fanciful, drawing him in. This was, after all, a dream we'd both shared before we were too tired, and too weighed down, to dream at all.

'You've been very busy,' he said, when at last he spoke.

'Yes,' I said. 'Look.' I cleared a space on the table and laid out the map that I'd made, clearly marked with the schools, the station and perhaps not quite so clearly with the position of the houses I was showing him. I'd sketched them in, complete with trees and old stone walls. David's a marketing man; he likes that sort of thing. 'I've looked up the schools,' I said. 'All the local kids go to them. The comprehensive is a quarter of the size of Sam's. They'd know who he was there. He wouldn't just get lost behind everyone else.' David looked at me, but before he could speak, I said, 'And just think, when you come home from work you'll come home to space, fresh air . . . we'll have room to move, we'll be able to go for walks, to really enjoy our lives.'

'You paint a very tempting picture,' he said. I knew he wasn't convinced, but that was OK; I hadn't expected him to be convinced at once.

I opened another bottle of wine. We talked late. In fact I talked, mostly, till my head was sore and throbbing. I wanted this like my life depended on it.

David listened, and he smiled, but he shook his head. 'It would be a massive change, Jane,' he said. 'You can't just pack up your life and move.'

He didn't dismiss it out of hand, though. Not that it would have made any difference if he had. I still wouldn't have given up.

For weeks I chipped away at him. For every negative he came up with I had an answer.

'You complain when I'm late home from work living here,' he said. 'I'd be late home every night if we lived there.'

'Yes, but you'd be late for a good reason, and not just because you'd taken hours getting home because of some delay on the underground or because you'd got stuck on a slow train out of Waterloo.'

'I might get stuck on a slow train out of Paddington.'

'No you wouldn't. It's the suburban lines that get delayed

and cancelled all the time, just because of the sheer quantity of them.'

He raised his eyebrows at this.

'It's true,' I said, though I didn't know if it really was or not. It just sounded true, to me. 'You'll know what train you need to get every night, you'll get it, then you'll come speeding home to us, waiting for you in our country retreat. And we will be so, so pleased to see you.'

He raised his eyebrows a little higher, and he laughed.

'I'll still have to get the tube, to get to Paddington,' he said, but I could tell he was weakening.

'Yes but you'll make sure you leave your office in plenty of time. You'll be looking forward to going home.'

We lay awake at night, talking it over. The whole idea took on a dream-like quality again in the dark, with sleep lapping at the edges of our minds. I lay in his arms, warm, close to him.

'I don't know, Jane,' he said. 'It would be a hell of a commute.'

'But don't you long for space and peace?' I whispered. 'For weekends that really are weekends instead of just a stressful continuation of a stressful week?'

'Of course I do.' His chest vibrated under my ear as he spoke. 'But couldn't we look at somewhere a little nearer? Somewhere still out of London but with less of a commute; somewhere in Surrey perhaps. There are loads of pretty villages in Surrey.'

'I don't want to live just in Surrey.' I turned to face him, leaning up on my elbow. 'I don't want to live in any old pretty village. It isn't about that. It's about us living where we've always wanted to live, and we've always wanted to live there, where we've been so happy. Haven't we, David? If we move, I want us to move properly, not to some half-way compromise. Let's really live our lives as we want to. This is what we've dreamed about. Just imagine it: our time at home would be so special. We'd go for walks. You'd have time to really relax. And think how much better it would be for the children – for Sam especially. He'll be destroyed if he stays where he is.'

'You don't know that it would be any better for him out there,' he said.

'Of course it would be! It would be so much better. You only survive here if you're worldly and tough, and Sam isn't. He's so miserable here. And what about Ella? We'll have to go through it all again with her in a couple of years. This is our chance to really change things, David. Let's just do it – for all of us.'

David sighed, the fingers of his hand circling rhythmically on my hip. 'You build up a pretty picture, Jane,' he said. 'But it wouldn't be easy. You know that.'

'Yes,' I said. 'But it would be worth it. It would be our choice, our decision, our new life.'

It gave us something to talk about; something new and exciting, with the added edge of spontaneity, of risk. When David came home from work I greeted him eagerly, with a smile and a glass of wine, like I hadn't done for years. I told him every tiresome and irritating detail of my day, every worry about Sam, about the schools, but I put it to good use. I said, 'Well at least it won't be for long now. We'll soon be away from all this.'

I talked about when, now, not if.

We went out for dinner with our friends Ed and Karen,

to the pub down on the river. And we talked about it with them too. 'Guess what,' I said. 'We've something to tell you.' And I ignored the way David looked at me, the shut up glare.

'We're thinking of moving to the country,' I said.

And Karen reacted as I knew she would. She clapped her hands, said, 'Oh my God, lucky *you*!'

And the more we talked about it the more wonderful she said it would be. 'We'll come and visit you,' she said. 'Won't we, Ed?'

And they did come, once, that autumn after we moved.

I got the children on board. I sold it to them easily. When Sam came home tired and grumpy and screwed up with the effort of every day I comforted him. I told him how much easier it would be at a small school, a friendly school, far, far away from bullies and crowds and struggling to blend in. No more worrying about the bigger kids at the bus stop, I said. No more trying to be cool.

'In the countryside, kids don't bother with any of that,' I said. 'They just all get on. And when they've finished school they all just get out in the fields and play.'

'Do they?' he asked me, so hopefully.

'Yes,' I said. 'They climb trees and make dens. It's safe there. And they don't bother with all this extra tuition either,' I added, pulling my trump card. 'That's simply a London thing.'

I remember his big eyes staring at me in a mixture of longing and disbelief. He could barely imagine such a place; that is what London had done to him. That is what we were doing to him, keeping him here. My poor boy; we really had to move, if only for his sake.

To Ella I just said, 'You'll be able to learn to ride. There are horses everywhere in the country.' That was all it took. She couldn't wait to go. She started galloping around the house, tossing back her hair. She even dug her old My Little Pony collection out from the back of her wardrobe, and brought them downstairs.

When David came home she said, 'Will I be able to have my own pony when we move to the country? Will I? I want to have a chestnut one with white spots and call it Amber.'

How could David resist, then? How could he possibly let us all down?

So we went to see some properties.

My parents came to look after the children and I included them in on our excitement too. They could come and stay properly, when we'd moved, I said; we'd have the room. And won't it be so much better for the children?

Always, for the children.

'I think it's a wonderful idea,' my mother said to David. 'So much better than bringing them up here.'

My parents never liked London; our small house, the traffic, the planes. I had them on side, too.

And how strange, how intensely momentous it was, that trip, as if our whole lives hinged upon it. It was the first time we'd been there midweek and the hotel was almost empty and so quiet without the weekenders and day trippers who always piled in for lunch on Sundays. Yet to me it felt more real because of that; living here would be quiet. But that was OK. I wanted a true place, not just a chocolate-box cover.

I could see no wrong in anything.

And there is no wrong; not in the place itself. Not in the

hills and the fields and the sleepy little villages. It is still as beautiful as it has always been.

We looked at several houses. A converted chapel in the same village as the primary school. An old farmhouse on its own on top of a hill, looking down over sheep-strewn fields. A new-build, one of a cluster, in the sold-off grounds of a stately home.

And we found what was to be our house, a wide stone cottage in a tiny hamlet, just two miles away from the hotel.

I cried when we found it. Suddenly it was down to David to be the strong one, the sure one. He was the one talking to the estate agent, working out figures and details, churning it away in his head. How far were we from the station? How long would it take to drive?

I walked through the rooms and I knew it was where we were meant to be. The current owners had two children, a boy and a girl, just like us; they were relocating nearer to family, in Wales. So there was a bedroom for Sam and a bedroom for Ella, both ready for them to move in their things. Our bedroom was huge with two windows, one overlooking the front and another at the back, both with their beautiful views. Downstairs past the lounge there was a sort of annexe with its own bathroom, perfect for visiting parents, or as a den for the kids. And a huge kitchen, all long and low and fitted out with wood. A real country kitchen. It was this that made me cry. The windows looked out across the garden and the garden looked out across the fields, separated only by hedgerows and flowers. There was even a swing. And space, open, green space, for as far as the eye could see. Even when dreaming of my house in the country, I had not dreamed of this.

*

That night, over dinner, we talked it through in earnest. The only other people in the hotel restaurant were a couple of middle-aged American women and the one spotty young waiter who hovered nervously between our two tables. We talked quietly, almost whispering, and my eyes prickled with the constant threat of tears.

'I liked the house,' David said, as he had said already many times since we'd seen it that afternoon. 'I like it very much.' Yet the reservation was still there in his voice.

'We've got to do this,' I insisted. 'We cannot carry on living as we are. It's mad staying in London, spending all that money to live in a tiny house, breathing in all those traffic fumes, worrying about the kids' schools all the time. We do need to move here, for all of us.'

'I am worried about the commute,' he said. 'It would be really hard, Jane. It would be well over two hours altogether, each way.'

And I said, 'You cannot keep us all in London because of that. We cannot be your prisoners.'

I wonder how I could have said such a thing. I thought, at the time, that I loved David more at that moment than I had ever loved him; that it was like when we first met, and yet more so. Like starting over; the intensity, the fear of everything to lose.

But the truth is that I didn't really care what David felt. I can admit that now, to myself at least.

THREE

We moved in early July, when Ella was nine and Sam had just turned thirteen. I took them out of school a week before term ended, and how unreal it all seemed. I collected Ella from school and we left the playground in a fanfare of hugs and good-luck cards and tearful goodbyes. We walked back to the packed-up house clutching armfuls of artwork and exercise books and little, folded-up notes, the two of us so strangely, so giddily unbound.

'I will come back, won't I, to play with Rosie?' Ella kept saying, over and over. 'She will still be my best friend.'

When Sam came home he dropped his school bag in the living room, shrugged off his blazer, and tugged off his tie.

'You won't be needing those any more,' I said.

He looked at me with his wide blue eyes and said nothing at all.

I thought of all the people I had seen to say goodbye to, and then of those that I had somehow managed to miss; the familiar, everyday faces, the neighbours, the mums from school. There are so many people in London; they float past you like a tide. Each day, so many people, and I had lived here among them, in my own little corner, for the last sixteen years. Of course I was nervous, of course I had doubts.

*

We followed the van for the first part of the journey, but soon overtook it on the motorway, which meant we arrived at the house first. I'll never forget it, that first sighting, with all of us in the car, together. The anticipation; the communal in-drawn breath. David drove the last couple of miles slowly; the house was down a narrow lane, easy to miss. And he did miss it, and had to double back, turning and revving the car in the tightest of spaces, while the children complained in the back, their faces pressed against the windows, waiting, watching. It seemed further from the village than I remembered, and I sat next to David tense, with my heart hammering. Then we turned a corner and suddenly there it was, just ahead: our new home, nestling low and golden in the sunlight behind a profusion of climbing roses and cornflowers.

'Ha!' David said, and he looked at me, and smiled.

Inside, the house was strangely cold for such a warm summer's day, and bereft, without the previous owners' things. I felt like an intruder; I'd say that we all did. Sam and Ella roamed through the rooms, unsure. We'd stayed in cottages for holidays before, and somehow, I think, we'd expected it to be like that. The plate of cookies in the kitchen, the welcome note and the luxury soap in the bathroom; all this was missing. The place was stripped, right down to the absent shelves on the walls and the light shades. Throughout, there were shadows on the painted walls and chips of plaster missing where pictures and mirrors had been taken down, and ghostly yellowing stains marking where furniture had stood. The walls in the children's rooms were speckled with Blu-Tack and the half-scratched-off remains of posters. But it would all be all right when it had been painted; I knew that. We'd move our stuff in; make it ours. We had time to do this. We had for ever.

And we had that garden, filled with flowers and trees and so much space. Already the children were out there; through the open windows I could hear Ella whooping and every two seconds Sam crying, 'Wow!' and 'Look, Ella, look at this!' It was overwhelming; the elation, the slow dawning that this was real. That this was ours.

That summer was like a dream. I look back and I see us all, hazy, blurred around the edges like figures on an old cine film. I see as though I am staring into the sun; it hurts my eyes. I see David, with his shirt stripped off in the heat, arms raised, battling to pin the wild, spindly roses by the front door back behind their trellis; I see him again, standing outside the front of the house late in the day with a beer in his hand, just looking at the view. He loved it here. He did. He loved it just as much as I did. And I see my children, sometimes near, their faces bright and animated, saying look at this and look at that, and sometimes in the distance, running, climbing. I see them playing in the field that rises up gently from the back of our house then steepens into a hill, dotted with gorse and trees; I see their tiny figures, arms outstretched, spinning round and round, till they collapse, dizzy on the ground.

To the front of the house, just a little way up the lane, there is a small pond that often spills over into the grass around it during the rainier months of autumn and winter, and then shrinks back again with the arrival of spring. That summer it had shrunk to almost nothing, and the ducks and moorhens that nested there jostled and squawked for space, splashing their wings dramatically in the water, and chasing each other away through the grass. Sometimes the ducks wandered as far as our garden. Always, always, I will remember Sam tiptoeing up the lane after them in the impossible pursuit of catching one, just one, so that he might, for just a moment, hold it in his arms.

If I paint an idyllic picture it's because it was idyllic. David took two weeks off work and we decorated the rooms, scrubbed down the floorboards, hung curtains, and gradually sorted through our things. The furniture was in place, and the boxes eventually unpacked. We met our neighbours; the sweet old couple in the house next to ours and the man from down the lane who walked his dog past our house every morning and always stopped to say hello and check on our progress. And we found our way around locally. It was about a forty-minute walk across footpaths and fields into the village and this we did, quite often, to buy bread and basic supplies. We even had lunch at the hotel a couple of times, that first summer. The local town was a twenty-minute drive away, where there was a supermarket, several shops and even a Saturday market. And a couple of cafés, three pubs and Sam's new school, set back off the main road out the other side.

I felt like I was living on holiday. Even shopping for food became fun. The supermarket in town wasn't up to much but there was a butcher's selling local meat and the market was amazing; lots of suppliers from the area selling locally grown produce. It was such a far cry from London. I could even buy fresh eggs from a farm half a mile from our house.

We got a sofa bed for the spare room downstairs – the den, as we now liked to call it – and over the summer we had a succession of visitors; my parents, David's father, his sister and her kids. There was always something going on, and we were busy, so busy, but happily so; so proud to show off what we had come to. And although David was back at work the weekends were just as I imagined they would be, with long walks and long lunches and lazy afternoons. We had done the right thing. We had.

Even David's commute to work wasn't a problem, not at first. The novelty made it worth it. It took him fifteen minutes to drive through country lanes from our tiny hamlet to the station, if he put his foot down. And trains were hourly, two hours and twelve minutes to Paddington, as long as they ran without delay. At first, it was worth getting up at 5.30 every morning to catch the 6.15 train, and not getting home again until nearly ten o'clock at night. It was worth it because we'd moved in summer, and those early mornings were beautiful, the air outside our front door so incredibly soft and peaceful. I'd get up with him, at first, to make him coffee, and see him off. And when he'd gone I'd walk about my garden in my nightdress, revelling in the contrast between this place, this life, and the one we had left behind.

Getting home so late wasn't a problem either, at first, even though he could never leave work in time to make it across London to catch the 6.20 train from Paddington, and therefore had to get the next one a whole hour later. I'd have supper ready, and a bottle of wine open and poured for him. And because our kitchen was so big and our new oak table so big too, and because this was the country and this our new idyllic life it wouldn't be just any old supper. I'd cook something special with meat from the butcher's and vegetables from the market; I'd put flowers on the table – wild flowers, picked from the garden and stuck artfully into an earthenware jug instead of a vase, and a basket of bread.

Often, I'd make a cake. I didn't have an AGA yet, but it was just a matter of time. And I'd sit with David while he ate, and drink wine with him, and talk with him, and laugh with him and I loved him. I loved him, because he was doing this for us.

And if, over time, the novelty wore off a little, that was only to be expected. The children missed their old friends. They settled into their new schools fairly well, considering, but still it was hard, especially for Sam, who is naturally shy. It was hard for all of us. I missed my friends too; conversations on the phone and promises to visit left me painfully aware of the wrench I had made. Sometimes, particularly on rainy days, when David was at work and the children were at school and I was in the house for hours on my own, I felt horribly alone. I missed the presence of other people, and, in truth, the shops. And for David, getting up so early on dark winter mornings soon lost its appeal, as did driving back again on wet, black nights. When he was at home, he was tired. Quite often, meetings kept him late at work and he wouldn't be back till nearly midnight. I stopped waiting up for him. I stopped getting up in the mornings too. Sometimes I'd be asleep when he left the house and asleep when he came home again. Some weeks I hardly saw him at all.

I told myself that was just the price we had to pay. After all, nothing is ever completely perfect. Life is not a dream.

FOUR

I met Melanie that first autumn, just outside the main entrance of Ella's new school. It was a damp, misty morning and she was coming out of the school gates just as I was rushing in with a tearful, anxious Ella in tow, ten minutes late because the 'new' car wouldn't start again. I'd seen Melanie before, briefly and in passing. I'd seen lots of the other mothers briefly and in passing, but until then I'd managed little more than the exchange of a smile, a quick hello.

I hadn't appreciated how difficult it would be to make new friends, especially in a place where everyone is spread out so. There were no people with same-age kids just up the road or just around the corner. I didn't properly consider how incredibly hard it is to uproot your whole life and come into a place an outsider, knowing no one. I'd simply seen the four of us, transported as a unit, complete in our idyll, and I'd assumed everything else would just fall into place.

I knew that the school playground was the most likely place to meet people, for both me and the children, and I knew also that it would take time. But what I hadn't factored in was the sheer rush it would be every morning and every afternoon getting Sam and Ella delivered and collected from their separate schools on time when those schools were located a good four miles apart. It hadn't occurred to me that there would be traffic, not on country roads.

We'd had to buy a second car. We hadn't thought of this, either; hadn't budgeted for it, in the general excitement of moving. But David had to drive to the station, and there our car languished all day, no use to anyone. We'd tried to see a way around it, but ended up arguing instead.

'You could give me a lift in the mornings,' David said. 'And pick me up again at night.'

And I said, 'Don't be ridiculous. What about the children? I'm not leaving them on their own every day, especially at night.'

'They'll be fine,' he said. 'Sam's old enough.'

'But Ella isn't.'

'You'll have to bring her with you then,' he said.

'Oh come on, David, she'll be asleep!'

'Jane, I'm telling you that we can't afford another car,' David said again, emphasizing the words as if it would make a difference somehow.

'I heard you the first time,' I said. 'And I'm telling you we have no choice.'

So we bought one, reluctantly, and in too much haste, from a second-hand dealer two villages away; just a small, cheap old thing that would do for getting David to the station and back. Within weeks the cam belt went and the exhaust needed replacing. And on cold and damp mornings it took forever to get it started. I'd lie in bed in the dark listening to David trying desperately to rev it up while the engine repeatedly choked and spluttered and failed. And then I'd hear him get out of the car again, slam the door, swear and curse the day that we'd ever moved, and take the Renault instead.

And so, more often than not once the weather turned colder, I was stuck with that old banger to drive the kids to school in, which meant that it was my bad luck to have the battle of getting it started. And I cursed David for his impatience, and his selfishness in taking the Renault, and leaving me to this. And the children would become agitated and I would get stressed and we never left the house on time. I'd thought country roads would be quiet but at rush hour in the morning the one road that ran through the town was solid with traffic because it was just that, the one road. I had to drop Sam off first at 8.45 but his school was right through the town and out the other side; even if I managed to get him there on time I still had to contend with the traffic coming back through again to get Ella to her school which was, ironically, in the same village as the garage that the godforsaken car came from. For her, school started at nine, and that should have been fine but it never was, not in the traffic. I usually ended up pulling up outside the gates in the car and letting her out just as the bell went and the other kids were all going in. At best, I'd manage to park up somewhat haphazardly round the corner and rush her there on foot, but it was never easy, it was never the relaxed and tranquil experience that I had dreamed of and so wanted it to be. Every morning we parted tense and fraught. The smile that I pinned to my face in the hope of making friends among the other women coming and going probably looked more like a grimace, and anyway, there was certainly no time to stop and chat to anyone.

Sometimes, when I pulled up in the car, there'd be a group of women still clustered around the gates, but they'd have dispersed by the time I actually came along, on foot, in the hope of meeting them. And to be really honest, women clustered in groups have never been my thing. Here, in the country, they looked just the same as they had in London; huddled against the weather in their ill-fitting clothes, bored, gossiping. I couldn't help thinking they were gossiping about me, the newcomer, always last, always parking the car so badly on the corner, delivering that poor child, late again, into school.

Afternoons were no better. For Ella the school day ended at 3.15, for Sam it was 3.30. The caretaker at Ella's school opened the playground gates when the bell went, and not a moment before, and the small mob of women congregating outside would shuffle their way through just as the children started exiting the building. This section of the playground was ridiculously narrow; more like an alleyway up the side of the school, and at home-time even a handful of people made it seem crowded and chaotic as small children dressed in bright blue sweatshirts swarmed among the dawdling bulk of mothers, locating their own. At least that is how it felt to Ella and me, to whom all this was still new. She panicked if she couldn't find me, and I panicked too, knowing that she would be upset, and knowing also that we would be late picking up Sam. Often, I wouldn't find Ella till the crowd had cleared, and she'd be standing there on her own or with the teacher, and I would have to comfort her and console her, making us later still.

'You know I'll be here,' I'd say to her. 'Why don't you just wait with your friends?'

To which she would tearfully reply, 'Because I don't have any friends.' Or, worse still, 'Because my friends are all at St Mary's,' which was her old school, back in London.

I knew she was exaggerating. I knew she was just playing up the whole situation to make me feel bad, and I really did feel bad. After all, I had uprooted her, and put her here in this strange place. And of course it takes time to make new friends. But I also knew that it would happen, for Ella at least. She is a lively, outgoing child. And she is a girl; she knows how to fit in.

It was Sam I worried about.

By the time we got to his school everyone else would be gone. I'd see him in the distance as we drove up, loitering outside the school by the roadside railings. Sometimes he'd be leaning against those railings, staring at the ground, or idly kicking at his bag. And sometimes he'd be peering into the oncoming traffic, looking out for our car and I'd see his face, anxious, his eyes pinched, straining to see. He seemed so small and forlorn and my heart ached for him. And when he saw that it was us he'd look so relieved that I wanted to cry. I wanted to wrap him up and put him away, safe. He'd pick up his bag and bundle himself into the back of the car, saying nothing while Ella would still be going on about the awfulness of her day or her mother or something or other, non-stop, relentless.

I'd look at Sam in the rear-view mirror, slumped down, face to the window. I could smell him, the mustiness of the damp air clinging to his hair and his jacket, and beneath that the warm, precious scent of boy.

'You OK, Sam?' I'd ask

'Yes,' he'd say, automatically.

'Good day at school?'

'Yes.'

That was all he ever said, and he said it not so much because he knew it was what I wanted to hear, but because it put an end to further questions. And while Ella would complain all the way home he would stay silent.

I worried about Sam constantly. I have always worried about him. With girls, in many ways, it is so much easier. I have been a girl; I know what it's like, what to expect. Girls are so much more socially aware, at least Ella certainly is. She is more communicative about her emotions too; I always know what is going on with her. If she isn't happy about something she doesn't hold back in telling me about it. And although it was taking time, I knew that she would make friends. She would find her place among her peers, and settle in.

But Sam is so quiet, so shy. Again and again I told myself that we had done the right thing in moving; that he would fare infinitely better in this smaller school, away from what I had come to perceive as the social thuggery of the London school system; first the competitiveness of getting a place, and then the strain of simply surviving under the opposing threats of either hot-housing or failure. In my head, the flaws in all that we had left behind were magnified. How else could I justify what we had done; what I myself had made us do, in moving here? There was no point in looking back, nothing to be gained from regret. And anyway, wasn't it worth enduring the inevitable struggle to begin with in order to live in such a beautiful place?

And I'd always only wanted what was best for Sam, my dear, sweet, darling Sam. That was all I ever wanted; to do my best. I say this now and my heart is clamped, tight as a vice.

I did not stop to think that the transition to secondary school was always going to be a struggle for a boy like Sam, or that maybe he would have adjusted, given time back in London. That at least there he had some friends; in fact a good number of kids from his year at juniors had gone on to the same comprehensive as him. I did not consider the possibility that by moving him away to a place where nothing and no one was familiar I might actually have made things harder for him. That in effect, I was making him go through it all again, only this time he was on his own. I didn't think of that at all.

And so the school run, both morning and afternoon, was stressful and fraught. The anxiety of it took up the bulk of my day; worrying about it, worrying about the children. In the hours in between I shopped for food, I tended the house and the chores and became accustomed to my own unanticipated and prickling loneliness.

Most days, I made sure to get to Ella's school before 3.15, with the intention of infiltrating those groups of women gathered at the gates, yet getting to really know anyone proved a painfully slow process. It is not easy for me to go up to strangers and introduce myself. I am not the most outgoing of people. Like Sam, I am shy, and shyness is both an excuse and a prop. I loathe it; it infuriates me, in both Sam and myself. And those women all knew each other, and they stood so close together, talking so busily. I could feel the curiosity in the glances thrown my way. I forced myself to smile; I made every effort to be friendly. And sure, they were friendly enough back. 'Hello,' they said. 'How are you? Are you settling in?' But it never seemed to go any further.

Meeting Melanie changed everything.

She was still there when I came back out of the school that morning after taking Ella in. She'd waited for me.

'You're the new girl's mum, aren't you?' she said.

'Yes,' I said. 'Hi. I'm Jane.'

'I'm Melanie,' she said. 'Your daughter's in my Abbie's class. I hear you're from *Lon*don.' She said it like that, with the emphasis on the first syllable. I wasn't sure if she was impressed or mocking me. I wasn't sure about a lot of things, when I first met Melanie.

'Afraid so,' I said.

She pushed her fringe back from her face and looked at me intently for a moment, brown eyes narrowed. It made me a little uncomfortable. But then she smiled. 'So do you like it here, then?'

'Oh *yes*,' I said, and she nodded, and smiled a little wider. Her front teeth were incredibly even and straight, apart from her eye teeth which were larger than the rest and protruded somewhat, giving her a slightly canine look. Yet she was strikingly good-looking, in a natural, rather unkempt kind of way; tall, with long, thick dark hair that fell in heavy layers around her shoulders. 'I just can't get to grips with the school run,' I said. 'That's why we're late again. My son has just started at Renfree Park, and getting from one school to the other on time is a nightmare. Lots of people must have children at both schools. How do they all do it?'

Melanie laughed. 'We help each other out,' she said pointedly, as if this was a concept we might not have heard of in London. 'You know, pick up each others' kids. Lift share.' And then she said, 'I've got a boy at Renfree Park, in Year 9. But it's easy for us because our house is near the school.'

'My Sam's in Year 9,' I said, perhaps too eagerly.

She gave me that intent look again. 'Mm,' she said. 'Don't know if Max has said anything about a new boy from *Lon*don.'

'Oh. Well. Sam's quite shy. I'm not sure if he really knows anyone yet,' I said, and straight away I wanted to kick myself. I'd said it almost as an apology, as if I was apologizing for Sam. And I'd labelled him, again.

We stood there, awkward, for a moment. At least, I felt awkward. Melanie, quite clearly, was weighing me up. Then she said, 'I'm organizing a football tournament at Renfree. You can help if you want. Get your boy involved.'

'Really?' I said. 'Thanks. That'd be great.' I was so pathetically grateful. I'd never helped organize anything in my life before – I'm just not that sort. But that could all change. And Sam wasn't particularly interested in football, but that too could change.

'It's the first Sunday in December,' she said. 'We make a day of it. You could help with the food.'

'I'd love to,' I lied, and Melanie's eyes narrowed just slightly.

'Good,' she said.

Quickly, before I lost my nerve, I said, 'I don't suppose you've got time for a coffee?' and immediately realized my foolishness because there was nowhere to go for a coffee. The village contained a handful of streets lined with beautiful old cottages, the church, a miniature council estate (which was absolutely nothing like the council estates I was used to in London), a post-office-cum-general-store, the primary school and that regrettable second-hand car dealer.

Melanie's eyes narrowed a little more and I knew exactly what she was thinking. *You can forget your Starbucks on every corner, here.*

'Or a walk,' I said. 'If you like.'

She carried on looking at me. Under her stare, I felt utterly exposed.

'Tell you what,' she said. 'Why don't you get in your car and follow me back to mine?'

She drove fast, as people who are used to country roads often tend to, and I struggled to keep up with her. Her little red car kept disappearing and it was down to me to speed up, much more than I was happy with. She didn't slow down. She'd told me she lived near Sam's school so I knew we were headed for the town, but it wasn't until we hit the queue for the main traffic lights that I could relax. Then, when we'd slowed right down, she wound down her window, stuck out her hand and jabbed her finger over the roof of her car to the left a couple of times, and gave me the thumbs up.

She lived in the centre of the town, in the same street as the butcher's. Her house was tall and narrow, the second one in a terrace of four, with a small living room downstairs onto which a kitchen and a bathroom had been added at some point, and just one room on each of the three floors above. I'd never been in a house quite like it before. The front door opened straight into the living room, and stored in there among the usual furniture of the sofa and TV were various outdoor things such as bicycles and skateboards and, on that particular day, the broken-up parts of her oldest son Jake's motorbike.

'Oh excuse this,' she said, as we climbed over the various pieces of metal. 'It's my boy Jake's. He's got a problem with the fuel pump. He's waiting for a part. Told him he could keep it in here out the rain.'

When Jake was there, and his girlfriend was staying too, they slept on a mattress on the living room floor, squeezed in between the bikes and the sofa. 'Jake used to share with Max,' Melanie told me. 'But I don't want Kelly up there too. That wouldn't be right.'

That day, the mattress was propped against the wall behind the TV, out of the way, but sometimes it was left out. Later I'd go round to Melanie's house and quite often I would step right onto it when I came in through the front door, and have to walk across the heaped-up duvet, abandoned clothes, Kelly's hairdryer, and, on more than one occasion, the sleeping couple themselves.

If I make this sound like a ramshackle way to live, it wasn't. It was just different. Different things mattered, to Melanie.

Where most people might have a picture or two painted by their children stuck on a wall or a door perhaps, Melanie's children had painted directly onto the walls. All through the living room and the kitchen, little drawings and paintings, mostly by Abbie, each one named and dated, many of them going back years. Smiley round faces with an arrow pointing at them saying *Mummy*. Little black cats with long whiskers and long, long tails that stretched out across the wall. Here and there some words too, mostly Max's contribution: *Smelly McWelly had a big jelly belly* and *Maths is for morons*.

On the kitchen windowsill, lined up in a row of old take-away dishes, was Abbie's mould collection. Some items I could recognize; the green-spotted bread, the furry cheese. Others were unidentifiable, lost under a kaleidoscopic growth of green and orange and blue. The smell up close was indescribable, but Melanie simply leaned over and opened the window. Then she pushed the remains of the breakfast things out of the way and put on the kettle for coffee. Someone had started to make pastry, or maybe it was bread, on the counter next to the sink. The dough sat there in a cracked, drying-out lump, with the imprint of a fist knuckled into the middle of it.

'Max loves baking,' Melanie said. 'It's good for them, isn't it, all that kneading? Gets rid of the aggression.'

We sat on the sofa in the living room to drink our coffee and Melanie quizzed me systematically and thoroughly about where we'd come from, and why we'd come. She was measuring me, like one of those cats scrawled upon her walls. Naturally I played along. I said how awful life was in London, how crowded and expensive and rushed. So much better to live out here, I agreed. So much better in every way.

Whatever she learnt about me that day, I found out a lot about her, too. That her house had belonged to her grandmother. That she'd had Jake, who was twenty, when she'd just finished school. Colin, the father of Max and Abbie, was still around though she didn't live with him. 'I wouldn't want to live with any man,' she said. 'Sooner or later you'd end up hating their guts and rowing all the time, and I'm not doing that to my kids. I'm not sharing them with some man wanting his dinner on the table and his ego pandered to all the time. No, it's much better this way.'

She worked part-time at the primary school, as a dinner lady. 'Not much of a job,' she said. 'But you do get to see what's going on, and it fits in with the family. That's how I knew about your daughter and you, coming from London. And what Abbie told me, of course.'

Melanie loved her kids. We all love our kids, but she loved hers with a fierce, almost animal aggression. You could see it on her face, her complete approval of everything they did. In her eyes they were perfect; no one would dare tell her otherwise.

It's funny, even then I sensed that Melanie wasn't someone to cross. She had such a sublime innate confidence, a complete lack of apology about herself or her life. She didn't care what people thought of her, and I envied her that. Melanie assumed popularity; she didn't need to court it. And she seemed to know everyone; she'd walk down the street saying hello to this person and hello to that person, and whoever she spoke to seemed almost grateful for the acknowledgement.

And here's the thing. When you move away to somewhere new where no one knows you it gives you the chance to re-invent yourself. You can start anew, be who you want to be. And if I suspected that Melanie was the sort of person that it is better to be on the right side of than not, I didn't let it worry me. The truth is I found it quite thrilling to be befriended by a person like that.

FIVE

'Guess what?' I said to the children over supper that night. 'I made a new friend today.'

Neither of them paid me any attention, but I didn't expect them to. Why would they be interested in their mother's friends when they were both so preoccupied with the painful lack of their own? They carried on eating, methodically, morosely, eyes downcast on the table.

'Abbie's mum,' I said, to Ella. 'You know, Abbie in your class?'

'Oh,' Ella said.

'You like Abbie, don't you? You'd like her to be your friend? We could invite her round for tea sometime.'

'OK,' Ella said, a little uncertainly.

And to Sam I said, 'And Abbie has a brother in your year. Max Wilkins. Do you know him?' Predictably, Sam shook his head. 'He's a tall boy apparently, with dark hair. He's into football.' Again, he shook his head. 'Well his mum said she'd get Max to look out for you. That's good, isn't it? And won't it be nice if we're all friends with the same family?'

How cosy I made it sound. How easy. They both looked at me for a moment, then, their faces a mixture of apprehension and wistfulness. I smiled back at them indulgently, feeling so pleased with myself. Now, I look back and I want to grab my old self by the shoulders and shake, hard. I want to slap the smug smile off my face. I wasn't just complacent; I was blind.

Ella became friends with Abbie readily enough; girls do at that age. A connection was all that was needed, and now, connected as they were through Melanie and me, they ran out of school together at 3.15 each day, the best of friends. For Ella, things changed pretty much overnight. She forgot all about Rosie and her old friends in London, and talked about Abbie all the time instead, and Hannah and Izzy and the other girls in her class.

But for Sam and Max it was never such an easy alliance. The fact was they couldn't be more different. Max was big for his age, dark-haired and dark-eyed like his mother, and confident like her, too. He was exactly the sort of boy that Sam would normally take care to avoid, not out of fear exactly, but through the automatic deference of the weak. I do not say this to be cruel. Sam has always been someone to whom life happens. In the jungle hierarchy of the school playground he was a natural victim; for Sam it was a good day if nobody noticed him. He expected his bag to be kicked; he expected to be left out of games. This aspect of his character filled me with despair and frustration in equal measure. I wanted to protect him; I wanted also to push him out there, to force him to stand up for himself and be seen. In truth, the thought of him skulking around the corridors of his new school, being known, if he was known for anything at all, as the new boy from London with no friends, filled me with a sense of deep shame.

And so, as far as I was concerned, Max was a gift. Melanie

assured me she'd have Max look out for Sam, and how much better to have a boy like Max on your side than not? I didn't care that Sam was less than keen – in fact his reticence exasperated me. He didn't want to make the effort to be friends with anyone; he'd be on his own forever if it wasn't for me. I thought Sam should be pleased that I'd engineered this opportunity for him; I was pleased, certainly. And as far as I was concerned Sam's forced association with Max was a good thing. Through Max, Sam would get to know the other boys at school. He would be included; more importantly, he would be protected, too. And maybe, with a bit of luck, some of Max's confidence might rub off on him too.

Having Melanie for a friend made all the difference to me. The loneliness that had been creeping around me like a mist since we'd moved here dissipated. We came to an arrangement whereby Sam would walk back to Melanie's house with Max after school, and I would pick him up from there after I'd collected Ella. Sometimes I'd collect Abbie too, but quite often Melanie and I would both go to the primary school. We'd meet there, and chat, not just with each other but with the other mums too. I got to know a few of them a little better, now that I knew Melanie; with her, I had no qualms about walking up to and joining their little groups. Being with Melanie gave me confidence. And I noticed the way she automatically steered the conversation, without any apparent resistance from anyone. She dominated things, but she also infected them with fun.

After school we would all meet back at Melanie's house. Usually, the boys arrived first, but a couple of times I managed to get back with the girls just before them, in time to see them coming up the road, Sam with his shoulders slumped, eyes on the pavement, dragging his feet two clear paces behind Max. I saw this, and found myself prickling with anxious dread, and, if I am honest, more than a little embarrassment that I covered up by slapping on a smile, and greeting them with a bright 'Hi Max, hi Sam'. Yes that's right, 'Hi Max' first as an acknowledgement of the favour Max was doing us, and as an apology for Sam's shyness, and apparent lack of grace.

And when we went into Melanie's house, which usually we did, for tea and squash and biscuits, I would be grateful for the general chaos into which Sam's shortage of social skills could be absorbed or overlooked, depending on your viewpoint. Melanie didn't care how quiet Sam was, I'm sure, and nor, I realize now, did Max. Sam posed no competition for him; there was no vying for centre-stage. Out would come the skateboard or the guitar, and Max would show off his skills. Or he'd get out the PlayStation controllers and thrash Sam at some game or other. He taught Sam how to balance on the up-ended skateboard. They went out into Melanie's small backyard, where he showed Sam how to dribble a football less clumsily, and how to strike a shot with the side of his foot instead of kicking at the ball with his toes. Sam was a biddable audience, and over time he became less shy. I watched this progress with relief. I took it for friendship.

David put up a goal net in our garden. It was my suggestion, though David was happy enough to oblige. He rigged it up between the apple tree and the side fence, carefully positioning it to make the most of the space. Now, Sam could practise for the tournament.

Between us, David and I leapt upon Sam's inclusion in the football tournament. I say inclusion, because I don't think it ever really stretched to proper enthusiasm for Sam. It never got quite that far. Sam enjoys kicking a ball around just as much as the next boy, but he isn't competitive, not in the least. He really hates pressure. He just played along with us because he knew it was what we wanted, and we charged at it, all guns blazing; me, because I was just so desperate for Sam to be popular, to fit in with the other boys, to be what I considered normal, and David because Sam's lack of any particular talent at sport had always been a slight disappointment to him. David of course is a fine all-rounder. We have, in our sideboard, umpteen photos of the schoolboy David with his football team, his rugby team, and the inter-school athletics relay team, along with countless rusting medals. Before Sam was even born David had visions of cheering him on from the touchline, fantasies of teaching him all that he knew, of reliving his own life through his son. Wrong, I know, but are we not all wrong, one way or another, in the dreams that we have for our children?

I look back and I see Sam dutifully kicking his ball into that net on Sunday mornings and my heart aches. I see him trying so hard to please his dad, to please us both; the puppy-dog light of gratitude in his eyes every time David called out, 'Yes, Sam, good shot, Sam, well done!'

Melanïe and I altered our usual arrangement so that on Fridays after school we'd all come back here, me bringing the girls and she coming along soon after with the boys. Friday being Friday, we swapped the tea-drinking for wine, cracking open a bottle as soon as she arrived so she'd have time to sober up again before the drive back home. They'd stay quite lat
which suited me just fine as I found Friday night waiting
David to come home the hardest night of all; that sense
weekend being both delayed and diminished, the kn

that when he did get home he would be tired and grumpy from the week's commuting. I was grateful to Melanie and her children for being there. They took away the quiet; they took away our isolation. I'd stick fish fingers and chips in the oven for the children; lazy food, that I would never have stooped to in London. In London, I would never have drunk wine at four o'clock. But it was fun; Melanie herself was fun. She had a wicked sense of humour; so wicked in fact that I often thought myself lucky not to be on the end of it. While the boys kicked their ball around in the garden, making the most of our new net, and the girls collected sticks and leaves from outside and cushions from inside to make their little dens, Melanie and I, we sat on the sofa together, we laughed, and we drank our wine.

The friendships I'd had before had taken years to evolve; they'd formed gradually, subtly, over time. In London there were so many people all around me, people I knew on varying levels of intimacy. In London, you really can pick and choose, even if you are on the shy side, like me. But I took it all for granted, and then I moved here, and I threw it all away. I went from knowing so many people, to knowing none. I cannot tell you the starkness of being faced with just yourself every day; the fear of being always alone. In my newly narrowed existence my friendship with Melanie mattered more to me than any friendship ever had before. I was so glad to have met her. If it had not been Melanie but someone else who had approached me that day outside Ella's school I would have been the same with them. Had it been a dog-walking woman, I'd have been into dogs. Had it been a worthy, dedicated mother-type I would probably have become more worthy myself. That Melanie was Melanie; that she was so relaxed, that she liked a drink and a laugh, and had those two children the same age as mine, seemed like an enormous stroke of luck.

Yet there is a memory from this time that flickers in my head, bothering me. I cannot shut it out. It's of the Saturday morning before the football tournament, and the first time that David met Melanie and her children. Max and Abbie had both slept over the night before, and Max and Sam were already outside playing football when David eventually got up and came down to the kitchen, where I had been for quite some time, slicing up tomatoes to go with the burgers for tomorrow.

'Who's that?' David said, watching them through the window.

'That's Max,' I said without looking up. 'Sam's friend. He stayed over.' David had come home late last night, on the last train out of London. All of us, Ella, Abbie, Sam, Max and me, were asleep when he got in, though surely he would have noticed the extra shoes in the hall.

'You didn't tell me Sam had a friend staying,' David said, a faint note of accusation in his voice.

'You didn't ask,' I said.

David was watching the boys intently. I followed his gaze, out to where Max was kicking the ball at Sam, who was in goal. Max was big and strong; he slammed that ball at Sam repeatedly. Sometimes Sam saved it, sometimes he didn't, and when he didn't Max laughed at him, a high-pitched drill of a laugh that split through the morning quiet. 'You'll have to do better than that, Sam,' he yelled. 'How could you miss that one?'

It was just banter; it was just what boys do. Sam didn't seem to mind too much. 'Sorry,' he said, and braced himself for the next one.

'Doesn't seem much of a friend,' David said, and I took this personally. I took it as criticism.

'Well he is,' I said. 'And Sam's lucky to have him. He wouldn't have any friends at all if it was left down to him.'

David looked at me. He was about to speak but just then Ella and Abbie came running in, chattering, clattering about as they opened the fridge, ran the tap, grabbed cups, poured drinks.

'Hello, Ella,' David said, but Ella didn't hear him. 'Hello, Ella,' he said again. 'And who's this?'

Ella glanced at him, and giggled, and Abbie giggled too, and they scampered off again, bursting into laughter in the hall.

'Well that's a nice welcome,' David said.

'What do you expect?' I said. 'She's got her friend with her.'

'So I see. She might say hello to her dad, though. I haven't seen her all week.'

'That's not her fault.'

David picked up the kettle, shook it to check for water, put it back down and flicked on the switch. 'You're in a bad mood,' he said.

And I said, 'It's not me, it's you. You seem to object to the fact that the children have got friends. I thought you would be pleased.'

'Of course I'm pleased they've got friends. I'd just like to know who's staying in my house, that's all.'

'If you'd come home earlier last night you would have known.'

'Jane, I couldn't come home earlier. I had work to finish.'

'You've been late all week,' I said. 'I hoped that last night, for the beginning of the weekend, you'd be home a bit earlier.' I could hear myself, petulant, complaining. How had it come to be like that? And yet it had, too often, too soon; the strain of waiting for David to come home, the disappointment that waiting entailed.

'So did I,' he said. 'I'm completely shattered.'

Just then, there was a howl of pain from outside. Sam was crouched on the grass, head in his hands. I could see blood from his nose seeping between his fingers. Max had hit him smack in the face with the ball.

'*Jesus* – ' David said and flung open the back door. 'You there,' he shouted at Max. 'Enough!'

'David,' I called, running out after him. 'It was an accident.'

'That boy has kicked that ball non-stop at my son,' David said. 'That is not what I put that net up for.' He said it to me, but Max could hear him well enough. He stared at David, and stepped back as we approached.

'I didn't mean it,' he muttered.

'It's all right, Max,' I said. 'I know.'

'It's not all right,' David said and he bent down to help Sam to his feet. Sam was crying properly now, and the blood was mixing with the snot, and running down his chin. David led him in to the kitchen, and I followed with a reluctant Max.

There was no harm done, not really. Sam's nose wasn't broken. I cleaned his face up at the sink and if David hadn't been there that would have been that. It was an accident; Sam knew that, I knew that. The boys would have got over it and got on. But David was there, making a bad situation worse, and the tension between us caught and flared.

'It was an accident, David,' I said. 'Just an accident.'

'Yes, I know it was an accident.'

'Then why are you making it into such an issue?'

'I am not making it into an issue.'

'The poor boy's mortified.'

'I haven't even heard him say sorry.'

'Sorry,' Max said.

And Sam, who really was mortified by hearing his father tick off his friend, wailed, '*Dad*!'

The girls came running in to see what was going on. They crowded around us, gawping at Sam's face, squealing at the blood.

'What happened? Let's see. Is Sam OK?' asked Ella.

'Yes,' I said. 'He's OK.'

'Did Max do that?' Abbie said.

And yet again I said, 'It was an accident.'

Then into this atmosphere Melanie arrived to pick up her children. She came around the back, tapped on the back door and walked straight into the kitchen. This was normal practice for Melanie, as it is for many people around here. The front door is for delivery men and strangers, unless of course, you live in the town. But it wasn't normal practice for David. He stared at her, appalled.

'Hello,' she said. 'Have I caught you at a bad time?'

'No, no,' I said brightly, wiping my hands on my thighs and sticking a smile on my face. 'Come on in.'

In one glance Melanie took in the room, her eyes both watchful and amused. And straight away her kids went to her, like cubs to a mummy bear, wrapping themselves around her body, even Max, who was a good foot taller than her, and had to stoop to fit under her arm. Melanie looked at David, and then at me, curious.

Quickly, I said, 'This is David. My husband.'

I could feel the tension coming off him in waves.

'Hello,' he said, somewhat curtly.

'And this is Melanie.'

'Hello,' Melanie said cheerfully. 'Everything all right?'

'Max kicked a ball in Sam's face,' said Abbie in a stage whisper.

'I didn't mean to,' Max said.

Melanie laughed. 'Of course you didn't,' she said. 'Let's have a look at you then, Sam.'

Sam, who was still holding a bloodstained tissue to his nose, did his best to smile.

'Oh you'll be fine by tomorrow, won't you, Sam?' she said. And to me she said, 'Kids, eh?' and again she laughed.

And I laughed too, probably too loudly.

'Did you have to be so rude?' I said, the minute Melanie, Max and Abbie had gone.

'I wasn't rude,' David said.

'Yes you were. I was so embarrassed!'

'She walked straight in through the door to our kitchen,' David said. 'As far as I'm concerned that's rude.'

'She's my friend,' I said. 'That's what friends do here.'

It was lunchtime now. The children, who had disappeared to escape the atmosphere, came back in search of food, then changed their minds and skulked off again.

'Can we not argue,' David said. 'Please can we not?'

'We're not arguing.'

'I just want to be at home at the weekend and relax with my family, that's all. Can we please not spoil it?'

But it was already spoilt. The tension lingered around us, unspent.

The next day was as bad. Sam's nose was swollen, and a bruise had appeared half-moon-shaped under his left eye.

'I can't play!' Sam wailed at breakfast. 'Everyone will laugh at me.'

'No they won't,' I said, and I tried chivvying him up like I used to when he was younger. 'Think of it as a war wound,' I said. 'Real football players get bashed all the time. You look like a proper player now. Like – ' I searched my head for the only footballer I could think of ' – David Beckham.'

'No I don't,' Sam said, and his eyes filled with tears.

'Eat some food, Sam,' I said. 'You can't play on an empty stomach.'

'I don't want to play. And I can't eat.'

'Maybe we should have got him looked at,' David said, as Sam dabbled his spoon about in his uneaten cornflakes.

'Where?' I snapped. The nearest hospital was thirty miles away. There was no handy walk-in centre nearby, like we'd been used to before. 'It isn't broken. It would be a lot more bruised than that if it was broken.'

'Eat up, Sam,' David said. 'We need to get going.'

'I can't do it, Mum.'

'Oh for God's sake, Sam,' I said. 'Stop making such a fuss and eat your breakfast. You can't pull out now. I'm doing the burgers with Melanie.'

I did not see Sam playing football. I was busy putting burgers into buns. Nor did I see him shivering on the sideline between games, quivering with the cold, and with fear, his pale face forever close to tears. I did not see, but I could imagine it well enough. I did, however, catch him at lunchtime. I left Melanie for a minute and sought him out, to make sure he had something to eat. I took a tray of burgers, and found him standing on the edge of a small group of boys, looking as miserable as I'd feared.

'Burger anyone?' I asked holding out my tray like a waitress.

Several grubby hands reached out and snatched at the burgers, but not Sam's.

'Wait!' I laughed. 'Leave one for Sam,' though no one did. I had to grab one back, from a boy who'd taken two. 'Here you are, Sam,' I said, holding it out to him. I said it gently, kindly, and he looked at me warily with his anxious blue eyes, the left one now as bruised as if he'd been thumped. 'Take it,' I said, and like the good boy that he is, he took it. I wanted to cry for him. I wanted to cry so much that there were needles stinging my eyes and a lump the size of a fist throbbing in my throat. 'See you later,' I forced myself to say brightly, and I quickly turned and walked away.

Melanie's on-off partner Colin came along to the football tournament. I had met him before, once, at Melanie's house, but David obviously hadn't. Colin was a carpenter by trade and came to watch the football in his dusty work clothes, with a beanie hat pulled down low on his forehead, and fingerless gloves that left his fingers free to constantly twist and smoke his roll-ups. He was a quiet man, not shy so much as brooding. That day, he stood near David on the touchline, while Melanie and I tended to the burgers, though they didn't speak to each other much. They were brought into proximity because of Ella and Abbie, who'd wanted to meet up, and had since run off to play with the other younger kids, across the field, leaving their fathers alone. I imagine that David took one look at Colin, and realized immediately that they'd have absolutely nothing in common and would probably never see each other again anyway, which, as it turned out, was true. And I imagine Colin looked at David with his neat hair and his pristine wax jacket and thought the same. But it was awkward, or so it seemed to me. When Melanie and I joined them we stood between them; two women chatting between their unsociable men. Not that Melanie seemed to care; if anything she found it amusing. But I was still embarrassed, after yesterday. It's not that David wasn't polite; he was, to Colin, to Melanie, to me, unfailingly so. It's just that whereas I had regarded the football tournament as an exercise in furthering friendships for myself and our children, for David it was about Sam. He was there to watch Sam play football. It was as simple as that.

SIX

At the end of January we signed Ella up for riding lessons at the local stables, just a few miles away across country lanes. It was her tenth birthday on the nineteenth and we'd given her the hat, the boots and the jodhpurs for her presents. I will never forget the utter delight on her face when she put them on for the first time. How proud she looked, and how proud we were of our fine little girl.

David and I both went with her for her first lesson. It was a cold, crisp Saturday, the sun slow to rise. The stables were part of a farm, accessible up a long, sloping track, a good mile away from the road. David bumped the car over stones and pot holes, the engine grinding in second gear, and all around us we could see field upon field shrouded in a low, floating mist. In the weak morning sunlight it was surreally, almost spookily, beautiful.

The farm was on quite high ground; we could see it as we approached, and the stables, too, across the courtyard. Beyond, they'd a huge field set up with jumps and flagpoles, as if for a gymkhana.

'Will I be doing that?' Ella asked eagerly from the back of the car. 'Will I be jumping?'

'Perhaps not straight away, sweetie,' I said, and beside me David laughed.

'Better learn to sit on a horse first, don't you think?' he said.

We'd brought the camera, and a flask of tea. I remember jiggling from one foot to the other with my hands clasped around my plastic cup of stewed tea, trying to keep warm, while David took photo after photo. I remember Ella's face alternately petrified and euphoric as she first led her small horse from the stables, and was then helped up on to it, gripping the reins with all her might, her breath fogging out in front of her face in short, fierce puffs. There were about eight girls there that morning, of various ages. The woman running the lesson was a caricature of everything I'd ever imagined a riding mistress to be; tall, thin, with a large, prominent jaw, huge brown eyes and a deep whinny of a voice that I swear you could hear right across those fields. I tried not to laugh. I looked at David, hiding behind his camera, and I knew that he was trying not to laugh too.

We watched as Ella was led away by one of the older girls to a nearby field – not, thankfully, the one set up with jumps. She tried to look back as she went, to smile at us, and nearly slid off her horse.

'Ella!' I yelled, before I could stop myself.

'Eyes on the road,' called David. 'Eyes on the road.'

Ella clutched at that horse, her little bottom sticking up behind her.

'Jesus,' I said as I watched her go. 'How many broken bones do you think this will end with?'

'None,' David said. 'She'll be fine.'

Ella could only have been on that horse for fifteen minutes at the most. The rest of the time she was in the stables, learning the etiquette, the things to do, and not to do. Don't enter the stables if the horse has his tail to you, don't run, hold your arm out straight when you lead him; that sort of thing. David and I stayed there the whole hour, though we saw little of Ella. It didn't matter; we were glad of the excuse just to be there. We wandered over to the far side of the courtyard, with that view stretched out around us. What a place to spend a Saturday morning. This was what it was all about, moving here. David's long commute, the hours we spent apart, it was worth it just for this.

It is a strange thing, when you finally achieve something that you have always wanted; when you are in the place you have always wanted to be. You are balanced on a peak. You daren't look down lest you fall. Is this it, you ask yourself, again and again. Are we really here?

Those Saturday nights during our first winter here, when our children were safe inside the house, and we, David and I, were curled up in front of the fire, were some of the happiest of my life. Sometimes I would go to the kitchen to fetch us some wine or make us some tea, and open the back door for a moment and put my head out into the cold night air, just to feel the contrast, the stark graveyard chill of the silent, black night outside, when we were so snug, so cosy within.

That first year, we had a whole stream of guests; at Christmas, at Easter and all through the long summer holidays.

'Come up,' I'd say on the phone to my friends back in London, and to family. 'You must come and stay.'

I bought in extra food, and towels and linen in soft cotton checks of yellow and blue. I placed eggs from the farm in a ceramic dish on the side in the kitchen, and arranged apples from our tree in another. At the front door I lined up our wellies, along with a couple of spare pairs for other people, and I stacked chopped wood in the living room beside the fire. At Christmas I decorated the house with holly from the garden and twigs that I collected myself and painted red and silver and gold. I planned; I created the dream. It hurts me now, to think of it. I see myself, before guests arrived, putting out a cake or fresh bread on the table, pouring milk from its supermarket carton into a white, old-fashioned jug. I wanted it all just so. It was imperative that people should see what a great life we had here. I wanted to send them home again wistful, envious even; such reactions reassured us that we really had done the right thing in moving. David played his part too. He took the men outside, showed them around. He said how great it was to be out of town every weekend, to wake up to just the sound of the birds, with no planes, no cars driving by. He even made jokes about catching up on his sleep on the train.

I remember my friend Karen, on the one and only time that she and Ed came to stay with their children, saying, 'Oh my God, you're so lucky. It's just so gorgeous here.'

We were sitting in the living room with a glass of wine at the time, in front of the fire which I'd lit though we really didn't need it. The children were still playing outside with their fathers. We could hear them calling to each other from far out in the fields; the sweet carry of childish laughter.

'I know,' I said, and how pleased with myself I felt, back then. How content. 'I could never go back to London. Not now.'

And when my parents came to stay, and I overheard my mum saying to Sam, 'Oh aren't you lucky having all these fields to play in? That's where a boy should be: outside, running around,' it validated what we had done. It made it seem so right. The same when we walked through the woods with David's sister Nicola and her husband Tom and their kids, with Sam and Ella leading the way, showing off to their cousins the giant tree with the foxes' lair burrowed under it, and the little stream gurgling out from under the stones in the bridleway. Then, too, I felt that everything really was good with our world.

People drift off, though, over time. They find it harder to get away. Not family of course, but friends. People like Karen and Ed; they are now names inside a Christmas card. We'd made the break: what more could I expect?

The thing about moving your life, as we had done, is that you must move it in its entirety. You cannot look back. You cannot do it in half measures, keeping an open door. It will never work if you try to do that.

SEVEN

Yet there were times during that first year that I felt myself to be very much on trial. Perhaps it was my imagination, but I was aware of the eyes upon me when I walked through town to do my shopping or approached the school gates, all those people looking at me, waiting to see me fail. I wonder if it is a peculiarly British thing, that desire to see others fall flat on their face, but it is there all right; that 'who do you think you are?' attitude directed towards anyone who dares to attempt to do something different with their lives, the hand-rubbing delight when it all goes wrong.

I'm sure no one meant me malice as such. I was more of an object of sport. 'How are you finding it here?' people would ask me in a perfectly friendly manner, but they'd follow their enquiry with 'Bit different from London, isn't it?' or 'Do you think you'll be staying?'

Once, I'd had what I thought was a really successful chat with two women outside Ella's school one afternoon, talking about all the usual school-mum things from class cake sales to the stress of the morning rush. I even had them laughing, though I can't remember what about now. But when I walked away from them to meet Ella I couldn't help overhearing one of them saying to the others, 'How long do you think she'll last?'

These things just made me try harder. I thought of it as a bit like joining a club; the initiation period, if you like. Pass that and you're in.

I remember a particular conversation with Melanie, at my house, one Friday evening over a bottle of wine. I must have been complaining about David getting home so late every night, and she said to me, 'What exactly does your David do in *Lon*don?'

'He works for a magazine company,' I said, and I named it, expecting to see recognition in her eyes. *Everyone* had heard of it. But Melanie's eyes gave nothing away. 'He's the new-business manager,' I said, 'which is sort of marketing. They're based in Soho. I used to work there too, once.'

Melanie drank down the last of her wine, watching me levelly over the rim of her glass. She said nothing. The truth is, I had expected her to be at least a little impressed by all this, and the fact that she clearly wasn't threw me; it made me work all the harder.

'I didn't work in marketing, though,' I said quickly. 'I was a designer.'

'You told me before that you were an artist,' she said and I immediately felt as if I was being picked up for boasting, which I hadn't meant to do at all. But those magazine days were a big part of my life and at times I missed them hugely. I didn't want to forget them and have them shunted into the distant past of life before children. Sometimes I felt envious, resentful even, that David was still so much in that world whereas for me it had ended years ago.

'Still,' I said, putting myself down before she could, 'the only painting I get to do these days is decorating the house.'

'It's a nice house,' Melanie said. 'Marketing managers must earn a lot of money.'

Was that a dig? I wasn't sure.

'Not enough to buy a decent house in London,' I said.

'Is that why you moved here?'

'Well, and for the schools,' I said. 'And the space. Just to find a better life.'

Melanie laughed. 'Well let me know if you find it,' she said.

Nothing impressed Melanie. That was one of the things that I liked about her, most of the time. Other times I didn't like it quite so much; it unnerved me. I always had the feeling she could see straight through me. Still, I was certainly in no position to take offence at anything Melanie said.

It was thanks to Melanie that I became friendly with a few other people. It would have taken me an awful lot longer on my own, had I ever managed it at all. I couldn't get used to the sheer strangeness of having everyone spread out so far and wide. In London my friends had all been a quick walk or drive or train ride away; to reach them was fast, safe and street-lit. The prospect of driving for twenty minutes or so along pitch-black deserted roads on my own was as great a deterrent for a night out as I could ever imagine. But Melanie would have none of it.

'You've got to come,' she insisted, when now and again there was a school mums' night out. If ever I objected on the grounds that I couldn't leave the children she'd send Jake out, often with Kelly, to babysit. She had no worries about leaving Max and Abbie alone, but then they were in the town, and Max was a whole nine months older than my Sam. And on the Friday of the Renfree Park quiz night she got Jake to pick me up in her car and drive me home again afterwards while Kelly stayed with my children, so that I didn't have to drive and could therefore have a drink. That night felt like a huge step forward to me, laughing with the others over the absurdity of the questions and our combined lack of general knowledge. On our team we had Lisa Staples, whose son Will was in Sam's class, and Melanie's friends Angie and John, and another couple whose names I forget now, and we all drank far too much wine. It was just a shame that David couldn't get home in time to come too.

It was Melanie who suggested I should offer to go into Ella's school, to help with art. Melanie knew everything that was going on in both schools; she made it her business. News never came to Melanie second-hand.

'Put your art to some good use,' she said. 'They're crying out for help.'

And I loved it; sitting with the children, showing them different techniques using different materials and helping them to develop their skills. It was infinitely more rewarding than making those cards at home on my own, cards which cost almost as much to produce as I could ever make by selling them. And as Melanie pointed out, where would I sell my cards around here? Besides, going into Ella's school once a week made me feel part of the community, and less like 'that woman from London'.

I embraced my new life with enthusiasm, and integral to it all was Melanie. Sometimes, especially on all those long dark nights waiting for David to come home, I thanked God that I had met her. Because how lonely would I have been stuck out here, in our house miles from everywhere, had I not?

*

I hardly ever saw David during the week. The times he managed to leave work in time to catch the 7.20 train from Paddington were all too rare now, and most nights we were all in bed asleep before he got home. It seemed there was always some reason for him to stay late at the office, work to finish, meetings to be had.

Things were harder these days; in these tough economic times the magazine world was suffering. There were redundancies already announced, and more on the way. The fear of this kept him awake at night, and had him counting the cost of our mortgage. The stress of the long journey added to the stresses of work; it became a constant issue, wearing him down.

'Couldn't you just change jobs?' I said to him once, trying to be helpful. 'Find something closer to home.'

But he said, 'I can't just change jobs. What would I do out here?'

'I don't know,' I said. 'But I'm sure you'd find something. And you could spend more time at home then, and less time travelling.'

He looked at me incredulously. And he said, 'Be realistic, Jane. How many marketing agencies or publishing houses do you suppose there are scattered around these fields?'

I flinched when he said that. Out here. These fields. That was how he'd started referring to this place that we both, once, so loved.

When we first moved here, the weekends were our focus; the time we would be together as a family. I shopped ahead, and I tidied the house so it would be lovely for all of us. I prepared for each weekend as if for a holiday, planning long walks through the woods with the children, and romantic evenings, just the two of us, snuggled up by the fire. All week, my hopes were raised; the children's too. We lived for the weekends, back then.

The children missed their dad. If they saw him at all in the week it was by accident: a nocturnal meeting on the landing on the way to the bathroom; a glimpse of him cursing outside on a black morning, trying to start the car. When they complained that he was never there I'd say, as though it was Christmas coming and not just another weekend, 'Soon be here now. Not long to go.' We'd count down the days, starting with each miserable Monday. Only four/three/two more to go.

But the expectation, month in, month out, became too much; the intensity somehow crippling. It rendered the children gauche. They'd be too boisterous, too shrill in their excitement, clambering all over David when he was tired, fighting for his attention. He'd snap at them and they'd retreat, wounded, like actors off a stage.

'Just give me a minute,' he'd say, guilty then. But what use was a minute to Sam and Ella, who'd waited all week just to see him?

I missed him too. I missed the closeness we used to have; the chats late into the night. He slept beside me but I hardly ever saw him awake. There is something odd, something invasive about having a person creep into your bed at night and then out of it again in the morning, ghost-like, without you even knowing they are there, even if that person is your husband. It made me cool towards him. I missed the affection, the closeness, of falling asleep in his arms. Most nights he saw me sleeping, naked, vulnerable. I saw him not at all.

On the rare occasions that I did still wait up for him he would come in smelling of the train and the city – a smell both familiar and alien to me now – and I'd see him moving about my kitchen in his suit, still a part of the world I had left behind, and he seemed like a stranger. At times I felt awkward in his presence. It was too difficult to keep adjusting, and adjusting back again. By the weekend I'd have a thousand things I wanted to talk to him about, just little snippets stored up through the week that I wanted to pass on, or gossip to share, but when it came to it I found myself oddly silent. He was too tired; too preoccupied with his own concerns. Some weekends we'd end up barely talking at all, our time snatched away before we had the chance to properly reconnect.

EIGHT

Our first winter here the worst of the weather came in the form of rain and sleet and fog, bad enough to deal with on dark country roads, but last year it snowed, hard. The first fall came one night in mid-December, and so tenderly I look back and see my children yelping with delight in the morning, hurling themselves out into the fairytale whiteness of an untouched, blanketed day. Theirs were not just the first footprints crunching into the snow down our lane, they were the only footprints. Ella stamped out her name; Sam ran in random circles, shaking off the constraints of adolescence, and finally throwing himself to the ground and rolling like a puppy. They climbed the hill, with much difficulty, and skidded back down again, using the dustbin lids as sledges, the pitch of their voices so excited, so full of delight, knifing through the stillness. They had never seen snow on such a scale before. There was no chance of school, no chance of going anywhere in the car. For them it was wonderful.

But not for David.

Doggedly, he got up at the crack of dawn as usual while the snow was still falling, went out to get the spade from the garden shed, and tried to clear the area beside the house where the cars were parked. I watched him from our bedroom window. With futile, angry determination he shovelled the snow away from the front wheels of the Renault, trying to dig a path down onto the road, while the flakes kept on falling, settling on him, and still settling, almost as fast as he cleared it, on the ground. He looked so comical with snow all over his head and his shoulders, one man and his spade against nature. Eventually he flung the spade down to the side and stood there, defeated, just staring out at the snow. Then he got in the car and started it, the engine juddering coldly, unwillingly; the sound so at odds with the stillness of the morning. He got back out, wiped the snow off the windows, then got in again, and, incredibly, started rolling the car down onto the road. I watched this with disbelief. He so obviously wouldn't get very far. As well as our drive, he would have to clear the lane, and all the roads beyond.

He made it perhaps five hundred yards up the lane. Then perhaps intentionally, perhaps not, he slid the car to the side of the road, right up into the bushes. And there he left it. I watched him get out of the car, slam the door, and start crunching his way back to the house. I ran downstairs to meet him.

'We should have got a four-wheel drive,' he snapped at me, forgetting he hadn't wanted to get a second car at all. 'Why didn't we get a four-wheel drive?'

He stamped the snow off his shoes, shook it off his head.

I put my hand on his arm and wiped the snow from his coat. 'There's no point in trying to go anywhere in this,' I said. 'Why don't we just go back to bed?'

'I can't go back to bed,' he said. 'I've got to get to work somehow. I've got a big meeting today.'

'Look,' I said. 'I doubt if the trains will be running anyway.'

David stared out at the snow, his face tight with frustration. 'God,' he said. 'This is impossible.'

'It's beautiful,' I said. 'Can't you just stay at home and enjoy it?' I said. 'It's only one day.'

But it wasn't one day, it was several. Each day, with increasing agitation, David got up and walked down the lane, inspecting the road. The snow had fallen a good ten inches deep, and it was frozen solid. It would be madness to try and drive anywhere. It was fine for me and the children; we all thought it was huge fun, setting off on expeditions across white, untrodden fields to the village to buy provisions, like explorers across the Antarctic. We really loved it. But for David it was hell. I did understand his anxiety. His is the kind of profession where it is important to be seen, more so than ever these days. Be missing from your desk too long and there is always the danger that someone else might fill your place. He worked from home as much as he could, using the computer and the phone and getting irritated if anyone accidentally interrupted him with their presence, but it wasn't the same as being there in the office.

And the novelty of having him at home quickly wore off when he was so irritable and on edge all the time. When he wasn't working he prowled around the house as though caged, or stood outside just staring up the lane at the snow, as if willing it to disappear.

I felt blamed in some way, as if it was my fault that it had snowed; as if it was my fault that he was stuck at home, trapped. After all, although he never quite spelled it out, it had been my idea to move here.

*

After the snow came the ice, and in many ways that was so much worse. The main roads were pretty much clear but the smaller roads, such as the roads around our house, were treacherous. Between our house and the main road were a good three miles of twisting, narrow, unlit lanes made deadly by black ice, especially early in the morning and late at night. When I went out, I drove at a crawl, but David, of course, was in a hurry every morning, rushing to catch that train. I'd listen to him leave, to the car disappearing, too fast, up the road and my heart would tense, and stay tense all day. I worried about him getting to the station in the morning, and I worried about him again coming home at night, and I assume that he worried about me, too, driving the children back and forth to school. Yet when I spoke to him at work, that concern did not properly manifest itself. Our conversations felt distant, perfunctory, like him, back there in the land of the sharp-suited marketing man, the land that I had long left behind. He sounded a million miles away. Down the phone I could hear the background throb of the office; the occasional raised voice; laughter. Sometimes he would have to break off from me, to speak to someone else. And when I put the phone back down after saying goodbye, the silence of my home slapped against me, thick in my ears.

Several times, that winter, David couldn't get home at all.

The snow had spread from us to London and the trains were running a reduced service, with frequent cancellations. He did get to work, eventually, but then he couldn't make it home again.

The first time, he phoned me from Paddington.

'You're not going to believe this,' he said straight away,

shouting over the background noise of the station. 'There are no more bloody trains.'

I did believe it. It had only been a matter of time till this happened, in weather like this. When we lived in London, the mere possibility of snow would disrupt the trains. Of course it would happen, living out here. 'Don't go in,' I'd said. 'You'll spend most of the day travelling. And what if you can't get home again? Work at home. You've got to.'

But oh no. David had to struggle on in to the office; a soldier in the field of marketing.

I said nothing. What could I say, to make things any better?

'Now what the hell am I going to do?' David shouted down the phone and I could hear the anguish, the utter frustration in his voice. 'I don't fucking believe this.'

He spent that night in the office, sleeping on a sofa in HR. I do believe this to be true. He was so angry, so ratty and unshaven when he got home the next night, that it couldn't really have been otherwise.

It happened a few more times over the course of that winter; more bad weather, more cancelled trains. The strain it put on David was unbearable; like the strain it put on us.

The second time it happened, he managed to get a room in a hotel near the station, but it was money we could ill afford. And he had no spare clothes with him, and no razor. 'I go to work in the morning and I don't know if I'm going to get home,' he ranted on the phone to me. 'I can't do this, Jane.'

And yet he'd no choice. It happened again, and again.

*

He started talking about renting a flat, in London. At weekends he'd sit at the computer, scrolling through the internet looking at grotty little bedsits and studios. But we had no money for renting flats, and even the cheapest offerings in London were extortionate. The frustration made him angry. He sat there, picking over the details of tiny, bleak rooms in tower blocks, or above takeaways in grim depressing streets, snapping, 'For God's sake!' and, 'This is ridiculous!' Words bitten into the air in desperation.

Had we left our lovely part of London for him to have to go back and live in a soulless damp cell in some godforsaken post code with drug dealers for neighbours? This is what he said. Did he work like a dog to live like a dog too? Was that part of this country dream?

The idea of him renting a flat in London was abhorrent to me. It was a step on the slippery slope, a dangerous separation. I couldn't bear the thought of David becoming one of those men that stayed in the city all week while we, the family, resided elsewhere. That had never been part of our plan. Of course I felt bad that his journey was so hard and his day often hideously long, but wasn't it worth it for us to be together, as a family? Wasn't it worth it, for us all to be able to live out here?

'I'm trapped, Jane,' he said. 'I can't see any other way to make this work.'

'It's down to us to make it work,' I said.

But he said, 'That's what I'm trying to do. I can't bear the constant stress hanging over me, not knowing if I'll get into work, not knowing when, or if, I'll get home again.'

'It was only a few times,' I said. 'When it snowed.'

'And what about next winter, if it snows again? What about leaves on the line in the autumn, or any other disruption? It was ridiculous to think I could commute from here. What about the evenings I have to stay late for something – I can't be watching the clock, thinking I've got to leave to make the train. How unprofessional do you think that looks?'

'We'd never see you,' I said simply.

And he said, 'You don't see me very much now.'

It seemed to be all we talked about at weekends, now, and if he wasn't talking about it he was thinking about it. The subject hung over us like a persistent, lowering cloud.

I remember one Saturday morning we'd been invited along to the stables with the other parents for a show day; Ella was so excited but nervous too, chattering away in the back of the car all the way there. It had been raining solidly the last few days but at last a pale sun was slanting its way through the clouds. The field was pretty much waterlogged but the show went ahead anyway; no one was put off by a bit of mud around here. We watched Ella, her cheeks as red as apples, trotting around the field on her pony. Well, David watched Ella, and I watched him. I saw the wistfulness, like pain, cutting tight across his brow.

'She would never have done this if we'd stayed in London,' I said.

He said, 'I know.'

'This is why we moved here,' I said. 'For things like this.'

Again he said, 'I know.' Still without looking at me he put his arm around my shoulder, and squeezed.

One evening during the long, dreary months before spring started lightening up the days David and I were sitting at the kitchen table, finishing our supper and drinking our wine. It was a Saturday night; Max and Abbie were staying over and the children were all in the den, watching a film. Outside there was the best part of a storm going on, the rain battering against the windows and streaming through the gap in the drainpipe, the wind rattling the guttering above. That drainpipe would need fixing tomorrow; another task to be done.

'Do you regret moving here?' I said suddenly. Sometimes, when I drink a lot of wine, sorrow sweeps down on me and makes me pick at my mental sores. It makes me say things I know I'll regret but can't keep inside.

'Oh, Jane,' he said.

'Do you? I want to know.'

But David knew, as I knew, that I was fishing for answers that I didn't want to hear. He looked at me, carefully, measuring his response.

Before he could answer I said, 'I think you do. I think you can't wait to get away.'

'Jane, don't be like this,' he said.

'All you ever talk about is getting a flat, and how terrible your journey is.'

'My journey is terrible. That's why I want to get a flat, not to get away from you.'

'But then you'd be one of those awful people who live in London all week and treat the country as some sort of holiday laid on, to just dip in and out of.'

'No I wouldn't.'

'Yes you would. You'd swan in at the weekend like a stranger. And what if there was an emergency? What if we needed you?'

'Look it was just an idea,' he said. 'We probably can't afford it any way.'

'Of course we can't afford it. So why do you have to keep talking about it all the time? Do you do it just to make me feel bad?'

It was the wine that made me so defensive. That, and fear.

'Of course not,' he said stiltedly. 'I won't talk about it again if you don't want me to.'

'Good,' I said. And we sat there in silence for a moment, but the issue of the flat still remained, like an elephant in the room.

'So do you regret moving here?' I asked again, unable to let it go.

'I do not regret moving here,' David said guardedly. 'But I'm not sure I would have agreed to it if I'd known quite what it would entail.'

That wasn't what I wanted to hear. Tears sprang into my eyes instantly, as quick as the flick of a switch.

'We used to love coming here, remember? All those weekends we used to visit and imagine what it would be like to live here. We dreamed about it, remember?' My voice rose, too sharp, too full of regret.

'Yes,' he said quietly. 'I remember.'

David didn't get a flat in London, but he did come to some arrangement with a colleague. This colleague lived not far from the office and had a room going spare. It made no odds to him if David crashed there from time to time.

How easy it was then, how convenient: late meetings, drinks after work, just a night, here and there. I do not remember every individual reason, I just know that every time David had to stay in London it felt, to me, like a severing. Whereas before we were undoubtedly stretched too thin, and too taut, now we were starting to tear.

Whatever happened to him rushing to catch the 7.20 train, or even the 6.20, to come speeding back to the love of his family, waiting for him here in our country escape? Even if that train was cancelled, couldn't he just get the next one, or find some other way to get home to us? Couldn't he at least try, or make it feel, to me, as if he tried? Part of me, a very deep, very fundamental part of me, wanted David to race over hot coals to be with me. I wanted him to run to the ends of the earth, further; after all, he would have done, once upon a time.

I could sense him moving away from me, and as I came to feel deserted, I in turn rejected him.

I stopped including him in our plans for the weekend. On Saturday mornings when David wanted to lie in bed, I would just get up and out, on with my day, taking Ella to the stables, perhaps dropping Sam in town to meet up with Max and some other boys from school. They'd started going to the rec near the school to play football; it had become a regular thing. And after I picked up Ella again we'd go back into town and do some shopping at the market. She and I might stop at the tea room, or we'd go round to Melanie's for lunch, to wait for Sam. Quite often, the three of us would be gone for most of the day.

And when we got back home again David would be in the garden or at the door, looking out for us. A little agitated perhaps; missing us. And that is what I wanted, that he should miss us; that he should be the one stuck at home waiting for us, for a change, instead of it being forever the other way around.

'Where have you been?' he'd say. 'You've been gone for ages.'

'Just into town,' I'd coolly reply. 'You were tired. I thought you wanted to rest.'

He was anxious to see his children at the weekends, but as they became busier with their own lives here, they were no longer quite so desperate to see him. I manipulated this. I left him out of things.

I thought all I wanted was for him to miss us, but looking back I see that I just pushed him away.

NINE

My mother's birthday is in April, and last year I arranged to meet her in London for a day, to have lunch and go shopping. It was a novelty for me as much as her, something we'd never done together before. But we didn't get to see each other very often, now. Cambridge had proved to be more of a journey, for all of us, than we'd hoped.

I dropped Sam and Ella at school, and went straight to the station. Melanie was going to pick Ella up for me later, and look after the children at her house until I got back. There was no hurry; I could take all day.

'Stay all evening if you like,' she'd said when I asked her. 'You could go and meet your husband. Surprise him. Go and have dinner somewhere nice.'

She said this to be kind. She knew I hadn't even told David I was going. I'd told her that he and I had had a row at the weekend, as we seemed to too often these days, all the tensions between us slammed together into two short days and overflowing. The trouble with not seeing each other properly all week was that there was no time to make it up again, and no time just to be at ease with each other, to be close and familiar. Any bad atmosphere on a Sunday night would still be there the following weekend, however suppressed. I cannot even remember what that particular argument was about now, but the result was that I didn't tell David I was going to London. For him it was just another Tuesday, up and out the door.

I saw his car in the station car park when I parked mine. How strange it seemed, buying my ticket from the machine and then standing on that little platform, knowing that David had been standing there earlier that day, as he had done so now on so very many days. In nearly two years of living here this was the first time that I had ever caught the train. I even had to check which side of the track was the right direction for London.

I boarded the train and sat by the window, staring out at the countryside whizzing by. Fields, trees, farm buildings and here and there the ugly blemish of a rail-side scrap yard flashed past me, like markers along the way. You see the best of the countryside, and the worst of it, from the window of a moving train. I tried to recognize the view; to become familiar with it, but I felt strangely disorientated. The last train I'd been on was a packed commuter train within London; now I was going into London, from this very different place. It made me aware of how far away I had moved, both physically in terms of location, and within myself, too. And I started thinking back to when David and I used to come here for weekends and stay in our favourite hotel. And about how we used to walk for miles and talk and dream. It was a long time since David and I had been off on our own on one of those long, rambling walks. And these days we talked about practicalities when we ever had the time to talk at all, not what ifs. For all that we had gained in moving out here, we'd lost something too. And there is the irony. We'd lost our dream through the living of it. And then what do you do? What do you talk about? What fills the space in your head and your heart where your dream used to be?

I met my mother off the Cambridge train at King's Cross, so that she didn't have to negotiate the underground on her own. Yet after all this time I too felt a little uncomfortable, rushing up and down those escalators, navigating my way through the crowds. I could feel my heartbeat picking up and sweat prickling the back of my head as people jostled past me, hurrying me along. I'd forgotten just how crowded it could get. For years this had been normal for me; the rush and the shove of all these people. Not so very long ago I had loved the buzz of the city; I had been a part of it. Now as the crowds pushed past me I felt stuck in slow motion, left behind.

We went to Oxford Street, starting at Selfridges and then moving along to John Lewis, where my mother felt more at home. After browsing around the security of women's wear for an hour or so we squeezed back out through the crowds, and found a café down a side road near Marylebone High Street to have lunch.

'This has all changed since I was last here,' my mother said. 'Mind you, that must be getting on for twenty years. I don't think I've been down here since we came to choose your wedding dress.'

I smiled. 'That would be eighteen years then,' I said. 'It's changed since I was here last, too.'

'I do find it tiring in those shops, though,' she said. 'It's always so hot. And far too busy.'

'Perhaps we should stick to the side roads. It's lovely just here.'

'Yes,' she said. 'It's all very expensive, though, isn't it?' She poked at her chicken salad with her fork, and whispered rather loudly, 'You know I could have made this at home for less than a quarter of the price.'

'That's not the point, though,' I said. 'The point is it's your birthday.'

She asked about the children, so eager to know every detail. How was Sam doing at school, and Ella? Had Sam grown since she saw him at Easter, because my goodness hadn't he shot up then! And Ella; was she still hoping to have her own horse one day?

'Such a lovely life they have,' she said. 'So much better to bring children up in the country air.'

She asked after David too. 'How is he finding the commuting?' she said. 'Is he still coming home so late?'

'It isn't easy,' I said, not really wanting to talk about it.

'No,' she said. 'I'm not sure your father could have coped with a journey like that. He was home for his dinner at half past six most nights. Still, things change, I suppose. It's very good of David to make that sacrifice for his family.'

I think perhaps we both pretended to enjoy the day more than we really did. My mother because she had never really liked London, and me because being there highlighted both what I had left behind and the change in me. When I lived in London I'd have dashed around those shops, as impatient as the next person. Now I felt like a tourist, and I minded that. I felt like I'd lost my right to be there; my sense of ownership had gone and in its place was an unwelcome timidity. I found myself speaking almost apologetically to the waiter at lunch and to staff in the shops, saying 'excuse me' too often, too grateful for being served. Several times, walking along the street, I bumped shoulders with someone hurrying past the other way. My mother and I seemed to block the pavement, moving slowly along like people from another world.

By three o'clock she was anxious to get home to Cambridge.

'Well,' she said when we were back at King's Cross. 'That was a lovely day.' She could relax now that she was going home. 'Now you take care getting back,' she said. 'Ring me when you get home. And give my love to the children, and to David. Tell the children I will see them very soon. And Grandpa sends his love.'

I watched her bustling down the platform to her train, anxious to be gone, and I felt overwhelmed with sadness. My mother would so much rather have visited us all, at home, where she would have spent time with my children, and travelled in the car beside my father. But such visits were confined to school holidays now, and as my parents grew older it would become harder still. I missed my parents these days in a way that I hadn't when I was younger. When I lived in London I was too busy even to think about them most of the time.

But now there was often too much time, and too much space.

I checked my watch, making a thing of it, trying to look as if I needed to be somewhere. It wasn't even half-past three yet. I couldn't face going back around the shops on my own, but it was far too early to go home. Ridiculously, the thought of Melanie seeing me come back so soon made me feel obliged to stay in London. I could just picture her raised eyebrows, her knowing look. 'Go and see your husband,' she'd said, and of course I should do that, but in the middle of the afternoon?

I wandered out of the station thinking I'd get a coffee

somewhere but there were no pretty side streets here, no fancy cafés as far as I could see. I ended up in a sandwich bar that was filled with travellers killing time between trains. But that was OK; I too was a traveller filling time.

I thought about phoning David while I scalded my mouth on too-hot coffee, and then I thought of all the reasons why it would be better not to. He might be in a meeting; I might need to leave a message. What would I say then? I should have told him I was coming to London; it seemed so petty now that I hadn't. He might not want to see me; he might be too busy. 'But if I'd known you were coming . . .' he might say.

No; far better, as Melanie had said, to just turn up and surprise him.

It did, I have to say here, occur to me as wrong that I would even think twice about phoning or stopping by to see my own husband, yet I was struck by a sudden loss of confidence. Actually, not so sudden; I'd been aware of it all day. I felt out of place, so different from the last time I had been there, and it was the thought of David seeing that difference that worried me.

For my day in London I'd made a bit of an effort; it was mild for April and I'd put on a skirt that I'd bought from one of the catalogues that came through the post, with just a long cardigan over the top. These clothes would have passed for quite smart the way I lived now. Normally, at home, I went around in jeans and a sweatshirt; there were no shops to buy anything else, and no need to dress up. How ridiculous would I look traipsing across the fields in the latest fashions anyway? Things were more practical in the country, and I liked it that way.

Yet how dowdy I suddenly felt, as so many people from

so many countries dressed in so very many different styles rushed past me on my way back down to the tube. How dowdy, and how invisible. I'd worn comfy, flat shoes, so sensible for walking around town; women half my age and twice my height charged past me in heels the likes of which I have never worn. And I didn't actually want to wear them – I just didn't want to feel so . . . insignificant. The tube was crowded but I managed to get a seat. I tried not to stare at the people sitting opposite me so I looked past them at the window instead; at the blackness of the glass streaked with blue and white and orange as the lights in the tunnel whizzed by. And then I saw myself. At first, I didn't realize it was me; I didn't properly focus. There was just this ghostly haze, but then it took form; the pale face, dark-eyed, distorted like in a mirage; the shock of shortish, untamed, bleached-out hair. I had been absently staring for quite some time before I realized that I was seeing myself.

Most of all it was the hair that shocked me.

The last time I sat on a tube train – before Ella was born, before she took those scissors and so innocently lined them up within the length of my hair, and cut – my hair would have been the first thing that I saw reflected in any tube train window; in any window at all. Oh yes, I would have recognized myself then. Anyone would have known me back then, by my hair.

After the disaster I tried to grow it back. Believe me, I tried. I missed it as much as if I'd had my face removed; my features all rubbed out. To me, my hair was my one defining feature.

But it wouldn't grow. It got as far as my shoulders, no more, then the ends split and broke off in a mass of rats' tails. Eventually I gave up, and had it cut into a short, manageable bob, so much more practical, so much more sensible with the children my priority now. So much easier to look after; so very wash-and-go.

I'd taken to bleaching my hair at home. Just some kit from the chemist, a little lightener, to brighten up the mouse; so much more convenient than trying to get to a hairdressers out where we lived. I'd thought it looked OK.

And then I saw myself. Who was I trying to kid? And how did I ever think there was any merit in a hair cut that was wash-and-go?

Sitting on that train I felt cheated.

It was the discrepancy that shocked me most. You think you are one thing. You go about, falsely secure in the confines of your own making, blind. And then, so unexpectedly, you are tipped out of your comfort zone and forced to see. And what I saw, right at that moment, was a woman just over forty who was starting to let herself go.

If I hadn't been on a crowded train I would have cried. I wanted to cry. I wanted to grab back all those years that I'd so casually let filter by and be what I used to be; I wanted to be young, confident, oblivious. Failing that, I'd rather be walking across fields with the wind and the rain in my face, with no need to think about such things, no *point* in thinking about such things. I didn't want to be here, in London, reminded.

The magazine offices are in a large building just off Old Compton Street, a five-minute walk from Leicester Square tube. I remembered the way, easily enough. Just ten minutes, cutting through the side streets, and you could be in Covent Garden, at lunchtime, or for drinks after work. For me, that was the best bit about working here.

I am actually three years older than David, and I started

on the magazine before he did. I remember him, the new boy fresh out of university, squeaky clean in his brand new suit. I remember when we first got together, in a pub on Neal Street one Friday night after work; I remember the crush at the bar and the noise of all those people, and having to reach up to him on tiptoe to hear him speak. I remember his hand gently moving my hair away from my neck as he bent down to me; and his breath against my ear, sending goosebumps breaking out across my skin. And I remember the drunken kiss, outside, on the way back home.

The office had been practically rebuilt since I last saw it. It now had a huge glass frontage, with revolving doors, through which an endless stream of trendy, young, creative types slipped seamlessly in and out. I watched them a while, from just across the street, and I seriously regretted my choice of clothing, particularly my sensible shoes. It had been hot on the underground, and I felt grubby from my day. I hoped my face wasn't too shiny, but I'd no mirror in my bag with which to check.

How silly that I should feel like this. David loved me for myself; that's what I'd always believed. He'd love me if I was dressed in a sack. We were married, after all. He'd seen me giving birth; what difference would a bit of lipstick and mascara make after that?

But as I stood before the unfamiliar office I found myself taunted by the memory of my younger self. I didn't mind being small back then; I was cute, and I knew it. I flounced around with my long hair flowing behind me, letting the bangles on my wrists jangle like bells, forever announcing my approach. I had David wrapped around my little finger. Most of our courtship – for want of a better word – went on here, at work.

I crossed over and pushed myself through those doors. The reception had been completely transformed since I worked here; I'd thought it plush back then but that was nothing to the way it looked now, all minimalist chic, a bank of steel-doored lifts ahead, a line of framed front pages of the various magazines on the wall to the left, and to the right the sweeping desk behind which sat an off-putting security guard and an even more intimidating, extremely pretty receptionist.

But I was not to be deterred; I used to work here, after all.

'Hi,' I said to the receptionist. 'I was hoping to see David Berry.'

I smiled my brightest smile, and she smiled back, but not before I saw her eyes give me a quick, almost imperceptible once-over.

'Is he expecting you?' she asked.

'No,' I said. 'I thought I'd surprise him. I'm his wife.'

I saw her double-take, the surprise on her face. Was it really that shocking that I could be David Berry's wife? Or was I just being paranoid, my own self-consciousness getting the better of me? I thought of David, waltzing into this building every morning in his smart suit with his hair all short and neat; I thought of what his colleagues saw of him and knew of him. He was a good-looking man, my husband; that woman behind the reception desk, every woman in the building for that matter, would no doubt have noticed that.

I felt a needle of jealousy right under my ribs, sharp, unexpected. Still, he was married to me.

The receptionist pressed some buttons, spoke into her headset, and then ignored me. I stood there, trying not to feel in the way, while people hurried past me on their way from the lifts to the door and vice versa, all of them looking straight out of the pages of the very magazines that they worked on.

After a moment I said, 'Shall I go up?'

She looked at me as if she had forgotten I was there. 'No, no,' she said. 'He's coming down.'

And that annoyed me a little; as if I couldn't be trusted to find my way up to the fourth floor where the marketing department was. I felt excluded, waiting down there, when I'd hoped to breeze into David's office with a big smile, receive his warm, pleased-to-see-me kiss and perch myself jauntily on the edge of his desk. Just like I used to, all those years ago.

The lift doors opened, and there he was.

'Jane,' he said straight away. 'What are you doing here?'

'I've come to see you,' I said, pointing out the obvious.

He looked confused. 'Is it one of the children? Is something wrong?'

'No, no they're fine.' I laughed a bright quick laugh, more for the benefit of the receptionist than him; she was watching us, clearly entertained. 'I was in London for the day and I thought I'd surprise you.'

'Oh,' he said. Just that.

'I met my mother,' I said. And I lied, 'I thought I told you.'

'No,' he said, frowning. 'No, you didn't.'

That receptionist was quite openly staring at us. I swear I heard her snigger.

'I thought you might show me your office,' I said coyly, tilting my head slightly to one side, much the way that I used to do.

But he said, 'There's a meeting going on up there at the moment. I came out when they said you were here. I thought something must have happened.'

'Oh,' I said. 'I'm sorry.'

'No, no, I'm sorry,' he said. 'If you'd let me know you were coming I'd have – I don't know – ' He was anxious to get back to his meeting. He glanced at his watch, and mirroring his actions, I looked at mine. It was twenty past four.

'Well,' I said. 'It was a bit spur of the moment.'

'I'm sorry I can't ask you up for a coffee or anything.'

'No. Well. Never mind. I'd better get back for the children anyway.'

He smiled. 'It was nice to see you,' he said, so terribly polite.

'It was nice to see you too.'

'I don't know how long this meeting will go on for but I'll try and get back on the 7.20 train,' he said, as if that was consolation, as if I thought for a moment he'd actually make it. These meetings, they go on and on. 'I'll see you later,' he said.

'Yes,' I said. 'I'll see you later.'

Back outside, I took a deep breath. I watched all those London people dashing about in their busy, London lives.

What had I hoped for? That he'd just abandon his work and whisk me off somewhere in the middle of the afternoon?

This was the real world.

I thought about David on the train home. I couldn't think about anything else.

It was a long time since I had seen him in his work environment, and it had made me realize that I knew so little about his daily life these days, away from us. All I knew about life in that office in London was what I remembered from when

I had worked there, nearly eleven years ago. In my head, the other people who worked alongside and around David were the same old people who had been there back then, but of course that wouldn't be the case. Most of those people would have moved on by now, and still more would have joined and since left too, in their place. The chances are I wouldn't have known anyone. I never kept in touch with anyone from work after I left; I was too busy with my children. And I knew that, certainly in my department, people came and went all the time. My memory was stuck in a time warp. The truth was I knew nothing about David's working life. I didn't even know the name of the colleague whose flat he sometimes stayed at.

And yet I could have known. I really should have known. I should have asked him. But I realized then that I had stopped talking to David a long time ago.

I stared out of that train window at the monotony of houses, trees, and fields flashing by, and I was struck by a wave of remorse. And worse than that: of uncertainty.

Visiting him there at his office, it was I who was the misfit, and yet that was how I had come to view him these days at home. Inwardly, I had felt some perverse satisfaction at the sight of him getting things wrong with the children; getting the names of their new friends muddled; not knowing that Ella had been on a school trip to Bath; that Sam had moved up a set in maths. I had come to see it as his fault that he did not know all the little details of our daily lives – after all, he had chosen to remove himself even more from us by frequently staying in London. It wasn't down to me to have to tell him everything, to fill in the gaps caused by his absence.

I felt smug too when I watched him trying to horse around

in the garden with Ella, insisting on giving her piggybacks when she was far too old now to want to play, or when he had to badger Sam to kick a ball with him, pleading, 'Come on, Sam, I'll be in goal.' And Sam, whose football skills had improved no end under the tutelage of Max, would say, 'Aw, Dad,' and smack a ball straight past him, and laugh.

Once, just recently, I caught him staring out the kitchen window at Sam and Ella as they played on the swing, Ella standing on the seat and Sam half-hanging by his hands from the top with his feet propped on the cross bar of the side frame. They were mucking around, taking it in turns to sing some daft rhyme, using words from a teenage language unknown to us.

'They grow so fast,' David said to me and there was a note of bewilderment in his voice, and of melancholy, as if it had happened overnight, as if he really hadn't noticed before. 'They're my children,' he said. 'Sometimes I think I don't even know them.'

What I should have done was wrapped my arms around him. I should have cuddled him and laughed it off, or given some reassurance. But instead I moved away from him in the kitchen. I slammed on a pan to start cooking supper.

'Wonder whose fault that is?' I said.

I got back to Melanie's at about a quarter to eight. I did think about going home first for a while to make it seem as if I'd stayed in London longer and had gone out with David after all. But what was the point of that, really? I have never been any good at lying, and Melanie was too sharp, too quick for me. She'd soon have it worked out, and then I'd have her contempt to contend with as well as her pity, and I couldn't face that.

Besides, I was tired. I wanted to gather up my children and go home.

She opened the door to me and said, 'I didn't expect to see you back so soon.'

'It was a long day,' I said.

The kids were still eating, munching on slices of pizza while they watched some American sitcom on TV. Sam, Ella and Abbie were squeezed onto the sofa. Max had got Jake's mattress down even though Jake wasn't there, and he was sprawled out on it, propped up on one elbow, legs stretched full-length and crossed at the ankles. I climbed over him and followed Melanie into the kitchen.

As if knowing it was what I needed, she grabbed a glass off the draining board, opened the fridge and poured me some wine from the box she'd got wedged inside the door next to the milk.

'Thank you,' I said, and she poured another glass for herself. Then she opened the back door and we went out into her tiny yard, and sat down on the upturned metal buckets that she used for seats out there.

'Well then?' she asked, pointedly. 'How was your day?

'Fine,' I said as casually as I could. 'It was nice to see my mother.'

'Hmm,' Melanie said. It was quite cold out there now, and I pulled my cardigan closer around me, so avoiding the intensity of her stare. 'Did you go and see David?' she asked.

'Yes I did,' I said. 'I felt a bit guilty because I dragged him out of a meeting.'

'Did you go somewhere?'

'Well, no,' I said. 'He didn't know how long his meeting would go on.' This was the truth; I wasn't just making excuses for David, but it did feel that way with Melanie's calculating eyes fixed upon me.

'Didn't you want to wait for him till it had finished?'

'I couldn't really,' I said. 'I might have been hanging around for ages.'

'Hmm,' she said again, but she didn't look convinced. 'So is he staying in London tonight?'

'No, no, he's coming home. Sometime.'

'Shame you couldn't have come home together then.'

'Yes, I suppose it is.' To change the subject, I said, 'Thanks for having Sam and Ella.'

'That's OK,' she said. 'That's what friends are for.' She sounded slightly hurt. She wanted me to talk more about David, but I couldn't, not then. I felt too vulnerable, too exposed under her stare. And I knew she judged him harshly; she made little effort to hide it. Now she said, 'What does your David do on the nights he stays in London?'

'Oh you know,' I said. 'Meetings. Drinks with clients.' I laughed, a little unsteadily. 'It's just the nature of the job.'

'You want to watch him,' she said. 'You know what those city types are like.' Then she laughed too, baring those teeth, sharp as a wolf's. 'Of course you do,' she said. 'You're married to one.'

I tried not to flinch when she said this. After all, wasn't any man working long hours in London a 'type'? Any man with a long commute home, doing his best to get on in his career, doing his best for his family? And wasn't any woman like me a type too, wanting to escape the city for a purer, simpler life in the country? We are all types, surely. Even Melanie, living her casual life on an income of peanuts, and having her dig at me.

What happened to me could happen to anyone. Please bear that in mind, all you out there who would judge me.

TEN

I started thinking more and more about those precious weekends that David and I used to spend here at the hotel in the village, without the children. Away from the stresses and chores of everyday life, I saw the best of him, and he of me. No wonder we both loved it here so much. When we moved here, I'd expected it to be the same. I'd thought that the romance would come with us; that somehow we would escape the grind that any marriage must endure. It would be like living within a permanent romantic weekend; that's what I believed, stupid, foolish me.

We had not been away on a proper holiday, either with or without the children, since we moved here. Our holidays had all been taken up with other people coming to visit us or by going to visit family, or just with time spent at home working on the house. Besides, there was no spare money for holidays, not after doing up the house as we wanted; and installing the AGA and the wood-burning stove. And in some strange way, it felt almost disloyal to want to get away so soon, especially as the reality was that David spent so little of his time here anyway.

And I couldn't ask my parents to look after the children. When they came to stay they came to see all of us. And after they'd had to travel such a distance to be with us, we couldn't then go off and leave them just with Sam and Ella; it would feel wrong. It would also give them reason to suspect that maybe all was not well, and I couldn't bear to do that.

They were so excited by our move to the country; my mother especially, even though it meant we were further away from them than we had been. In London, she had understood my need to get away now and again only too well; she couldn't see why I had ever wanted to live there in the first place. But what would she think about us wanting to get away on our own now, from here, when we had not even been here for two years yet? She'd pry. She wouldn't mean to, but she would. And she would worry.

Besides, I didn't want to get away from our home. It wasn't the place that I needed a break from; it was what it was doing to us. To David and me.

I had this idea. At the time it seemed a little crazy, but in a good way; in a wild, spontaneous, let's-just-do-it kind of way. We needed not to go away as such, David and I, but to go away together right here, to stay in the hotel in the village again, and retrace the very steps that had led us to wanting to live here in the first place. We'd see it all with those eyes again, renewed.

How brilliant my idea seemed. It fizzed inside me like angel dust and I paced the solitude of my house, unable to be still. And oh how I plotted and schemed. I would arrange it all in secret; I would book the hotel, pack the bags. And I wouldn't tell David till the very last minute – it would be the perfect surprise. I clapped my hands together at the thought of how thrilled he would be.

*

'I've got something to ask you,' I said to Melanie at the school gates the following morning. I'd made sure I was early dropping Ella off, in order to catch her.

'Oh?' she said, curious.

'Not here,' I said. 'You got time for a coffee?'

Melanie loved a mystery. 'Meet me back at mine,' she said straight away, as I knew she would. And I got back into my car and she got into hers, and I followed her all the way to the town, just like I had on the first day that I met her.

Jake was lying on the floor on his mattress when we got back to her house, watching TV and eating Jaffa Cakes from the box. Melanie pushed open the front door and it hit the mattress, blocking our way. 'Hey!' he called from the other side of the door. 'Careful!'

She shoved the door harder and we squeezed in. 'Aren't you supposed to be at work?' she said. 'I thought you'd be gone by now.'

'Don't have to be in till ten,' he said, not taking his eyes off the TV. He was watching some children's puppet cartoon and clearly loving it.

'It's nearly ten now,' Melanie said, ripping the duvet off him, and switching off the TV.

Jake was wearing just his boxer shorts. 'Mum!' he yelped, grabbing back the duvet, and going bright red.

Melanie laughed. 'That'll teach you to lie in bed when I'm bringing home guests!' she said.

He slammed upstairs with the duvet wrapped around him, then slammed down again five minutes later fully dressed and headed for the door.

'Bye, my lovely boy,' Melanie said, grabbing him in a hug on his way past, and planting a kiss on his cheek that made him blush again. When he'd gone she said to me, 'Right. Now we can talk in peace. What's the big secret?'

But I waited until she'd made the coffee, shoving the breakfast bowls and cereal boxes out of the way to make room on the counter for the cups. I loitered in the doorway, thinking maybe we should have gone back to mine. I wasn't sure where to sit. Jake had left the mattress and his clothes from yesterday on the floor, and what looked like the week's dirty washing was piled up on the sofa. If it had been my house I'd be rushing around, embarrassed, doing a quick tidy-up. But not Melanie. You took Melanie as you found her.

'Here,' she said and she handed me the coffee cups. Then she grabbed that heap of clothes, dropped them on the mattress and settled herself into one corner of the sofa, legs curled up cat-like underneath her. She took her coffee and looked at me expectantly. 'Well?' she said.

'I need to ask you a favour,' I said, sitting down next to her. But suddenly I was having doubts. Suddenly, sitting there in the chaos of Melanie's living room it didn't seem like quite such a good idea. 'I was wondering if you would look after Sam and Ella for the weekend.'

'*This* weekend?'

'No, no. Sometime soon. I haven't booked it yet.'

'Haven't booked what?' she asked impatiently. 'You're being very mysterious.'

'I was thinking of booking a weekend away with David.'

'Ah!' she said, really interested now.

'So I wondered if you wouldn't mind having Sam and Ella. But it's a lot to ask,' I said, half-hoping she'd say no.

'Of course I'll have them,' she said straight away. 'You know that. Where are you going to go?'

'Well,' I said. 'You know David and I used to come out

here for weekends sometimes before we moved here? I want to do that again. I want us to stay in the same hotel.'

She burst out laughing, spluttering coffee down her chin. 'What would you want to do that for?' she said. 'Oh my God, I thought you were going to say Rome or Venice. New York perhaps. Not the local hotel, ten minutes up the road!'

I looked at her looking at me, her dark eyes so incredulous. And at that moment I felt a million miles from everything familiar. A multitude of images clocked through my head like photos on a reel: the nursery that Sam used to go to in London with the length of string draped across the window onto which the children's finger paintings were pegged to dry; the café that David and I used to walk to for brunch on Sundays, where we'd prop Sam up in the wooden highchair and feed him croissants; those blissful nights when the kids were a little older and we could leave them easily with a babysitter and go out to any one of so many restaurants nearby; and, bizarrely, the view from the A4 on our route back home after a weekend spent here, the cars and buildings crowding in, the billboards, the concrete rise of the flyover.

What was I actually doing here?

I opened my mouth to speak but there was a rock in my throat, blocking the words. My whole head was swimming with tears.

'Oh, sweetheart,' Melanie said and she grabbed my arm. 'I didn't mean to upset you. Stay at that hotel if you want. I hear it's very nice.'

I shook my head. I tried to smile but couldn't.

Melanie looked around. She picked up a T-shirt from the pile of clothes on the mattress and gave it to me. 'Here,' she said. 'Use this.'

And I wiped my eyes on it, and again I tried, and failed, to smile.

She moved closer to me and stroked my arm, gently, as if I was one of her children. 'Now then,' she said. 'What's wrong?'

'I don't know,' I managed to say. 'It's just since we moved here things aren't the same – between me and David, I mean. It was fine at first. It was really perfect at first; we were so happy . . . but lately . . . it's probably just because of his work, but even at weekends . . .'

I rambled on.

And she listened, and she sympathized. And even though I knew full well what she thought of David with her view of city types, and that she and Colin probably had a laugh about him when they were out together down the pub, she didn't pass judgement. She just said, 'It sounds a great idea, then. Dead romantic. It'll be just what you both need. And of course I'll look after your kids. Don't you worry about that.'

ELEVEN

Our wedding anniversary is at the end of May, and that year it fell on the Friday of the bank-holiday weekend, before half term. I phoned the hotel and managed to get us a two night booking for the Friday and the Saturday, and I cannot tell you how excited I felt, hanging up the phone. What could be more perfect? I had two weeks to keep it secret, to plan every detail, to make sure David would come home early from work.

He was working so hard. Not a week went by when he didn't have to stay in London at least once. Usually he'd stay there on a Tuesday, when they had their team meeting in the late afternoon which would invariably overrun, but quite often he'd stay on Thursdays too, if there were projects to be finished, or drinks to be had with clients. I'd got used to it. I really didn't like it. I especially didn't like the loneliness of sleeping in the quiet, dark house without him there, but what difference did it make when most nights I'd be asleep before he got home anyway? At least he didn't complain so much about the travelling any more.

The weekend before, I told him I'd booked the hotel just for dinner. 'For our wedding anniversary,' I said, in case he needed reminding.

'I thought we might go out on Saturday,' he said.

'But our anniversary's on Friday.'

'I know,' he said. 'I just thought Saturday would be less of a rush.'

'But you could come home from work early,' I said. 'I thought we could make it really special.'

He hesitated. 'I've got a presentation at two,' he said.

'But that won't go on all afternoon, will it?' I said. 'You could leave straight after. You could come home a *bit* early, couldn't you, just this once?'

He looked at me, and I stared back, willing him to say, 'Of course my darling, I'll come racing home, for that, for you.'

'I'll do my best,' he said after too long a moment.

The dread of him not coming home in time hovered over me all week.

'You will be home, won't you?' I said to him again, and again, when I spoke to him. 'I've booked the table for eight. We can't be late.'

I could hear the threat in my voice; the fear of being let down. I heard it in his weary replies too.

'I will do my best,' he said. 'I can't do any better than that.'

It took the shine off a little. It became yet another pressure between us.

I wanted him to catch the 5.20 from Paddington. I'd planned to meet him at the station, with our bags packed, though he didn't know that, of course. He thought he would be rushing home to get showered and changed to go out for dinner.

On the day, I had things organized like clockwork. I packed

a case for us both, picking out the shirts for him to wear for dinner, remembering to put in his pants and socks. The night before he had stayed in London, the better to finish things up at work so that he could leave earlier that day, and so he had with him his overnight bag containing among other things his toothbrush and shaver. I packed shorts for us to wear walking, and dug out the old backpack he used to wear to carry our drinks in. For myself, I took a long time planning what to wear. I did not exactly have a huge choice; I'd hardly bought anything new since we moved here.

I packed up the children's weekend things too, and their sleeping bags, and put them in the car. And in the afternoon I drove to Ella's school to collect her and Abbie, and went straight on to Melanie's. The girls chattered in the back of the car all the way there, and as soon as we arrived they ran straight upstairs to Abbie's room to carry on.

'All ready to go?' Melanie asked. 'Have you got time for a cup of tea?'

'No, not really.' I said. 'I'll just wait to see Sam. Thank you so much for having them.'

'It's no trouble,' Melanie said. 'You know that.'

Suddenly I was nervous, my stomach massing up with prickles. It was silly; the kids had stayed at Melanie's before, though not for two nights. They'd be OK; I knew that. What difference was an extra night?

'Relax,' Melanie said, astute as ever. 'The kids will be fine. They'll have a great time. And so will you.'

When Sam and Max got back I looked too intently at Sam's face, as I always did, searching for some new ease of being in his features that would tell me that he was OK, and that I could leave him freely for these two nights at Melanie's, without any need for guilt. But I didn't see it there; I never did. Guilt, it seemed to me, had always been at the centre of my relationship with Sam; the guilt of a mother for the anxieties of her son. Guilt over his struggles to fit in at school and with his peers; over the fact that he was too small, too shy, too sensitive. I worried, he worried, and thus came the guilt. And what a vicious circle that can become.

He never voiced his concerns, my Sam; nor his doubts, or his fears, about anything. He just hoarded them up in those wide blue eyes for the rest of the world to see, and that made it worse. At times it frustrated me, at other times it simply broke my heart.

'Hi, darling,' I said brightly when he walked in, hot and tired under the weight of his school bag. 'How was school?'

He mumbled a typical, nothing reply. And he wouldn't meet my eye. He never did when Max was there.

Melanie asked Max much the same, and Max replied with long, drawn-out detail; the two of them instantly launched into conversation, leaving the silence between Sam and me so much more intense, and painful. How I longed to have him to myself. How I longed to have him 4 years old again, when he was so blissfully free of his awareness of the world.

'You'll be all right, won't you, Sam?' I said, and Sam scowled, hating me for asking.

Melanie answered for him, disturbingly able as she was to listen in on us as well as talk to Max. 'Of course he will,' she said. 'Max will look after him.'

Sam's cheeks flushed, agonizingly red. Still he wouldn't look at me. And I could say nothing else. But how torn I felt between my desire to protect him, and my desire to have him not be like this at all. Surely he would be OK. He liked Max, or liked him well enough. If it wasn't for Max Sam wouldn't know anyone. His life here would be hell; he had to be as aware of that as I was. Yet there would be no break, staying here for two nights and two days. He would be in Max's charge, full on.

I fussed about, knowing that I shouldn't. I made too much of passing over their things, their sleeping bags, and of telling Melanie to call me if she needed me while all the time she watched me with somewhat amused, tolerant eyes. And finally, I had to leave.

'You could have had that cup of tea after all,' Melanie said.

I called upstairs to Ella. 'Bye, sweetie, I'm going now.'

Vaguely, over their general giggling, Ella called back 'Bye' in reply. Suddenly, stupidly, Melanie's lack of a smoke detector and the sheer steepness of her stairs leapt into my head to taunt me. But this was how I punished myself. This guilt at letting go.

I could feel Melanie watching me, reading my every thought. She made no secret about her opinion that I came from that middle-class place that is somewhere in London, where we agonized over our children's chances of reaching grade eight on the piano, but wouldn't so much as let them walk to the shop round the corner on their own. Where we fretted if the juice in their lunch boxes wasn't organic, but wouldn't let them loose in the kitchen to cook whatever they wanted, however they wanted, with all those sharp knives around. She made such observations with a laugh, of course, saying, 'I know you're not like that, but . . .' and so I made desperately sure that I wasn't like that, at least not when I was with her. The details that bothered me were superfluous to Melanie; they distracted from the real purpose of actually loving your kids, and simply letting them be. Yet if I was uptight, she really was quite lax, though I would never have dared to judge her as such. She loved her children, I've no doubt about that, just as I loved mine. But the leash by which she reined them in was elastic beyond belief.

'Bye, darling,' I said to Sam. 'See you Sunday.' And I went to kiss him – he was taller than me now, by a good couple of inches, though still the shortest among his peers.

He tipped his head away, but not quickly enough, and beside us Max coughed on a laugh.

I drove back to my empty house, to shower, wash my hair and get dressed. I wanted to be ready for the evening when I met David, to save time. But my anxieties about leaving my children were combining now with my anxieties about David getting back in time. It was just after half-past five; hopefully he would be on that train. Yet when I called his mobile he failed to answer. I called his office number, but he didn't answer that. Either he was on his way home, or he was still stuck in that presentation. And I swear, from the leaden sinking of my stomach, I knew which it was. I left him messages. 'Where are you? Just checking you're on your way home.' And I got myself ready, taking my time as I had planned to. In the week I'd had my hair done, at the only place in town; a much-needed trim, and I'd had proper hi-lights put in, for the first time ever. David hadn't seen it yet; he hadn't seen me, awake, all week. I carefully blow-dried my hair; I polished and I preened. And intermittently I phoned him, and still he wasn't there.

In my heart of hearts I knew this would happen; that was the worst part of it. I called him and called him again, my stomach churning with apprehension. I was ready to go by six-thirty. I had more than half an hour to spare before I had to leave to meet him off the train, if he was on it at all.

So I made a cup of tea, and watched the clock as I drank it. And then he rang me.

'Jane,' he said, his voice weary and defensive and distant against the background noise from the train, 'I couldn't get away. And there was a delay on the bloody underground – I nearly missed this train too. I had to run all the way to the platform and now there's nowhere to sit.'

'You said you'd catch the 5.20,' I said.

'I tried,' he said. 'I couldn't get away in time. I had to rush to get *this* train.'

'But you'll be an hour late,' I said. 'Why didn't you phone me?'

'Because I was hurrying for the train.'

'But earlier; you could have phoned earlier.'

'I was in the middle of a presentation,' he said. 'I left as soon as I could.' He sighed in my ear, his breath crackling down the phone. In the background I could hear some other man, talking into his phone, presumably to his wife. 'See you in an hour or so,' I heard him saying. 'OK, darling. Sounds good. See you then.'

Tears stung my eyes.

'Look,' David said, 'just call them and put back the table. Please, don't make this any worse than it is.'

He didn't know that I was going to meet him at the station. That was part of the grand surprise.

I'd had it all planned. I was wearing a dress – just a simple dark blue thing, straight up and down with thin straps on the shoulders, but a dress nevertheless. I'd be standing there on the platform with our suitcase beside me when David got off the train. In my dreams of course I'd spun us back a few decades, half a century at least. My dress would have been tighter, my heels higher, my lips painted a bright vermillion red. He'd step off the train to the sound of the whistle, banging the door behind him, and as the steam from the engine cleared he'd see me. He'd take the trilby off his head, drop the leather briefcase from his hand, and wrap me in his tender arms.

Earlier in the day it had been quite warm for the time of year but as the evening settled the temperature was dropping rapidly. I'd put a cardigan on over my dress but my skin still puckered up with goosebumps in the chill air. There were a couple of cars waiting with their engines running by the station exit, and literally only one other person on the platform. I stood just inside the gate, with my suitcase down beside me. David would see me as soon as he got off the train. He couldn't possibly miss me.

And yet he almost did. He almost walked straight past me.

It was as if he simply didn't notice me there, positioned as I was outside of my usual domain. He got off that train along with just a couple of other passengers and walked towards the platform gate, carrying his overnight bag in one hand and his laptop in the other, and looking right at me at the same time as he looked straight through me. His eyes simply didn't register. Not for one, two, three . . . a good ten seconds at least. And then when he did see me it wasn't pleasure that spread across his face so much as a look of shock.

'I didn't expect to see you here,' he said.

I smiled, but my face was tight from the chill of the air and from the tension of waiting. 'I thought I'd come and meet you.'

'Oh,' he said. 'Right.' Then, 'But I've got my car. I was going to quickly get changed.'

'You don't need to,' I said. He was about to start walking on to the car park, but I stayed where I was, and so he stopped and looked at me again.

'You've changed your hair,' he said after a moment.

And I said, 'Do you like it?', one hand automatically reaching up to touch it, to feel, even after all this time, the absence of its length.

'I do,' he said. 'It's very nice.' We both stood there, looking at each other, me with that suitcase still unnoticed down by my side, and how awkward it suddenly felt, how unlike I'd hoped it would be.

'Well aren't you going to kiss me hello?' I said, and I tipped up my face to him. Thus prompted, he kissed me on the cheek. He smelled of the train and of the heat of travelling; the fumes of the city clinging to his suit, and on his skin the faint remains of that morning's cologne.

'We better get going,' he said, and then, at last, he saw the suitcase. Strangely, he glanced around the platform, as if expecting it to belong to someone else.

'We're going away for the weekend,' I said.

He laughed; a confused, doubtful laugh.

'What? *Now*?' he said.

'Yes, now.'

'Where?'

'To The Lamb,' I said. 'Just us. For two whole nights.'

I watched my words sink in.

'The Lamb?' he repeated. 'We're staying there?'

'Yes.'

'But – how come?'

'Because I booked it,' I said. 'As a surprise.'

He looked around the platform again, bewildered, so hesitant to believe me. 'But what about the children?' he said, as if expecting them to pop up suddenly from wherever they might be hiding.

'They are staying at Melanie's.'

'At *Melanie's*?'

'Yes.'

'Are they OK with that?'

'Of course they are.'

He handed me his laptop to carry, and picked up the suitcase. And we started walking towards the car park.

'I thought you'd be pleased,' I said.

'I am,' he said. 'I'm just . . . shocked. Surprised, I mean. Two nights at The Lamb. Wow.' And then he said, 'Do you think we can afford that?'

I stopped short, my feet grating on the gravel. 'David,' I said, 'we haven't done anything nice together for ages. I want it to be special, different, a treat for us. We have to afford it.'

'OK,' he said. 'OK.'

I'd parked my car almost next to his. There was plenty of space; the car park was never very full, least of all at this time on a Friday night.

'We'll have to take both cars,' he said, putting the suitcase and his overnight bag in the boot of his.

'We can leave mine here,' I said, 'and pick it up Sunday.'

'Do you think that's a good idea?'

'Of course it is. It'll be fine.'

He looked around, not convinced.

'You leave yours here in the week, David. What's the difference?'

'I suppose we could drop one off at home, first,' he said.

And I said, 'We can't. It'll take too long.'

In such detail I remember all of this. Small, random things

such as the raspberry-streaked yellow of the light starting to dip behind the trees; and the white, dimpled skin of my knees as I got in the car beside David and my dress hiked itself up, tight across my thighs. The knuckles of his hand clenched on the gear stick, and the faint line of red biro spread like the trail of an aeroplane across the cuff of his shirt. The shuffling of his body in the seat next to me as he twisted to get comfortable; the creak and catch of his seat belt as he pulled it too hard. And my awareness of his tiredness, and of our conversation, so struggling, so wrong.

TWELVE

It was nearly nine when we eventually pulled up into the tiny car park at the back of The Lamb Hotel, a whole hour later than I had wanted it to be. I cannot tell you how much I had dreamed about staying there again. Since moving here, we had had lunch a couple of times in the bar, and on each occasion I had looked about me so longingly and taken in every little change; the rearrangement of pots above the fireplace, the new wallpaper in the ladies' loo, the addition of a blackboard marked up with the daily specials propped up against the bar. And I had noted all the familiar things too, the comfy, slightly worn old furniture probably in need of a little re-upholstery; the enormous settle by the fire that David and I had sat together on countless times over the years; the ancient, uneven dark red tiles of the floor. Noted them and loved them. This small old hotel had played such a part in our lives. All those times we had stayed here, David and I; all those dreams that we had shared.

I'd booked us the Barn Room, overlooking the courtyard at the back. It was our favourite; a large misshapen room with the roof on one side slanting right down to the floor, and a huge bathroom down a short flight of steps. The receptionist took us up there, and left us, and then we both just stood there in the middle of the room, looking around. Both of us, seemingly, overwhelmed. To me it was almost too much; I wanted to just look and look, to take in every single detail, to remind myself of what I knew and loved. The first time we had stayed here, David and I, in this very room, we hadn't even had children. We'd only known each other a couple of years. How young we were, how full of hope. And how we had clung together on that vast bed. To be there again, both in that room, and in that lost place in our lives, meant everything to me.

Did David feel the same? I thought so at the time.

He moved first, walking to the wardrobe and hanging his jacket inside it. He went into the bathroom to wash his hands, then came out again, opened one of the bottles of water on the tray on the dressing table, poured himself a glass and drank it down. And he spoke first too, while I was still motionless, still swamped with the memory of other times. He went to the window and looked out, and said, 'I wonder if you could see our house from here if there were no trees or buildings in the way. And no hills. You probably could if the land was flatter.'

He wanted to phone the children before we went down to dinner, to say hello, and then he needed to shower and change. I sat on the bed, waiting for him, wishing he would hurry up. I'd hoped we'd have time for a drink before dinner, perhaps a walk around the garden, but the evening was disappearing too fast. By the time we got downstairs and went straight into the restaurant the waitress was laying up tables for breakfast.

'Oh,' she said, taken off guard. 'I thought we were finished,' and she scurried off to the kitchen to warn the chef. We could hear their raised voices beyond the screen door, and the banging of pans.

We sat at an unmade-up table away from the kitchen, and soon the waitress reappeared with cutlery and glasses, which she hastily deposited in front of us along with a menu.

'I'm afraid the lamb's all gone,' she said apologetically, 'and the fish is plaice now instead of bream.' Quickly, she took our orders, and disappeared again to the kitchen.

'We're somewhat late,' I said.

'It's not even ten,' David said. 'It's hardly late.'

'Late for dinner,' I said. 'Late for here.'

'I got back as soon as I could,' he said defensively. 'But I had a presentation this afternoon, I told you.'

'Yes I know,' I said, hurt by his tone. 'I just meant we're lucky they're still serving, that's all.'

The waitress came with our wine then, and poured. Then she brought out our starters, and stood beside the screen door to the kitchen, waiting while we ate. We were the only people in the restaurant; no doubt she could hear every word that we said.

'How was your presentation?' I asked, making an effort to show interest.

'Oh you know,' he said vaguely. 'We put such a lot of work into the preparation; sometimes it's worth it, sometimes it's not. You can never tell at the time.' He took a long sip of his wine. 'I felt really bad having to rush off.'

'Oh,' I said. 'I'm sorry.'

'It's not your fault.'

'No.'

We put our forks down and the waitress cleared our plates.

Within seconds she'd brought out our mains and was back in position like a sentry by the kitchen door.

'How has your week been?' David said.

And now it was my turn to say, 'Oh you know.' I could not believe we were speaking like this, so politely, so remotely. Where was the intimacy? Where was the romance I had so very much wanted to recreate? 'I put my name down to help at Ella's school fete. They're having it on the green this year instead of in the playground, so it'll be a sort of village thing too. Oh, and I've found someone local to fix the bathroom radiator.'

He raised his eyebrows slightly, and nodded in acknowledgement, but I could tell he was only half listening. The stress of his day was still plain upon his face; his eyes were shadowed and guarded. I talked on, about this little thing and that, for the benefit of the waitress as much as him. I barely tasted my food. The sound of my own voice grated in my head, too forced, too bright.

When we used to stay there, we'd go back into the lounge after dinner, and snuggle up on one of the sofas by the fire. And someone would bring us a tray of coffee, and a dish of little hand-made sweets, and we'd sit there wallowing in the pleasure of it all. But not that night. David was too tired. And I was too disappointed by then, too sorely aware of the difference between how I'd wanted the evening to be, and how it actually was.

We went straight from dinner to our room, and to bed. I curled up beside him in that vast bed, but we did not make love. Yet nor did we go straight to sleep.

I lay awake long after we'd turned the light out, and I could sense that David was still awake, too, beside me. I could tell by the shallow sigh of his breathing. I could almost hear him thinking. Eventually he reached his hand across towards me underneath the duvet, and took hold of mine.

'This is all quite strange, isn't it?' he said. 'Staying here again.'

THIRTEEN

The next day dawned bright and clear, daylight breaking through the gap in the curtains, waking me early. I had not slept well, and my head was heavy from last night's wine. Beside me David slept on; I listened to the rhythm of his breathing, so familiar, so seemingly at peace. I could picture in my head every single time that we had stayed here over the years, all those fragile memories, stacked up, layer upon layer, like pages in a book. I could see myself so young, before children, drawing back the curtains, throwing myself down on the bed to lie next to David. 'What will we be like in ten, twenty years' time?' I could hear myself saying, so sure, so immune to the future. 'What will we be like when we're old? We'll still come here, won't we? We'll be like ghosts, haunting the place.'

I wondered if we would ever stay here again. I hoped we would, but how time moves, and how things change. Lying there beside David, I realized how much we had both changed. Back then, I never thought we would really be living here one day. We'd swapped those brief weekends for permanence. Would I do it again? Would I have done it at all if I could have seen so far ahead?

That day we went on our favourite old walk, the one that

started from a tiny village five or so miles away, down narrow, one-track lanes signposted to nowhere; it took us an age just to find the village again. We hadn't been on this walk since we'd moved here. If asked why, we would probably have said that there hadn't been time, that we simply hadn't got round to it but meant to soon . . . some poor, poor excuse. How quickly things slide if you let them.

But here we were again, at last, and how beautiful it still was; the stream rippling over pebbles under willow trees, the gentle rise of the hills and everything so green and verdant. Early summer has always been my favourite time of year here, when the whole world bursts into life, lush and full. With every breath my head was filled with the heady scent of the blossom on the trees and the cow parsley in the hedgerows, combined with the sharpness of dew-soaked grass, so fresh, so clean, so new. I never noticed anything like that in London. In London, at the first glimmer of a warm day, the overriding smell would be of the trapped fumes of the traffic; and, where we lived, barbecues. Oh my God the barbecues. That is what I think of when I think of the London suburbs in summer: the combined acrid stink of burnt fat, paraffin and traffic fumes. I didn't miss it. I didn't miss it at all.

The morning started quite cold but quickly the sun burnt through, slanting into our eyes, beating down on us, bright and strong. I should have brought a hat. There was no breeze; the air was still as can be, thick with so much pollen and so many spores. We walked slowly, especially up that hill. The exertion made my fingers swell up like sausages, and sweat prickled under my hair. I could feel my boots rubbing blisters on my heels; an irritation at first, becoming steadily more painful with every step. I wished I'd brought some plasters, or worn thicker socks. The discomfort consumed me. And I'd wanted to enjoy this so much; I'd wanted it to be so perfect.

In the past, when we walked here, we would talk so freely, about everything; about our lives, our hopes and dreams. The memory of those other times swirled about my head, snippets of long-ago conversations echoing clearly in my mind. Above all, how young we seemed, that David, that Jane. How at ease with each other, and how free.

Now, we talked about the children.

'What will they do at Melanie's?' David asked me.

'I don't know,' I said. 'The usual stuff. Go to the rec probably.'

'Where will they all sleep?'

'Ella will be in with Abbie and Sam will be in with Max. They've got sleeping bags. They'll be fine.' All these questions annoyed me. I felt as if he doubted my arrangements. 'They've slept at Melanie's before, David.'

'Not for two nights, though. And not both of them at the same time. It's a lot for her to take on.'

'They're good kids,' I said.

'Of course they are. I do know that. You don't need to tell me.'

We walked on in silence. Where were our dreams, now; where were those innermost thoughts that we used to share, so close, so in tune with each other? The strangest thing, the most disturbing thing was that I felt unable to talk with David as I used to. The words were in my head but there they stayed, unspoken. I wanted to talk, but I sensed a wall, silencing me.

It was a long walk, without our dreams to carry us along. My feet were killing me. I tried to ignore the pain. I breathed slowly, trying to absorb it. We still had a good couple of miles to go. I'd got the hotel to make us a picnic and we stopped at the top of the hill to eat it, sitting down in the long, damp grass. I took off my boots, though I knew that putting them on again would be agony. The skin on my heels was rubbed pink and raw.

'Haven't you got any plasters with you?' David said, as if he thought that maybe I had but for some bizarre reason had opted not to put them on.

I didn't reply. Everything was annoying me: my sore feet, David, just the fact of being annoyed was irritating me further. I'd hoped so much; *too* much. We sat there looking back down the hill at the village nestling below, and all I could think of was the last time we had been here; the last time and all those precious times before. We hadn't struggled for things to talk about then. We hadn't sat side by side like this, so close in proximity but as distant as strangers. What had happened to us to make so great a change? I'd wanted this walk – this whole weekend – to be just like it used to be. Yet I could feel the division between us as solidly as if it were a physical barrier.

Down below, in the distance, two boys were playing in a field at the edge of the village. We could see them in miniature, running around, so free in all that space. We watched them, and I thought of Sam, and I know that David did too. They represented all that we had wanted, space for our children, the room to move and grow.

Beside me, David sighed.

'I wonder what Sam and Ella are doing now,' he said.

I said nothing.

'I miss them in the week,' he said. 'When I'm in London, you all seem so very far away.'

He sounded so sad, so wistful. My eyes were brimming up with tears and I pinched my hands hard together so as not to let them out. I sat with my knees drawn up and rested my chin on them; I watched those boys playing and felt my heart would break. I knew that David would much rather have been with his children than sitting there on that hillside with me.

Later we sat in the hotel lounge, tired after our walk. We drank tea, and read our books. Someone had lit a fire, even though we didn't need it; one solitary log quietly smouldering away. We dozed in the heat, lost from ourselves, until it was time to go back to the comparative chill of our room and get ready for dinner. We phoned Melanie, so that we could speak to the children. I spoke to Melanie first, putting on that bright, tinny voice that I so often caught myself using around her. David sat on the bed and watched me, and he heard it too.

'Oh yes,' I said. 'We're having a fantastic time.'

There was chaos in Melanie's house. I knew there would be, at that time of the day, on a Saturday evening. I could hear it in the background; I could hear Jake, who had probably just turned up with Kelly, shouting over the noise of the others. But it was OK for Sam and Ella to be in that chaos, to be part of it. It was good for them; such a change from the quiet of our house. It was always so lively at Melanie's. I convinced myself that Sam and Ella enjoyed being there.

I said my brief hellos to the children. I could barely hear them over all that noise. David sat on the bed, waiting for his turn to speak.

And then I watched him as he spoke to them, though I

pretended not to. I saw how hard he concentrated, straining to hear the answers to his questions. 'What did you get up to today? I'm looking forward to seeing you tomorrow.' I saw how he frowned, trying to hear their replies. I saw how much he missed them. And when he hung up, he muttered, 'God.'

'What?' I said.

For a second it was on his lips to comment on the chaos of Melanie's house, and of his unease at his children being in that chaos. I saw the words as clearly as if they were written in a bubble and my defences rose. But he bit them back. 'Let's go and have dinner,' he said instead, his voice flat, denying all expression.

This time we did have time for our walk around the garden, and our drink in the bar. And we made a better effort to relax over dinner, planting smiles on our faces, talking about the children, the house; easy, safe topics. Yet absurd as it was, I felt self-conscious. I had put on some make-up, something I hadn't done for years. A little grey eye-shadow and mascara, and a touch of pink blusher on my wind-blown cheeks. I'd felt like a clown putting it on, so unnatural was it to me. I was wearing the same dress as the night before because it was the only decent dress I possessed, but I'd put a different cardigan on over it. Did I pass muster? Did I do? Or did I look as I felt; like someone who'd forgotten how to try suddenly trying far too hard.

That night, we made love, but I remember it for all the wrong reasons. Looking back, it felt just like payment due. Obligatory, almost. David went through the motions as if he couldn't avoid it after I'd arranged this supposedly romantic weekend away. Bad sex is worse than no sex but much, much worse surely is indifferent sex. Our bodies banged together but we could not connect, and when he rolled away from me loneliness engulfed me like a blanket.

I don't think he was really with me at all, all weekend. Not in mind, not in soul.

The next day we went for another walk and had lunch at a pub. Even to me the whole exercise seemed a bit pointless now, spending all that money to stay just ten minutes up the road from our home; to walk where we could walk anytime if we ever got round to it, to have lunch in such a local pub. Pointless, and more than a little bit silly. As soon as we reasonably could we drove back to the station car park to pick up my car, and then I followed David to Melanie's to pick up the children. I cried as I drove, alone now, in my car. I cried out loud, with my mouth open and my face all screwed up; angry, angry tears. I wonder if he looked in his mirror, and saw me.

David didn't go in to Melanie's; that was for me to do, even though he was so impatient now to see Ella and Sam. He waited outside, making some pretence of having parked the car in a dodgy spot and needing to keep an eye on it. David didn't much like Melanie but he liked her living arrangements even less. So I had to go in alone, clambering over the mattress just inside the door and all the sleeping bags and God knows what else, forcing a bright happy smile onto my face and saying what a good time we had had. Melanie, of course, must have seen straight through the pretence.

By the time I'd got Sam and Ella and all their things rounded up and outside on the street David was pacing up and down like a dog, so anxious to be gone. As soon as he saw his children I felt myself disappear from his consciousness like a puff of smoke. The three of them went back to the house in his car. And again I followed, and again I cried.

And when we got home I busied myself with sorting out the washing and getting it on, and cooking dinner. Sam and Ella disappeared to their rooms, both of them no doubt glad to be alone again in their own space, and David tended to his emails, and his post, and whatever else he had so missed while he was away. We hid behind the routine of domesticity. At home, we didn't have to talk. We could avoid each other, in different rooms, each of us busy with different tasks.

Later, much later, when I'd had my bath and was about to go to bed, I came downstairs to get a glass of water. Sam and Ella were both in bed, and David, I thought, was catching the end of the news on TV. But he wasn't in the living room, and the TV wasn't on. I don't know what instinct drove me, but suddenly I knew to be silent. He was in the den. I could hear him speaking, but not what he said. His voice was soft, low. Quietly, I walked across the living-room floor. The door of the den was open, and he was standing just inside, facing away from me with his phone to his ear, listening now. I stood in the doorway; if he looked round he would see me straight away. I wanted him to see me; I wanted him to smile and put his phone away and for this all to be normal. My heart was pounding so hard he had to know I was there and yet it seemed like an age before he realized. He spoke again into his phone. He said, 'Yes. Yes, I will. Me too.' And then, 'Goodbye.'

He must have sensed me standing there then because suddenly his shoulders stiffened almost imperceptibly, and the muscles in the back of his neck beneath the neat edge of his hairline tensed for a moment before he carefully turned around, holding that phone behind him, slipping it into his back pocket.

He smiled at me, too widely, too brightly.

'I just needed to check something about work,' he said. 'It's not important.'

I didn't question him. I didn't say, 'Who would you be phoning about work at gone 10.30 on a Sunday night before a bank holiday?' I didn't query him at all. Fear, and my need to believe him, held me back.

But that night, I lay awake, long, long into the early hours. I couldn't relax. I couldn't shut down my body or my mind. My senses were pitched on alert, every instinct screaming. I thought back over the weekend, picking it apart; I scrutinized every awkwardness, every silence, every difference so acutely felt. I thought of his guarded politeness over dinner and of his distance; the constant awareness of words unsaid.

I turned my head on the pillow and stared through the dark at David sleeping beside me. I listened to the heavy sigh of his breathing, to the irritating click at the back of his throat every second or third breath. And I thought of all the nights when he wasn't here; all those nights he spent in London, elsewhere. Suspicion crawled across my skin.

But I trusted David. I always had. It was inconceivable for me to do otherwise. He was a good man; decent, honourable and loyal. How offended he would be if he knew that I doubted him, how hurt.

David wouldn't cheat on me, surely?

Yet through my head came the sound of his voice as he spoke into his phone. I heard it like an echo, repeated over and over. It was the way he said goodbye, his tone so warm, so tender.

He used to speak to me like that.

FOURTEEN

I slept poorly and woke late with a headache. David was already up, and downstairs. I could hear the radio playing in the kitchen, and the banging of cupboard doors, the clunk of cups and plates. Ella was down there too; I could hear them talking to each other, her voice high-pitched and clear, carrying straight up to my bedroom, his a soft, low background burr.

I lay there for a long time, not wanting to be awake, not wanting to face the day. Last night's fears weighed heavily in my body, still there, like lead in my veins. I could smell toast, ordinary, comforting. Sunlight filtered through the gap in the curtains. I couldn't bring myself to move.

Soon the bedroom door opened, and David came in, bringing me a cup of tea. So quietly he crept across the carpet, so carefully he placed the cup on my bedside table. I could feel him looking down at me and opened my eyes. He was dressed in jeans and an old sweatshirt; gardening clothes. He hadn't yet shaved and his dark hair, which on weekdays he kept so neatly groomed, was ruffled and untamed. Yet still he was handsome. He smiled at me but I couldn't smile back.

'I brought you a cup of tea,' he said.

And I said, 'Thank you.'

David's eyes are blue like mine, but darker, and looking up at him in the dim room I couldn't read them at all. What was he thinking? What was he hiding? Doubt twisted inside me, a hard, tight knot.

'How are you feeling?' he said, and there in his voice was that tenderness, that same kindness, that he had used on the phone, last night.

I swallowed hard. I managed to say, 'Fine.'

He stood there for a moment more. 'Good,' he said. 'Well. I better get started.'

He'd planned to sort the garden. The bushes at the back needed cutting away and the patch beside the shed sorting out. When I came downstairs he was out there, digging over the flower bed. I watched him through the kitchen window. Ella was out there too, sitting on that rusty old swing and idly rocking from side to side, chatting to her dad and watching him work. I could hear the murmur of their voices through the open window; hers rambling non-stop about everything from horses to Abbie's new pet mouse to favourite pizza toppings and back to horses again; his offering replies when required and chiding her to get off the swing and come and help him. Eventually she did, rocking the swing up high first and then leaping off to land almost on top of him. She had her own spade; a pink-handled thing my parents had given her for her birthday. She picked it up from the ground where it was lying and dug it into the mud, scooping up the dirt and flinging it, any which way.

'No, Ella, not like that,' I heard David say. 'We're turning the mud over, not digging holes.'

'But I like digging holes,' Ella said, and she carried on, no help at all.

David stopped, to stretch his back. He rammed the spade into the ground like a spike, put his hands on his hips and arched backwards slightly. Ella did the same, copying him, exaggerating every move. David wiped his forearm up across his forehead; she did the same. He yawned; she yawned. He shook his head and laughed; she shook her head too and then collapsed in a fit of the giggles as he grabbed hold of her in a hug, tickling her.

I watched them for a long time.

Then Sam came into the kitchen, and I moved away from the window.

'Morning, Sam,' I said. 'How are you?'

He grunted in reply. And he kept himself turned away from me, rummaging in the cupboard for cereal, opening the fridge for milk. By the set of his shoulders I knew he wished I wasn't there. What is it with boys? When he was little he was so sweet and so open, so loving towards me, more affectionate than Ella was. And yet now he could barely bring himself to look at me, and if I should dare to touch him he would shrink from me, prickly as a hedgehog.

He sat at the table, hunched over his cornflakes, willing me to leave him alone.

But I couldn't leave him alone. 'You OK, sweetie?' I said.

'Yes,' he said without looking at me. 'Don't keep asking me.'

He finished his cornflakes. As quickly as he could, he got away.

Soon Sam too was outside with the others, much more relaxed around David than he ever was with me. Was it because I was his mother, maybe? Was it because he thought mothers were for babies? What did I know about teenage boys? I'd no brother of my own and spent most of my teenage years in an all girls' school. I only knew how much it hurt to be rejected by Sam, and that I loved him and worried about him endlessly. Yet that love and worry were the very things that seemed to push him away from me.

It was another beautiful day, sunny and warm, but I stayed in the kitchen, busying myself with chores, with making lunch. I would have liked to have gone out into the garden and joined them but I couldn't bring myself to. I was too tense, too trapped with foreboding. So I watched them from the window, my husband and my children, out there in the sunshine. I watched them as though I was watching a film, and I took it all in; the laughter, the chat, the movement of their bodies in the bright light of the day. How idyllic it looked. How perfect.

David kept his phone in the pocket of his jeans. But later, when he came in from the garden, he put it down in the bowl on the sideboard, alongside his wallet and keys.

'I'm going to have a shower,' he said.

I should have left it at that. I should have wrapped up my life as it was, safe, and kept it so. After all, a guilty man wouldn't part with his phone so easily, surely?

'You should have come outside,' David said, hesitating in the kitchen doorway.

I was sorting Sam's football kit at the time, I remember, rinsing muddy socks under the tap. I shrugged a shoulder in reply, not meeting his eye. He stood there, watching me.

'You OK?' he said.

'Why shouldn't I be?' I said.

'I don't know,' he said. 'You seem to be in a strange mood.'

I said nothing, but I could feel the colour bleeding into my face. I concentrated on my task, willing myself not to speak. I dared not speak; one word and the demons would come tumbling out.

'Well,' he said eventually. 'I better go and get clean.'

I listened to hear his footsteps on the stairs, to the opening and closing of doors, and then the rushing of water through the pipes as he ran the shower. Sam had come in earlier and was now in the living room watching TV. Ella was outside still, back on the swing, singing to herself, rocking back and forth.

I picked up his phone. I unlocked it easily enough, though I wished that I couldn't; I wished I could be spared this. I wasn't looking because I wanted to find evidence; I was looking because I wanted to find nothing. I wanted to be wrong. I wanted to be ashamed of myself for ever so much as suspecting him . . . and I was ashamed, sneaking, prying like this.

I scrolled through his contacts; there were so many of them, all unknown to me. So many people in his daily life that I had never even heard of, but that is the nature of his work. I looked through his call register, at calls made, and up came a number for 10.35 last night, unidentified. I scrolled down, and there was the same number, so often, too often. I memorized it, saying it over and over in my head. I scrolled through his contacts, couldn't match that number. I checked his texts, found nothing. My heart was pounding now, banging against my ribs. I switched back to calls made, double-checked the number. I flicked to calls received, and there it was. Again, and again, and again.

My hands were shaking but I hunted for a pen, for a scrap of paper to write on. I scribbled down that number, and then

I threw David's phone back down where I'd found it, wanting it out of my hands. It could be nothing, I told myself. It could be nothing. But I felt as if I'd been punched. I didn't know what to do. I could hear the chatter and laughter from the TV next door, the floorboards creaking above. Outside, Ella slid off the swing and started walking towards the house. I stuffed the piece of paper with the number on under the fruit bowl, out of sight. And I went back to my washing, my head numb, my heart beating wildly in my chest, fast as a jack-hammer.

All week that piece of paper stayed there, hidden under the fruit bowl. I didn't touch it, I didn't look at it. But I couldn't stop thinking about it.

I told myself I was being paranoid, stupid. It wasn't unusual for David to make the odd work call at weekends, so why did this one have to be any different? It wasn't as if he said anything out of the ordinary to whoever it was he was speaking to, anything . . . incriminating.

But it was how he said it.

Half term was busy. I had not a minute to myself. I had to ferry Ella back and forth to the stables every day where she was helping with the horses, make trips to the town. Sam had end-of-term exams coming up and getting him to revise meant standing over him, checking that he got down to it, seeing that he wasn't just idling on Facebook instead. On Wednesday, Melanie came round with her kids. She quizzed me about the weekend, about our stay at The Lamb. She wanted to know all about the rooms, the food, what we did in the evening.

'I've never been in there, ever,' she said. 'Looks way too expensive for me. Still, I'm curious to know what it's like.'

How easy it was for me to wax lyrical about the hotel itself. I described it to her in detail; the open fires, the bedroom, the beautiful candlelit restaurant. I told her about what we ate, and what we drank, about the quality of the sheets that we slept on. Oh yes, with such passion I could talk about the hotel.

Thankfully, she didn't ask for details about us.

David came home quite early on Wednesday night, just before nine. I heard his car on the drive, surprised, not expecting him back so soon.

'I had a meeting that finished early,' he said. 'I managed to get away.' Then, 'How are you?' he said. 'How are the kids?' He asked about my day. He stood in the kitchen with me while I cooked him pasta, chatting about inconsequential, mundane things and I responded, politely, somewhat unnerved by the novelty of him coming home. Before he ate he went off to chat to Ella and Sam. I stayed in the kitchen and listened to them talking and laughing, each of them vying for his attention. How ordinary it seemed and yet how strange.

And later, when we lay in bed, he pulled me to him, wrapping his arm around my shoulders. So rarely we went to bed at the same time these days. He stroked his fingers along my arm, in time with the rhythm of his breathing, and I curled up against him, all thoughts suspended. He turned his head slightly, and kissed my hair.

'We had a nice weekend,' he said and right then I wanted to believe that he meant it. I wanted to forget how awkward and strained it had been, and convince myself that yes it *was* a good weekend. I wanted to swallow the lie, whole.

I closed my eyes, safe in the warmth of his body. I willed myself numb.

And then he said, 'I'm going to have to stay in London tomorrow. We've got a meeting with clients. It probably won't finish till late.'

I did not speak. I did not move. I lay there, rigid in his arms, as the fear that I had suppressed all week came racing back through my veins.

When you love someone, and are married to them, and have given birth to their children; when you have slept with them, night after night, and been so close to them, you think they will be there forever. You think that you know them and that you will always know them. You think you are bound.

By Friday I could bear it no longer. All night I had lain awake on my own, thinking about David staying in London, torturing myself with what ifs. I couldn't face the weekend, not knowing. I couldn't face being alongside David for two whole days with these doubts, these suspicions, gnawing away at me.

I needed to know I was wrong.

On Friday, Sam and Ella were both out. I had the house to myself for most of the afternoon.

With shaking hands I took that piece of paper out from under the fruit bowl and put it down on the table – not that I needed to see the number; I'd got it memorized in my head. I put my mobile phone on the table too. I wasn't going to use the house phone. I'd thought of that. If I used my mobile, whoever answered wouldn't have a clue who was calling. I sat there at the table for a while, bracing myself. What would I say? What would phoning this number prove, or not prove?

I still hoped I was being foolish, that I'd got it all wrong.

I took a deep breath. I keyed in that number, and pressed dial.

Straight away I was connected to an automated voicemail. The phone didn't even ring; whoever owned it was on a call. And that felt like a reprieve, a chance to cop out, to stop this nonsense. 'Leave it there,' I told myself, but I couldn't. I just couldn't. I had to know whose number it was. So I dialled again, and again I got that voicemail. I took another deep breath, and let it out slowly. I counted to ten. I dialled again.

This time I got through. A woman's voice said, 'Hello-o,' lilting the word slowly over three syllables. I dropped the phone as if burnt. She could be anyone, I told myself. She could be anyone. She was still there; I could hear her, faint and tinny, speaking into my kitchen. 'Hello,' she said again. 'Anyone there?' I held my breath, all plans of making excuses, of pretending to have dialled a wrong number, gone now. She muttered something, then silence. I counted the seconds till I was sure she had gone, my heartbeat booming in my ears.

She could be anyone, I told myself again, but I knew. I just knew.

I found myself hunting through his wardrobe like a mad-woman, checking his pockets for proof, for receipts, sniffing his jackets for the scent of another woman's perfume. I went through his underwear looking for I don't know what; I counted out the condoms in the drawer in his bedside table, examining the box for recent disturbance because apart from that disastrous occasion on Saturday night it certainly hadn't been disturbed recently on *my* account. *I* packed the condoms for our weekend away, grabbing a couple and sticking them in my wash bag – how many were left in the box then? Seven condoms I counted now but for how long had there been seven? I knew I was being ridiculous. He wouldn't use condoms from this box on *her*, sneaking them out of the house like a naughty school boy; my rational self knew that. But I wasn't feeling rational. I was possessed by a rage I didn't know how to deal with and rolling in and out of that rage was utter panic. How could he *do* this to me?

He kept his bank and credit card statements in the den, in a file underneath the computer. When I'd gone through absolutely everything I could think of upstairs I went down there, and dragged them all out. And I really scrutinized those credit card statements, and that's where I found what I was looking for: bills for dinner in restaurants, on nights that he was away from me. Not huge bills; those he would have put on his company card, when he was entertaining clients. Bills just the right size for a nice little dinner for two.

We did not have much money. We'd stretched ourselves financially, moving here, doing up the house. I couldn't bear that he was spending what little money we did have on some other woman. We never went out. He never took me to restaurants any more, but then how could he? There were no restaurants around here. Last weekend at the hotel was the first time we'd spent money on doing anything special together for ages, and even then when I met him at the station with my grand surprise all arranged he'd had the cheek to say, 'Do you think we can afford it?'

I sat on the floor of the den, howling out my rage. I scrunched up those credit card bills; I tore them apart. I wanted to be the one that my husband took to fancy restaurants in London. I should have been the one. And I would have been once, but here I was, stuck out in this farce of a country dream on my own, night after godforsaken night, while David . . . wasn't. The unfairness was unbearable; it bore into me like a drill. He had one foot in this dream of ours – of mine – but the rest of him was still there in London, with somebody else.

Now what was I going to do?

I wished I'd never heard him on that phone; I wished I'd never seen the way his shoulders and his neck had tensed so almost imperceptibly, so guiltily, when he realized I was there. I wished, now, that I didn't *know*.

There is so much to be said for ignorance, for wilful blindness, for just chugging on, obliviously, with your head stuck firmly in the sand . . . but actually knowing changed all of that. How could I talk with David now, how could I live with him, sleep with him, share my space with him? How could I wash his clothes, care for his children, be here?

He had betrayed me. He had rendered my whole life a sham.

I went to bed very early on Friday night, and pretended to be asleep when he got home. I didn't want to see him, didn't want to have to say, 'How are you? How was your day? And how did it go yesterday, with that meeting that ran on so late?' I didn't want to ask these ridiculous, false questions and hear his lies for answers. I didn't want to hear him sigh, and tell me how tough it was, all this commuting, all this crashing in London at his colleague's flat. I didn't want to hear him say that he *missed* us, when he was away. I lay in bed with my eyes pinned shut when he came up, *burning* with anger. I heard him come in, and undress. I felt him creep underneath the duvet beside me. But I did not move. I barely breathed. One word, one touch, and I would have ripped him to pieces. I would have ripped out his heart.

FIFTEEN

On Saturday I got up before David, and left him in bed still asleep. There was no riding lesson that day but I had errands to run; Ella needed new plimsolls for school, Sam some new trainers and PE shorts. Things we should have got in the week, only I hadn't been able to do anything useful with all these suspicions spiralling around in my head. But now that David was home I wanted to be out. I didn't want to be near him at all.

I drove the kids into town, but we shopped miserably, perfunctorily. They seemed to pick up on my mood and exacerbate it. And there were no plimsolls in Ella's size in the school outfitters, and of course there was nowhere else to try.

'I need them for Monday,' she wailed. 'I've got to have them.'

'Well you can't have them if they haven't got any,' I said, too eaten up with my own worries to care about a pair of plimsolls.

'I could try and order you a pair,' the shop assistant said doubtfully. 'But it will take a week or so.'

'A week!' Ella screeched. 'What am I supposed to wear till then?'

'You'll have to wear your old ones,' I said.

'They're too small,' she wailed. 'I'll get blisters.'

And she carried on moaning, all morning. We trudged about, trying to get the rest of our things, and then trawled around the market to buy food.

'Can't I just go and meet Max?' Sam said, but if he went off with Max I'd have to pick him up later from Max's house, and that would mean seeing Melanie. And I couldn't face the sight of her, not right then.

'No,' I snapped. 'I need you to help carry the stuff.'

'You don't normally need me,' he muttered.

'I do today.'

'I could carry the stuff then go,' he said.

And then Ella latched on. 'I want to go and see Abbie,' she said.

'Not today.'

'Why not?

'Because we've still got things to get. And I've got too much to do.'

'I haven't,' said Sam.

'Well I have,' I snapped. 'And I haven't got time to be ferrying you two back and forth. So no, not today.'

'Just because *you're* in a bad mood,' Sam scowled, dragging his feet up the street behind me.

And so we went home. My stomach sank as I turned the car down the lane to our house, dread lodged heavily inside me. I tried to concentrate on the things I had to do: putting the shopping away, getting the washing on, organizing lunch. But I resented all these chores now. David had put his clothes from the last couple of days in the laundry basket; I saw them in there among our things and I wanted to throw them at him. How dare he come from fucking *her* – whoever she was – then bring me back his dirty clothes to wash? How dare he? I didn't even want to touch his clothes – I flicked them out of the way, flinging them on the kitchen floor, kicking them aside with my feet.

He wandered into the kitchen.

He sauntered over to the counter, and started cutting himself a slice of bread. 'What are we having for lunch?' he asked, as if all in the world was normal.

I could not speak. My face was tight, my teeth biting into my screwed-up mouth. My heart was thumping, angry, hard and slow.

He opened the fridge. 'Got any ham?' he said. I turned to look at him. He stood with his back to me as he searched through the contents of the fridge. He was wearing a blue polo shirt and jeans. How relaxed he looked; how very ordinary in his Saturday clothes, his dark hair still damp from the shower. He prodded around at the food I had just bought, finding ham, finding cheese.

'What?' he said, when he turned around and realized I was staring at him. He plonked the food down on the counter beside the sink, having to step across his strewn socks and pants in the process. He looked down at the floor, saw those pants and socks and absently kicked them back in the direction of the washing machine and me.

And that did it.

'Who is she?' The words were out, thick and alien, my voice not my own.

He hesitated for just the merest fraction of a second, then carried on preparing his sandwich, his eyes on the task, as if hoping he hadn't heard me.

'*Who is she?*' I shouted this time, so that no way could he pretend not to hear.

He flinched. I saw the colour flash into his cheeks. Slowly his hands stilled and he forced himself to look at me. He tried to smile. His eyes hovered on mine like beads on springs, flickering, unable to hold. 'Who is who?' he said.

I slammed my hand down on the counter, so hard I felt like I'd smashed it. 'Don't insult me!' I screeched, the palm of my hand, my fingers, singing with pain.

The colour rose further in his face, then faded right back out. He folded his arms across his chest defensively, and tilted his head to one side, eyes focused somewhere on the floor. I waited for him to speak. I waited and waited. The house was silent but for the whir and click, whir and click of the washing machine going round and round.

'Well?' I said.

'It doesn't matter who she is,' he said quietly.

'It matters to me! And it obviously matters to you!'

'Jane,' he said. 'We'll talk about this.'

'Fine! Talk away!'

'Calmly,' he said.

'*Calmly?*'

'Jane, please.' He looked at me now, spreading his arms, imploring me. 'I didn't want you to find out like this.'

'You didn't want me to find out at all!'

He sighed. He half closed his eyes, as if he was the one in pain here.

'Who is she?' I said again.

He bit down on his lip, sticking out his chin, while he considered whether to tell me or not. 'Her name's Diana,' he said at last.

And just the sound of her name, the sound of her name

on his tongue, in his mouth, flicked a switch inside my head and I felt myself crumple. Diana. Diana. How tenderly he formed the word. I started crying, uncontrollably, sobbing so hard I couldn't get my breath.

'Jane, please, I'm sorry . . .'

He put his hand out to me but I slapped it away. I didn't want him to touch me. I'd wanted him to deny it. I'd wanted him to tell me there was no one, to insist, to lie. But to tell me her name, and to tell me it so easily, made it unbearably real. She might as well have been in the room. She might as well have been standing right there, draping herself all over him.

'Please, Jane, don't cry like this,' he said, but I couldn't stop.

'Where did you meet her?' I asked through a mouthful of tears. 'How long have you been seeing her?'

'Jane, don't . . .'

'Tell me!' And then it dawned on me; the obvious, the impossible. 'Is it her that you stay with when you stay in London?'

I sat on my bed. I'd cried myself into a thick, sore head, my eyes swollen and bruised. I could hear David, Sam and Ella downstairs in the kitchen, having their lunch. How could David eat? How could he move about in our house, talk to our children, function normally, now?

'What's wrong with Mum?' I heard Ella ask.

And he said, 'She's got a bit of a headache. She's gone to lie down.'

The liar, the liar.

I could hear them chatting. I could hear my children

laughing, with David, oblivious that he had ripped their world apart.

The daylight was dipping and our bedroom cast in shadow by the time David eventually ventured upstairs. I heard his footsteps on the landing, the creak of the floorboards, and I could sense him lurking out there, plucking up the courage to come in. The handle turned, and he slowly pushed open the door.

I'd stopped crying some time ago, but I was still sitting on the bed, numb. He shuffled in to the room, closing the door behind him.

'Can I get you something to eat?' he asked, speaking gently, quietly, as if I was ill.

'No,' I said, and he loitered there, the manifestation of concern.

'Or a cup of tea?'

'*No*.'

For a long time he stood there, in front of me. I kept my eyes fixed, firmly, on the knees of his jeans.

'Talk to me, Jane,' he said.

I kept silent, my mouth clamped shut.

He sighed. He shifted his weight from one leg to the other; I watched the denim around his knees alternately crease and ease. I bought him those jeans for Christmas.

Eventually he sat down on the bed beside me, with his elbows resting on his knees, hands propping up his chin. And he sighed again. His presence, so close to me, was like a magnet, simultaneously pulling, and pushing me away.

'I didn't mean for it to happen,' he said, and really, I could have predicted those words. Isn't that so often the way with men – they didn't actually mean for whatever it was to have happened? It wasn't deliberate; it wasn't their fault. Be it forgetting your anniversary, or not putting out the bins. Or fucking someone else.

'I didn't plan it,' he said, and I almost wanted to laugh. Did he really think that made any difference? 'You and me . . . we've grown apart, Jane. Since we moved here. I don't feel so close to you any more. You've got your life here with the children, and I suppose I feel . . . well . . . just not such a part of it any more.'

I didn't want to hear that. I didn't want any of this to be my fault. It wasn't me who'd gone screwing someone else.

'Don't try and twist things,' I said, still not looking at his face. 'It's not my fault that you're never here. But of course now I know why you always want to stay in London.'

'It's not like that. You know it's not like that.'

'I know you're fucking someone else!'

I sensed, more than saw, him flinch. 'Jane, it wasn't like that. I have to stay in London for work, you know that. Diana – ' There, he said her name again. I didn't want to have to hear him say her name '– Diana listened to me. We got on well. We just grew close.'

'Well that's all right then.'

'Jane, don't be like this,' he said.

'Like what?'

'So . . . cold.'

'What do you expect me to be like?'

'I don't know,' he said and he sat up straight now, hands spread open on his knees. 'I want you to try and understand.'

'*Understand*?' I said. 'You want my *sympathy*?' I looked at him now, square in the face. His eyes were dark, small, too familiar, too filled with what he had done. My heart set itself in stone. 'You want me to tell you it's OK?'

He stared back at me, at a loss now. He opened his mouth to speak, then closed it again, helpless. At last he said, 'It wouldn't have happened, Jane, if you hadn't pushed me away.'

And quick as a flash I said, 'I didn't push you away, David. You were just too weak to stay.'

We spent the rest of the day in awkward silence, moving around each other, moving around the children. He slept downstairs, slinking up to our room to remove his things. I sat frigid on the bed as he collected his pillow and the T-shirt that he slept in; as he took the spare duvet from the cupboard on the landing. He crept about quietly, meekly, and I hated him for his cowardice. I hated him for leaving me there, alone in our bed with my misery untethered. I wanted him to comfort me, to witness my suffering, to feel it with me . . . I wanted his remorse.

'Who is she?' I demanded first thing, when I went downstairs and found him buttering toast in the kitchen.

He looked at me, confused.

'Oh I know that she is called Diana,' I said, my voice rough and dry from too much crying and not enough sleep, 'but who is she beyond that? Diana who? Is she young, old? Younger than me? Is she blonde, brunette? Tall, short? Is she thinner than me, prettier than me, does she have bigger tits?' He winced, visibly. Oh that I could bring her down to that. 'Where did you meet her? Oh – she's a colleague. We've established that. By the coffee machine then, or the photocopier? Do you still have photocopiers at work? It's so long since I was in an office – goodness I must be out of touch.

Did you thrill her with your marketing skills? Did she thrill you with hers?' On and on I raged, my words, my whole self just an inch from hysteria. 'Is she married? Does she have a husband who might mind about this?'

He listened to my ranting in silence. He listened till I eventually stopped, dried up, and thus he gained the upper hand. He looked at me, so frighteningly detached from me, and suddenly I was aware of my grubby old bathrobe gone yellow round the collar and the sleeves, of my blotchy red cheeks and the mat of my unbrushed hair sticking back from my face. I was aware of the shrillness of my voice, and of my bare feet planted on the tiles of the floor, of my neglected toenails as misshapen as a dead man's teeth.

And when he was sure that I had finished raving, he said, slowly, and in a tone that suggested I was mad to consider otherwise, 'Of course she isn't married.'

'But you are!' I sobbed at him. 'You are!'

But who was she? I thought back to the days when I worked on the magazine; I painted all those faces back into my head. When I first met David, I looked down on him slightly, from a work point of view. We all did, in my department. Not just on him; we looked down on everyone in marketing, just as we looked down on everyone in accounts or HR. They weren't the real magazine people that we were; not journalists or designers. They were office workers of one type or another, lucky to have landed themselves a job alongside us. We pictured them, trawling through the situations vacant pages in the media section of the daily papers, aspiring to any position that sounded more glamorous than, for example, a job at the local council, or at an IT firm.

Oh yes, I had the upper hand, way back then. How smug

I was, throwing scraps of my creative favour his way. And he was enthralled.

Did I ever meet her? Was she there when I was there?

She can't have been. I bet no one was still there from back when I worked on the magazine. They'd have all moved on long ago. No one stayed put in that world for long, no one except David, that is. But might I have met her at some do, in the past? I hadn't been to any work parties for years, not since Ella was small. In my working life celebrations were the norm; it was part of the job to be always having a good time, to go to press parties, launch parties, fashion parties . . . there was always something. But all that changed with the slide in the economy. There were no parties to speak of these days, no more cash to flash. If I had met her at any kind of function it would have been a long, long time ago, and how unlikely that was. But still she hovered in and out of my memories, a cardboard cut-out of a cameo, a cartoon imposter, popping up at the edges.

We still had the rest of Sunday to get through.

Like cats, Sam and Ella avoided us, aware of the atmosphere, but unaware of what it might mean to them. They avoided me in particular, slinking out of a room if I walked into it, keeping out of my way. That made it all the worse: as if I had done wrong somehow, as if I was the bad witch. I hated to hear David talking to them; even more I hated to hear them still speaking to him.

'Do you know what he has done?' I wanted to shout at them. 'Do you know what your father has done?'

But of course they didn't know, yet.

'Why were you and Mummy fighting?' I heard Ella asking

David later on Sunday morning, and I stopped still, silent outside the kitchen door, awaiting his answer.

'What?' he said. 'Oh nothing. Just grown-up stuff. Don't you worry about it.'

The coward. Did he think he could keep it from her and Sam? Did he think he could just carry on as before, coming and going, as if everything was just normal?

Later, I saw him, out there in the garden, talking on his phone. He was standing about halfway down, out of earshot from the house. I was in our bedroom, and I watched him from the window. I watched how he stood with one hand in his pocket, moving from foot to foot, shoulders hunched. He had his back to the house but now and again he moved just enough for me to see his face. He was frowning so intensely, his expression painfully raw.

He was speaking to his precious Diana, obviously. I watched him with a lump in my throat so swollen I felt I would never swallow again. It was just coming up to five o'clock, and the sun, with which we had been so blessed for these last few days, had disappeared now, driven away by the arrival of grey cloud and drizzle. The day was passing grindingly slowly, full of threat, full of fear. Eventually he put his phone back into his pocket, but still he stayed out there, staring at nothing.

Something about him, about the expression on his face when I caught a glimpse of it, and the tense set of his body, hurt my heart more than anything. I loved David; his feelings, his quirks and the things that drove him and worried him had been part of my awareness for so long. I thought I knew him better than anyone. I felt as linked to him as if we were physically tied. How could it be that so much of him, his concerns, his secrets, could now rest with somebody else?

He came up to our room late on Sunday night. I had stayed there for most of the afternoon and all of the evening, lying low like an animal, nursing my wounds. Life elsewhere in the house had carried on, excluding me. Conversations had been had, meals, however haphazard, had been cooked and eaten. I had been missed hardly at all.

Now, late as it was, decisions had to be made, practicalities seen to. However you try to avoid it, life will still need to be lived. The fear of Monday, of tomorrow in all its forms and meanings, reared up, insurmountable, before me.

'Jane,' he said, creeping into the room and closing the door behind him, and how I hated the sound of my own name right then. Over and over inside my head I could hear the way he had said her name: 'Diana'.

He dared to sit down beside me. I felt the dip of the bed, his closeness so intrusive. 'Jane,' he said again. 'I am sorry. So sorry.'

In my head I thought, Sorry, sorry, what good is sorry?

I did not speak. Surely, he did not expect me to.

We sat there in horrible, agonizing silence. After an age, he said, 'What happens to us now?'

I forced myself to look at him. His face was tight and anxious, and helpless as a boy's.

'You have caused this situation,' I said. 'You can sort it out.'

He ran his hand through his hair, rested his elbows on his knees, his head in his hands; all these things have endeared him to me. But at this moment my heart was locked, solid as a wall.

'Do you want me to leave?' he said.

And I said, 'Is that what you want?'

He sighed. He ran both his hands through his hair. 'I have no idea what I want,' he said.

We sat there for longer, the silence going on and on. Eventually he said, 'I'll stay in London this week. I'll come home at the weekend.'

'The best of both worlds, then,' I said.

'I'll want to see the children,' he said.

And I said, 'Perhaps you should have thought of that before.'

'Jane,' he said, 'I love my children. You know that.'

My children, my children.

'I thought you loved me,' I said and there was a rock in my throat; hard, sharp edges, scratching me apart.

'Jane, I do love you.'

'Then how could you possibly do this to me?' I didn't want to cry, couldn't bear to *feel*, but there I was, ripped open, limbs, heart, soul, strapped on a rack with the wheel turning.

'Jane,' he said. 'Please don't make this any harder.'

'Don't *me* make it harder? You're leaving me for someone else but you still expect to come here at the weekends. How do you think I feel, David?'

'You're hurt, I know that. You're angry.'

'Yes I'm hurt. Yes I'm angry. Don't you dare make it any harder!'

'What would you have me do, Jane? I'll sleep in the den. I'll keep out of your way. You won't know that I'm here.'

I was crying now, however hard I tried not to, the tears bitter and raw on my face. 'Do you love her?' I said.

'Jane, *please,*' he said.

'It was supposed to be our dream living here, you, me, the children. It was supposed to be our happy ever after. How could you do this – how could you just smash it all apart?'

He sat there, with his head in his hands, saying nothing. After a while I realized he was crying, his breath coming tight and hard, his shoulders slightly trembling. Eventually he spoke, his voice thick and low. 'I can't live like this,' he said. 'I'm sorry. We should never have moved here.'

And I hated him, then. I wished him dead.

SIXTEEN

I heard him get up the next morning. I was wide awake, attuned to every sound. I heard the faint thud as he folded up the sofa bed in the den, and the hiss of the pipes as he ran the downstairs shower. I lay there, rigid in my bed, praying, willing for him to come upstairs and say something, anything at all, to me before he left. I couldn't bear that he would just be gone.

Not once had he asked for forgiveness, nor begged me to let him stay. So easily he'd packed up his things for the week last night, leaving too many words unspoken. I wanted him to tell me it was all over with her, finished, a stupid mistake. That he'd never see her again, that it was me that he wanted, that we would get through this somehow. I wanted him to plead with me; I wanted his regrets, his fear for all that he would lose.

Yet it seemed that the fear was all mine.

I heard the click of the front door as he opened it and my whole body was screaming to go to him, to grab him, to stop him leaving. I heard the closing of the door, the crunch of his feet on the gravel. I heard him start up the car, turning the ignition over once, twice, three times, then drive away. I listened as the sound of the car grew fainter and fainter. I listened till long after it had gone, listened to the silence, to the unbearable hush of being alone.

I could not imagine a life without David. However hard things had been at times since we moved here, however distanced we had become, I thought he would be here for me, always. I thought his loyalty to me was unquestioning.

I took it for granted.

It was Monday, and the children were back to school. No matter how wretched I felt I had to get up and on with the usual routine: making sandwiches for Ella who wouldn't eat school dinners, putting out breakfast, shouting up the stairs to Sam to hurry up and get ready. Rushing round at the last minute locating books and bags and finding PE tops still at the bottom of the washing basket, unwashed. The stresses, the complaining, the irritation of trying to start the car.

I'd had no sleep. Inside, I felt as if I'd had a layer of myself burned away. The children sat in the back of the car in silence. I looked in the mirror and saw them both staring out of their windows, their faces solemn. David had told them he'd be staying in London this week, but that he'd see them on Saturday. How vague was that? And how empty of the reasons why? They barely saw him in the week anyway, so what difference did it make? Yet they sensed there was more to it. Of course they did, they weren't stupid.

I dropped Sam off and then drove on with Ella, rushed, late as usual. I pulled up outside the school gates, and she got out of the car and ran in. And I drove straight off, home to my empty house.

The week stretched before me, hollow, without form. I felt robbed of the weight of my limbs, as if gravity had altered;

I walked but I didn't walk. I moved, but I moved without feeling. All over my body I felt as if I'd been slapped, that ringing numbness echoing on and on. What was I to do now? I didn't want to see anyone, or speak to anyone. I wanted just to hide away and pretend this wasn't real, yet I had to go about my life as usual. I put on an air of being busy, barely having time to stop and chat when I picked up Sam from Melanie's, or ran into her at the school gates. I avoided her in town; I avoided everyone. I phoned Ella's school, said I couldn't come in this week to help with art. I said I had the flu.

I couldn't stop thinking about Diana. What did she look like? What kind of woman was she? And oh how I hated her, as I drove my kids about, cleared up after them, and dragged myself through each day.

I felt so rejected, and that is a horrible, horrible way to feel. Self-loathing lapped at my edges. I felt utterly unloved.

David phoned me on Wednesday, from work. How strange it seemed that he should just call me up like on any other day, like we still had humdrum, safe things to say.

'How are you?' he said, concern, so familiar, so falsely comforting in his tone.

'Oh I'm fine,' I said, my voice brittle and sharp as cracked glass.

'And the children?'

Cruelly, I said, 'They haven't even noticed you've gone.'

He paused for just a second. 'How have they been back at school?' he asked.

And I said, 'I'm sorry, did you phone up for a report?'

He was silent then. I stood in my kitchen with the phone against my ear, listening to the beating of my heart. I wanted to hang up on him, but I couldn't. Nor could I say stupid, measly things like how are you? I wanted him to be hurting like I was hurting. I wanted him to be tormented by what he had done.

'This isn't easy for either of us, Jane,' he said, and the sheer unfairness of his words made my head buzz.

'This is your fault!' I said, and I did hang up then, slamming the phone down so hard on the table that its battery fell out.

It crossed my mind that I could try to stop him coming home at the weekend. How cruel I could be, if I put my mind to it. 'You've made your bed,' I could say; 'now lie in it.' But the thought of not seeing him at all filled me with cold fear, the finality of an ending. How do you sever a marriage? How do you just turn your back?

I still hoped that he would turn up at the weekend and that somehow, like the needle on an ancient record-player scratching backwards, this could all be erased. He could not love his Diana. He could not choose her over me.

If he turned up on Saturday morning full of regret, I could face this somehow. Otherwise life reared before me, without focus, unbound.

On Thursday evening, Melanie phoned me.

'You've been avoiding me all week,' she said. 'What's wrong?'

'Nothing's wrong,' I said automatically.

'Mm,' she said.

'I've just been busy.'

'Right.'

I could feel my heart swelling up, the need to talk, and

yet the dread of it, brimming in my chest. 'I had a row with David,' I said.

'Ah,' she said. 'Tell you what, why don't you pick up the girls tomorrow, and I'll bring the boys and we'll have a bottle of wine at yours?'

Melanie didn't like David, any more than he liked her. She never said as much; she didn't need to. It was all there in the look, and in the unspoken.

Several times, when I was first getting to know her, she suggested that we come to the pub in town with Colin and her and some other people that she'd known forever; locals, happy to play darts and have a laugh. On Saturday nights they had karaoke.

'Come and join us,' she said to me. 'Bring your David with you. We'll show him how to have a good time. Loosen him up a bit.' She laughed when she said it, of course.

But how out of place David would have been; how out of *Lon*don. And how hard it would have been for me to pretend that I was otherwise with him there by my side. So I never asked him. I never gave him the choice.

Our bottle of wine turned into two. I drank most of it, because she was driving.

'You need it,' she said, as I sat there sobbing out my heart.

I told her too much, with the alcohol hot in my face, loose on my tongue. I told her about his woman, about all those nights I thought he was stuck in London because of work, when really, he was seeing someone else; about how he'd made me feel guilty about the trains and the hardship of his journey when all the time it was he who was guilty. And how loose, how clichéd a picture I painted, glass in hand, for Melanie. The staying late after work; the shifty, double life.

She nodded her head as I spoke. 'It doesn't surprise me,' she said. 'What did you think would happen with him staying in London so much?'

I realize that I played to her. Even in my heartbreak, I described what had happened as she would understand it. I portrayed David as she expected him to be. As a two-faced, devious, London-bound cheat, as shallow as she'd ever imagined.

But did I paint him that way for her benefit or mine?

I didn't tell her that I'd pushed him into moving here; that on my account he'd had to endure a good five hours travelling each day on stuffy, crowded trains, never mind the drive either side. That for him, it had been day in, day out unrelenting grind, compounded with the subtle, progressive exclusion from his family. That he'd moved here for me; and that because of me, he'd gone from loving this place to hating it. I didn't tell her any of that, because I couldn't acknowledge it to myself.

As on most Saturdays, I was up and out early with the children, taking Ella to the stables, going on into town to drop Sam at the rec, then going back for Ella and back again into town for shopping. I could have hurried. I could have called Sam on his phone and given him an earlier time to be collected but instead I dragged it out. I knew David would be at home, waiting for us to get back. Well, let him wait. I picked up some bread and cheese at the shops and phoned Melanie; she was only too pleased to have the three of us meet round at hers for a late, impromptu lunch. And there I watched the clock, nervous, prickling up with dread. How slowly time passed.

'You should relax,' Melanie said to me, though there was no chance of that. 'Why hurry home?' she said. 'He can't expect you to put yourself out for him now. Make him sweat, I would.'

He rang my mobile three times while I was there, but I didn't answer. I would have stayed at Melanie's all day but for Ella's anxious, 'Will Dad be at home yet?'

We got back late afternoon, and there was his car on the drive. I unlocked the front door with my heart thumping, all my senses on the defensive. He was sitting in the chair just inside the living room, by the window. Just sitting there, waiting, as if he'd been sitting there waiting for hours. Well, good, I thought.

He said hello to the children, and they to him, and that took all of two minutes before they escaped and disappeared to their rooms. Children don't want to be around when there's an atmosphere, he'd learn that quickly enough. We both would. Sam and Ella wanted to know that their dad was there, but they didn't want to spend enforced time talking to him. 'What have you been up to, Sam?' David asked. And, 'How was school this week, Ella?' But all he got was a shrug, perhaps a mumble, in reply. How quickly children pick up on tension. David would be more of an outsider on their lives now than he'd ever been before; I saw the realization of that cross his face and age him a decade. And again I thought, Good.

He followed me into the kitchen, where I had started putting away my shopping.

'I tried to phone you,' he said.

I shrugged. 'Did you?'

He stood there, awkward in his own house.

'I was here just after eleven,' he said, accusation sharp in his voice. 'I wanted to see the children.'

'Well now you've seen them.'

I could feel him watching me. And I could feel his anger, but what right had he to feel angry? The way I saw it, he'd forfeited all rights. I filled the kettle with water, took a single cup from the cupboard to make a single cup of tea.

'You knew I was coming,' he said. 'Why were you out for so long?'

'I'm sorry,' I said. 'Did you expect me to drop everything on your account?'

Out of the corner of my eye I saw him push a hand back through his hair in frustration. 'Why do you do this?' he said. 'Why do you always, always do this?'

'If you remember, I haven't done anything,' I reminded him.

'You cut me out. You push me away.'

'You cut yourself out!' I snapped, glaring at him now. 'When you went off with *her*!'

'Well maybe I wouldn't have gone off with her at all if I thought I was wanted around here!'

The heat burst into my face, the blood roaring in my ears. I turned away from him, picked up the kettle and poured boiling water into my cup, spilling it all over the place.

'Look,' he said, deliberately calmer, and quieter now. 'Can we at least be civil to each other? Please. For the sake of the children, if nothing else.'

I ignored him, and poked at my tea bag with a spoon, tears burning behind my eyes.

Stiltedly he said, 'I've put my bag in the den. If it's all right with you I'll go upstairs and get some different clothes. I'll make up my bed later.'

'Don't think you can leave me your washing,' I shouted after him as he walked out of the room, 'nor your dirty sheets!'

Later, I cooked pasta for Sam, Ella and me, with my emotions still raging inside me, and then we three sat at the kitchen table to eat while David sat in the living room, left out.

'Why isn't Dad eating with us?' Sam asked, miserably prodding his fork about in his food.

'Because he's not,' I said.

'When will he eat then?' Ella asked anxiously.

They'd both stopped eating, and were looking at me, making it my concern, my problem.

'I don't know,' I said, irritated. 'You'll have to ask him.'

Then David came into the kitchen, and started rummaging around in the fridge.

'Is it all right if I get myself a sandwich?' he said.

'Do what you like,' I said.

Sam stared back down at his plate, poking his food around with that fork again. Ella switched her gaze from me to David, frowning.

'Why aren't you having pasta?' she asked him.

He stroked her hair as he moved from fridge to counter. 'Oh, a sandwich is fine for me,' he said.

'They had a fight, stupid,' Sam mumbled, raising his eyes just enough to glare at Ella across the table. 'Why else do you think Dad hasn't been here all week?'

'But you've made it up now, haven't you?' Ella said, looking at me. 'Dad won't stay in London this week?'

I avoided her stare and said to Sam, 'Eat your food.'

David carried on making his sandwich, slicing the bread I had bought that morning, using up all of the ham. 'Don't you worry about me, Ella,' he said over his shoulder, his voice so calm and easy. 'I often have to stay in London. You know that.' He turned around, sandwich completed. 'I'm here now though. All right if I sit down?'

The three of them looked at me, waiting for a response.

'No,' I wanted to scream, 'it isn't all right.' The hurt he had done me loomed over me, an engulfing monster of a shadow. I could not pretend. I pushed back my chair, left my plate where it was and walked out.

He spent the evening in the den with the children, watching some programme on TV while I drifted from the kitchen to the living room to the kitchen again, excluded. Later, when Ella had gone to bed and Sam too was making his way up, he came into the kitchen for a glass of water.

'I don't want you here,' I said.

'I'm sorry,' he said, misunderstanding. 'I just want to get a drink.'

'I mean I don't want you here, at all. Not just in my kitchen – I don't want you here in the house. I don't want you *sleeping here*!' I'd wanted to stay calm but my voice rose with every word, too loud, too shrill in the quiet of the house.

He stopped on his way to the sink, suddenly, like an animal caught in the lights, and spread his hands out helplessly. 'Jane, it's nearly eleven. I'm not going to get a train back to London now.'

'Then stay in a hotel! But just go!'

He stared at me, the colour rising in his face. 'I'm not going anywhere now,' he said.

'You can't stay here!' I shouted at him. 'You can't be here! I want you out!'

'Jane, this is my house too. And I came to see my children.'

'That's too bad.' I was crying now. 'You can't do this to me.'

'Jane, I'm not trying to do anything to you. I'm here to see Sam and Ella, that's all.'

'You can't be here! You can't come from her to me! You can't be in this house, acting like everything is normal!'

'Then what would you have me do, Jane?' he said, raising his voice now too. 'Not see my children?'

'I don't know. I don't care!' I screamed, and instantly I heard Sam slamming a door upstairs.

'Look,' he said, quietly now, lest Sam should hear more. 'I am sorry for all of this and I will try harder to stay out of your way. But you are not stopping me from seeing my children.'

And so it was and so it would be for all the miserable weeks that followed. He turned up on Saturdays and we bristled around each other, and always we ended up fighting. He wanted to stay over to keep things normal for the children, he said, to make it easier for them, but in fact we made it hell.

I couldn't stand it. Couldn't stand him sleeping down there in the den, while I was upstairs, too tense, too tormented to sleep at all.

We tried to talk, on those wretched Saturday evenings when the kids were in bed. Late, late into the night we talked, getting nowhere, getting more and more upset. He missed us, he said; he still cared about us, about me. But how could he care about me when he was still seeing her? When he was living with her, now, more or less?

'I'm not living with her in that way,' he said. 'I'm staying in her flat. She's a colleague. It's an arrangement.'

'You're sleeping with her,' I said. 'You're staying in her flat. You're living with her.'

'Jane, this is still my home,' he said with his head in his hands. 'You, the children, are still my family.'

'You want us both then?'

'I don't know what I want,' he said, the guilt, the anguish, clearly eating him up.

Well, let it eat away. Let him suffer. After all, what had he done to me?

One Saturday night we were sniping at each other in the kitchen when Sam burst in. He stood in front of me, fists clenched at his sides and shouted, 'Why do you keep going on at Dad?'

'I beg your pardon?'

'All you do – you go on and on. Rowing with him all the time. Why can't you just leave him alone? No wonder he doesn't come home much any more.'

I looked at Sam with his face all puffed up and angry and the utter injustice was like a slap in the face. How could he blame me, automatically and without knowing? And clearly he did blame me. Clearly he'd been stewing on that blame for quite some time.

'Sam,' I said, so calmly now, so coldly, 'do you want to know why your father and I are, as you put it, rowing all the time?'

'Jane—'

'Do you want to know why he doesn't come home much any more?'

'Jane!' David said again, much louder, and I heard the warning in his voice. I heard it, and ignored it.

'It's because he's seeing someone else.'

The colour fell from Sam's face. Now it was he who

looked like he'd been slapped. And right then I didn't care. I was too hurt that my son had automatically sided with his father.

'Sam, listen,' David said and he reached out an arm to Sam but Sam stepped away.

He looked from me to David and back at me again with such horror, such *disgust* in his eyes. His bottom lip turned right down in an arc, like it used to when he was younger and about to cry. But he didn't cry; he ran out of the kitchen, stormed upstairs and slammed his bedroom door behind him.

'Why on earth did you have to do that?' David turned on me, furious.

Equally furious, I said, 'It's not me, I didn't do anything.'

'How could you possibly say that to him?'

'What?' I said. 'You mean it's OK for you to sleep with someone else but not for me to tell him?'

'He didn't need to know,' David said, his face flushed with anger. 'You should not have told him like that!'

The next day I saw David try to talk to Sam, but Sam walked away from him out into the garden. I watched from the kitchen window as Sam kicked at the ground, kicking at sticks, imaginary or real. He looked caged, even out there. David followed him around the garden, his hands outstretched, beseeching. Sometimes, when they raised their voices I could catch what they were saying. I could just about make out David pleading 'You must understand . . . it makes no difference to us . . . to you and me and Ella.' Far more clearly I heard Sam say 'I don't want to know.'

Ella came into the kitchen and sidled up to me. 'What's the matter with Sam and Daddy?' she said.

And I lied, as I should have lied to Sam. 'Oh don't worry. It's nothing.'

'I hate everyone arguing all the time,' she said.

'I know,' I said. 'I'm sorry.' I put my arm around her to hug her but she slipped out from my grip, and left the room.

Long after Sam came back in David stayed out there, sitting on the bench with his head in his hands. As I watched, he looked up, as though pleading to the heavens, and I realized that he was crying. And I wanted to be pleased. I wanted to be glad that he was hurting too but I wasn't. I felt more wretched than ever.

Things changed then. They were never going to get better, but how quickly they went from bad to worse. His visits were agony, for me, for the children, for all of us. We told Sam and Ella we still loved them, that what was going on between us was no reflection on them. We were both there for them, as always, we said. We were still a family.

But still they were screwed up with it all. It was like we'd taken the ground from beneath them and thrown it into the air as freely as dust. Ella started having nightmares. Sam retreated into himself. Sam, my once sweet-natured, tender boy, pulled away from us both.

David reduced his weekend visits to a day; he'd come on Saturday morning, and leave again in the evening, going back to London and to her. It killed me to think of them spending Sundays together in London, going for walks along the Thames and for lunch in Soho or Covent Garden, doing things that we used to do. So the rows were even worse on Saturdays, two days' worth condensed into one. He wanted us to be here when he came on Saturdays and got agitated and anxious if we weren't. But why should we drop everything? Why should we change our plans? Of course the children wanted to see their dad, desperately, much more than they would admit and certainly more than I would ever acknowledge, but it altered the course of our Saturdays. No more trips to the market, no more seeing our friends. For Sam and Ella, just the bittersweet pressure of their father coming to visit, and with it the reminder of all that that meant.

So he switched his visits to Sundays. To fit in with us, he said, but to me that was worse. The thought of Sunday clouded Saturday; it shadowed the whole week. The ridiculous thing was that after all this time of looking forward to the weekend, to having David home and being a family, some tiny part of me still did look forward to seeing him, as if I was programmed that way, like a dumb dog, unable to change its ways. And it hurt and it hurt, the cruellest pain.

There was always something to do on Saturdays, so I could fill the space easily. I could avoid seeing him for much of the time. But Sundays dragged, an interminable pause. For the children it was better that he should come on a Sunday, but it wasn't for me. For me there was no escape; it was unbearable.

And because there were no trains to speak of on Sundays, he needed his car. He came by train one Saturday, and slept on the sofa bed for what I assumed would be the last time. And on the Sunday he packed up his car with the last of his stuff, and drove back to London.

And then I knew that he'd really left me.

SEVENTEEN

On those many, many nights alone, with nothing but a bottle of wine for company, I had plenty of time to take a good long look at myself. I thought I was lonely before, but it was nothing to this. At least before I knew David would eventually come home, if not every night then certainly most, and always at weekends. His presence punctuated our lives, gave us structure. I am loath to admit it, but I was like a three-legged table without him; unstable, and unable to be stable for my children. The days stretched before me, all of them the same, as vast and endless as the sea.

I looked backwards, critically. I saw myself wanting the right house, the right schools, like any woman, wanting what's right for her kids. Wanting, wanting, as if it was my due. I realized that the dreams that David and I shared were, for him, only ever that: dreams, a fantasy, a counter to reality. I could see that he'd never really wanted to move here, but then I gave him no choice. I wanted it, so I would have it, but at what cost to us all.

I had plenty of time for analysis on those long, long evenings, and plenty of time for regrets. But what do you do when faced with such a painful view of yourself? You turn away from it. You close your eyes.

*

I veered from anger to regret to utter despair and back again. There were days I couldn't face getting up in the morning, other days I couldn't bear to go to bed. Several times my kids missed school because I couldn't force myself to get up and take them. Sometimes I couldn't even bring myself to look at Sam and Ella because in their faces I saw David and the failure of my marriage. I resented their demands and their childish selfishness, always needing this, wanting that. Let them get their own meals, see to their own things. I saw no point now in keeping an orderly house. No point in maintaining the dream.

And I couldn't stop thinking about the other woman: about Diana.

In my head she was perfect, in a glossy, over-polished sort of way. She was my opposite. Not just physically, not just tall and dark and graceful, but in the abstract too. She was patient, understanding, amused at all his jokes. She tended his ego, soothed his treacherous brow. She was everything that I wasn't, nor wanted to be.

But she was with him.

Sam and Ella were distraught. In each of them, it manifested itself in different ways. Ella became clingy and whiny, making the biggest fuss about everything. Sam was more sullen than ever. I thought that now he knew about his father's affair he would be nicer to me, sympathetic even, but instead I felt unfairly judged by him. I wanted his support, but he was a child and he needed mine. They both did, but I couldn't cope with them. I couldn't face their grief and their worries as well as my own.

When your children are small you deal with their anxieties so easily; a cuddle for a nightmare, a plaster and a kiss for a sore knee. I treated them much the same in the face of this adult crisis. I relaxed rules, totally, for all of us. We ate pizza, and chips, from the freezer, and we ate when and where we wanted to eat. I had no space in my head for planning meals, nor could I bear their miserable faces around the table. Why force more misery upon them by making them eat vegetables when they didn't want to? What good was a bit of broccoli to us now? What was the point of enforcing structure, purely for structure's sake?

I let them stay up as late as they wanted, Ella as well as Sam. If I sent Ella to bed at her usual time she'd only keep coming back down again, wanting a glass of water, wanting comfort, like a small child again, fearing the dark. I stopped nagging about schoolwork, about getting off the computer, about tidying up. I stopped nagging full stop, and thus, all arguments with my children stopped too. In my head I could almost hear David saying to Sam, 'Have you done your homework, you've got GCSEs next year, don't forget,' just as I, deliberately, didn't say it.

And do you know what? I found life so much easier once I stepped back like this. Once I took my foot right off the parent pedal.

How zealous I had been before, how much energy I had wasted, fretting about everything. Now, I saw motherhood, and wifehood, and the whole great con of domestic sacrifice, as nothing but angst and failure. All that striving, and all that worrying, and for what?

I moved from day to day, numb. But within that numbness, in fact part of it, was a new freedom. The time of day no longer mattered, beyond the necessity of getting the kids to school and back but even there I stopped worrying about being late. 'Be grateful that I'm giving you a lift at all,' I said, if either of them complained. Most mornings we were late on their account anyway; the difference was that I no longer chased them. I couldn't care less if they couldn't find their books/PE kits/forgot their homework. That was their problem, not theirs to dump on me. I'd had enough of carrying everyone else's woes. I made Ella's packed lunch, and I drove them both to school. I collected them again. I fed them, sort of. That was it. I backed off completely. I felt the lightness in my hands. Numb. Free.

It's not that I didn't love them. I did love them, with all my heart, as always. But for the last however many years my life had been all about them, and David, and the servicing and facilitating of the family unit. I was housekeeper, cook, chauffeur, planner and PR, and how diligently I had tended to it all. I was the cement holding the family together and the donkey dragging it on. But did any of us really want that any more? I didn't want it, certainly; I didn't want the shabby remains. As for my kids, what good would it do them having me pretend that we were carrying on as normal, a family still, with all its ridiculous, unnecessary rules? Rules not imposed by David especially, any more than by me, but by our combined expectation of how family life should be for nice, middle-class people like us. You think you have no rules, but you do. What you eat, the way that you eat; where you shop. The language you use when you speak and the tone of your voice; even the way that you argue. The programmes you admit to watching on TV and the other programmes that you watch in secret. The programmes that you let your kids watch; the token division of chores, times spent on homework, the careful rationing of screen time. The way you line up your shoes in the hall and the colour of your toilet paper. The way you arrange fruit in that ceramic bowl on the kitchen table, and stick your flowers in that earthenware jug. They're all rules. And they no longer applied.

I was more grateful for Melanie's friendship than ever. Everyone seemed to know that all was not well between David and me, from old Mr Arnold up the lane with his wry nod of the head and his, 'Ah, well, ah well,' to all those women at the school gates. You can't keep secrets in a place like this. Once one knew, they all knew. I hated the looks and the comments, and the thought of them all talking behind my back.

'How are you managing?' was a question I heard too often, however kindly meant. 'Will you be staying here?' was another.

'Take no notice,' Melanie said. 'It gives them something to talk about, that's all.'

She took me under her wing, like a broken chick. She took charge. I didn't need to vent my hurt or anger about David in her presence because she understood how I felt, and boxed my feelings into manageable chunks. Whereas left to my own devices I would have swung from weeping on my bed with a clutch of David's left-behind clothes in my arms one minute to ripping up those same clothes with my bare hands the next, she simply gathered up a pile of his socks and T-shirts and oddments that had slipped through with the rest of the laundry and now languished like a bad reminder on the stairs, and stuffed them in the outside bin.

'Don't need that lot cluttering up the place,' she said.

And if she phoned on a Sunday evening after David had gone and could tell by my voice that I had been both drinking and crying, she'd get in her car and drive straight over. She wouldn't take my glass away, she'd pour me another. She'd tell my miserable children to give me a break and sort themselves out for the evening, close the living-room door on them and settle herself on the sofa with me and that bottle, and a film maybe; something funny or uplifting about women breaking away – you know the sort of thing.

On one such evening when she was round, Sam walked into the living room complaining that he'd got no clean PE kit and no clean uniform for school on Monday. Ordinarily, this would have lead to some sort of exchange of blame and guilt between Sam and me, but when I opened my mouth to speak Melanie beat me to it.

'Go and wash them then,' she said.

We were watching some corny road movie on DVD. The remote control was on the arm of the sofa by Melanie but she didn't pause the film, nor did she turn down the volume. She didn't even look at Sam as she spoke, but I did, and through my drunken blur I saw him hesitating there in the doorway with the colour creeping into his face, not sure what to do.

'I can't,' he said. 'They won't be dry by the morning.'

'Then you'll have to wear them dirty,' Melanie said brightly, still watching the TV.

Poor Sam. He stood there, so horribly uncomfortable. He looked at me – for what? A different answer? A solution to the crisis of the unwashed clothes? If it had been just me and him I might at least have tried to do something, but it wasn't just me and him, and so I sat there.

'Oh, Sam,' Melanie said, 'if you're going to the kitchen be a love and fetch us some more wine, would you?'

And when he left the room she looked at me, simultaneously laughing and rolling her eyes. 'How sweet is he?' she said. 'Worrying about his washing!'

I admired her blasé decisiveness. I let her prop me up.

It was Sam's birthday on 8 July, and in the general meltdown of family life there was a good chance that it might have been more or less overlooked apart from the false jollity of a few presents and cards and the agony of a telephone call from his father in London, but here, again, Melanie intervened.

We were round her house after school; it was the Tuesday, just three days before his birthday.

'So what are you doing for your birthday, Sam?' she asked over the background cacophony of shrieking girls and TV and Max's ambitious guitaring. 'Got to do something special for your fifteenth.'

Sam, as ever, blushed under her singular attention, and muttered an indecipherable reply.

'You want to have a party, Sam,' she said. 'Doesn't he, Max?' She raised her voice over the noise. 'Max! Sam wants to have a party for his fifteenth birthday!'

'Cool,' said Max. He rammed his fingers ear-jarringly over the guitar strings then flung the guitar to one side. Then he sat himself down on the arm of Melanie's sofa, right up close to her, and beamed at us with his wide, cat-like smile.

One of us – Sam, or me, I do not remember which – started mumbling stuff such as, 'I'm not sure' and, 'it's a bit short notice,' but our excuses were feeble, and hopelessly without effect.

'Go on,' Melanie insisted, steamrollering over any objections. 'It's just what Sam needs. Cheer him up a bit.'

Sam, who is not, never has been, and I am sure never will

be remotely the party animal, squirmed like a mouse in a trap. I felt for him. Inwardly, I was squirming too.

'Oh you two,' Melanie said, picking up on our unease. 'Don't you worry. We'll help you. Won't we, Max? Max will know who to invite.'

And Max grinned at us, 100 per cent his mother's son.

So that Friday, whether he wanted it or not, Sam had a party at our house. Max did the inviting; really, it was his party, with Sam as a sort of mascot for the night. I'd hoped they'd be outside but that night it was pouring with rain, and so there were probably fifty kids, boys and girls, squeezed into our den, spilling over into the living room, and some of them, as the night wore on, disappearing upstairs.

Ella was staying over with Abbie. I could, perhaps, have sat it out in my bedroom with a book, but I didn't want to be hidden away. I wanted a chance to see the kids, to put names to faces. Also, I thought my presence would ensure some order. So I loitered in the kitchen, in a state of tension. I remembered all too well the parties I'd been to as a teenager, and for that reason alone I never thought I would be hosting a party in my house, for my own teenager. But then I never thought I would be alone, either, while their father lived elsewhere with somebody else.

The kids brought their own alcohol and took it into the den with them, some quite openly, some half-heartedly hiding it under their jackets. Not too much, I hoped, but I didn't see how I could stop them. Sam was young in his year, and many of the others were closer to sixteen. Some of them wandered into the kitchen from time to time, but they didn't stay long, not with me sitting there. A few even helped themselves to the soft drinks that I'd naively stacked on the counter.

Midway through, Sam walked in, his face white with, I presumed, the effort of it all. I sent him back impatiently. 'Go on,' I said, 'just enjoy yourself.'

Steadily, I drank my way through one bottle of wine and the best part of another, and thus I loosened up a little. I made myself relax. They'd got the music cranked up frighteningly loud in the den but not loud enough to kill the screeching laughter of one girl from somewhere upstairs in my house, and the equally piercing weeping of another, nor the dreaded death-groan of vomiting from the bathroom. I told myself it was to be expected; it was no big deal. And I thought how uptight David would have been if he'd been there.

Gradually, they started pouring into the kitchen en masse in search of more drink, some of them in search of food. Somewhere around midnight I had the toaster on, popping up one round after another, while these kids I'd never even met before sat around my table tucking into toast and butter, toast and jam. They filled my house with their chatter and their laughter. Some were drunk; some quite hideously so. I made them drink water, I saw that they were OK. It is a horrible truth that it easier to be kinder to other people's kids than it is to your own. And besides, who was I to judge them when I was probably quite drunk myself?

Sam lurked in the background. I knew he was there but I don't actually remember seeing him. I was busy with his friends, or rather, Max's friends. Max moved around the kitchen beside me, totally at home. He passed me bread from the freezer, he passed me plates. He said, 'Oh thanks, Jane, you're too good to us,' as I turned on the oven for chips. He was more comfortable in my house that night than my own son. And, it would seem, more comfortable around me.

Many of them stayed over. They had no choice out there where there was no transport, no way home at all but for a willing parent, dragged out too late on those dark, forbidding roads. They slept on the floor of the den, mostly; some in the living room. Some migrated upstairs to the comfort of Sam's and Ella's beds; Sam himself was relegated to his bedroom floor. For a time, there were two boys and a girl fast asleep on my own bed. I told myself I didn't mind, that I was fine with this, as I moved them off good-naturedly, seeing them settled elsewhere. And then I lay down for a while with my heart pounding, exhausted. It seemed the party would go on all night. The music boomed out from downstairs, it stopped, it boomed out again.

I remember, vaguely, walking about my house in the early hours, checking that everyone was OK. I turned semi-unconscious boys onto their sides; I found blankets to tuck over girls. I didn't sleep; not at all. Too soon the sun rose in the sky. The wine that I'd drunk had shrunk my brain into a hard, dry nut, rattling inside my skull, yet I was still on a strange, fragile high. Slowly, they began to rouse, some more readily than others. Doors banged, toilets flushed. Again, they found their way to my kitchen, but oh so subdued now. Among the empty bottles and sticky spills and last night's toast plates I made tea, filling the cups on rotation. There was no more bread. Some ferreted in the cupboards in search of cereal and biscuits; they ate whatever they could find. Many didn't want to eat at all. Soon they started drifting off in threes and fours, squeezing themselves into the cars that pulled up outside to collect them, and then there were just Sam and me, the mess and the slight bewilderment that this had gone on in my house at all.

*

I thought the party would make Sam happy. I thought he would be grateful that I had done this for him. I especially thought so as I cleaned up the disgusting mess in both my bathrooms and struggled to remove dry vomit from the carpet in the den. What other mother would be so relaxed, so tolerant? Wasn't he lucky, that he had me?

Wasn't he?

'Your father would never have put up with this,' I said, feeling the need to ram it home.

He was tired, miserably so. He's never been good with late nights, my Sam. He staggered through the day like a zombie, no help at all with anything. In his tiredness he seemed angry with me; petulant, like a small child. And I felt irritated with him now that his friends had all gone.

Later, Melanie turned up, bringing Ella home. She had Abbie with her, and also Max, who'd got a lift back home earlier with somebody else. They arrived at just that point in the afternoon when I thought I might literally collapse with exhaustion, yet their presence tripped me over into a new lease of life. I was so wired I was shaking.

'Look at you,' Melanie said. 'I think you could do with a drink.'

She picked up a half-empty bottle in the kitchen, sniffed it, and poured us both a glass.

'I had no sleep,' I said emphatically.

She said, 'Max said it was a good party.'

Abbie had gone upstairs with Ella. I assumed that Max had gone off too, in search of Sam, but then there he was, joining us in the kitchen.

'Yes,' he said. 'Excellent party.'

Unlike Sam, he seemed remarkably together. He slouched against the counter by the sink, still in last night's clothes. I remember that; and I remember thinking how strange it was that I should notice. Max's hair is thick and straight; it fell across his forehead heavy and unwashed. His skin had a slight sheen to it, and above his top lip was the dark hint of the need for a shave.

'Was it OK?' I said, fussing now, unable to be still. I shoved all those empty cans into a bin bag, to stick out for recycling. The metal clamoured against my ears. The dishwasher was open. I squeezed in a couple more plates, a cup, the knives left lying around covered in jam, then stuck in a tablet and slammed the door. The machine cranked and groaned into life. Then I stood still and sipped my wine, suddenly light-headed.

'Excellent,' Max said again, so calm, so easy.

'I'm surprised you're not at home sleeping,' I said to him. 'My Sam's completely shattered.'

'No stamina,' he said with a smile.

'This is a good house for a party,' Melanie said.

'It is,' I agreed. 'They were in the den most of the time. It's perfect for them. That's what we thought when we bought this house – that the den would be perfect for teenagers.' I twittered on, hyper now, unable to stop. 'You should make use of it,' I said to Max. 'You and the others. Come here at weekends. Come and use our den.'

'Well it's somewhere for them to go,' Melanie said, clearly amused.

And Max lolled against my kitchen cabinets, grinning at me. 'I'll bear it in mind,' he said.

David came up on Sunday. He walked into the ongoing after-party lull, a cold judge of a man. I'd more or less finished clearing up by then, though the smell of booze hung heavily on the air still, clinging to the furniture and the carpet. The empty bottles and cans were stacked outside the front in the box for recycling and I'd stripped the sheets off the beds, though we, Sam and I, were still horribly tired.

'You've had a party,' David said, a faint note of reproach in the observation. And I wished then that it had been my own party; that I'd found myself a hundred local friends suddenly and that we'd had a wild, debauched time of it, drinking, dancing, and whatever else, but without him.

'Sam had a party,' I said.

'Sam?' He looked around him, bemused. 'But there are loads of beer cans out the front. And bottles.'

'I know.' I'd got myself a cup of tea, and I sat at the kitchen table, drinking it. The kids were both in their rooms. Neither of them had come charging to the door to greet him on his arrival. They used to do that quite often when he lived with us, back in London; here too, at first. Now, when he came, they slunk away like cats. They pined for him in the week, but come Sunday they'd have to be coaxed out of their rooms. They wanted to see him and then they didn't, for the simple reason that each visit would end with him leaving again. It would, always, end in tears.

Was David aware of this? Of course he was. It was there in the shadows around his eyes, and in the nervous, apologetic way that he moved within the familiar unfamiliarity of his own home.

'You've lost weight,' I said. 'Isn't she feeding you properly?' The sarcasm in my voice hit the walls and bounced back at me, sharp in my ears.

David ignored it. He just said, 'How many of them were here?'

'I don't know,' I said. 'I didn't take numbers.'

'But you let them drink.'

'David, they're fifteen. Some of them are nearly sixteen.'

'Was Ella here?' he said.

'No,' I said, wearily. 'She stayed at her friend's.'

I'd finished my tea now. I just wanted to go and lie down. I looked at David, standing there so out of place in my kitchen, his face tight with disapproval, and annoyance flicked its way up my spine. Who was he to walk in and take the moral high ground, now?

'Was Sam drinking?' he asked.

And I just said, 'I really don't know, David. Why don't you go and ask him yourself?'

EIGHTEEN

Over the summer, barely a weekend went by without at least some of Sam's friends turning up, for either the Friday or the Saturday night. Sometimes it was just Max, or Max and Tommy, or Max and Tommy and Will. Other times there were more of them, holed up out there in the den, having themselves a little party. Usually they'd stay over, piling onto the sofa bed, or crashing out in sleeping bags on the floor.

I bought them beer. After all, as Melanie said, it was better that they should drink in my den than out in a field somewhere. When she said that I was shocked, not so much by her words as by the ease with which she said them, her acceptance that that was just what boys did. As if at least at my house they'd have a roof over their heads, they'd be out of the rain. The thought of my Sam ever lying drunk in an open field horrified me. It wouldn't happen. It musn't happen. But if he was out with his friends, how would I know where he was? How would I know what he would have to do, to go along with the crowd? And how would I ever find him, if they left him out there somewhere, alone? Horror at the sheer endlessness of the night around here flashed through my head, the remoteness, the darkness, going on and on, blanketing the land.

So I bought the beer, in an attempt to feel control where I had none. And I heated them up pizza, and took it into the den on big plates. If they were watching a film I'd perch myself on the arm of the sofa and stay there a while, joining in. I might have a drink with them. They were nice to me, those kids. 'Oh thanks, Jane,' they'd say when I came in with a tray piled with snacks, or fetched them some cans. And to Sam, 'Your mum's so cool.'

I'd always wanted Sam to be popular, to be part of a group. I wanted my son to be the sort of teenager who had friends forever in and out of the house, not the sort that cut himself off and lived in gloomy isolation. And it seemed more important than ever now.

But Sam would never arrange anything without prompting from me. Round at Melanie's after school I'd say, 'So, are you guys coming round our house at the weekend?' I'd throw it out as a general enquiry, looking from Max to Sam and back to Max as I said it, but we all knew that the question was directed at Max. We all knew it would be up to him to tell the others, and to get them to come.

Sam hated me doing this. He thought I was interfering. He'd scowl at me, say, 'Mum,' in a shut up hiss.

But I'd laugh it off. I'd say, 'Come on, Sam. Max doesn't mind me asking, do you, Max?'

And Max, who was always entertained by Sam's awkwardness, would laugh too.

Whatever I did, I did it for Sam. I knew that he still struggled to fit in. I only had to see him with those other boys who'd all known each other all their lives to see that he was never really at ease. I'm not so stupid as to think that Sam was the big attraction when they came to our house. I knew that they were there at least partly for the beer, and the convenience of the den. But if they came here, it meant Sam was included. There was always the fear that if they went somewhere else they might leave him out. That was my fear at least, and I assumed it was Sam's too.

Having those kids here at the weekend was good for me too. They brought laughter into my house, and noise; I found their presence strangely comforting. They alleviated my loneliness, for a little while.

Because believe me I was lonely. A couple of times on a Saturday night I'd left both my kids at home and driven over to Melanie's and gone to the pub with her, but I'd hated every minute of it. I didn't know anyone there, apart from Melanie, and I felt as if everyone was looking at me. In truth, I felt they thought I was on the pick-up. Available again. This wasn't helped by the fact that Melanie had started seeing some guy and flirted with him all night. Not Colin, someone else. It seemed that Colin was fine with this, that they were all friends together. Yet I couldn't help feeling the intention was for me to pair up with someone too. 'Relax,' Melanie said. 'Go on, live a bit.' I'd avoided going to that pub with David, because I knew he would have hated it. Yet there I was without him, hating it even more. And I still had the dreaded drive home.

If Sam's friends were all coming to my house, it gave me an excuse to stay in. I don't think Melanie cared. I think she was too busy, by then, with her new man. In truth it probably suited her to have Max so much at our house, out of the way. Most weekends I'd have Abbie staying, too. That summer, her children practically lived with us.

*

Sometimes, when David turned up on a Sunday, a couple of boys might still be here from the night before. Max would often be here, loafing about the place as if he owned it. It amused me that Max could wander into the kitchen right in front of David, and casually help himself to food from the fridge, as relaxed as anything while David, in contrast, was totally *un*relaxed. David arrived like an awkward visitor, unsure of his welcome. There was no welcome. There couldn't be.

If Max was here, Sam would barely acknowledge his dad. In fact David's arrival made him uncomfortable. How could he perform for his friend in the required manner, and simultaneously perform for his father? He couldn't. The two objectives were incompatible for a self-conscious 15-year-old. And it was Max that Sam needed to get along with, day in, day out.

And Ella took the lead from her brother. If he was cool towards David, then she was too. If Sam acknowledged David with just a bored, no-eye-contact hello, she'd do the same. If he answered, 'Fine,' when his dad asked him how he was, so would she. A shrug of the shoulder; an end to the conversation before it had even begun. Poor David. That left him with me.

'How are things?' he'd say, as if he really cared, but I didn't want his charity, his blood-money concern. 'Is there anything I can do while I'm here?' he'd ask, looking out at the garden, at the overgrown lawn. He'd look at the state of the house, full stop. He'd register how much things had changed. The towels left hanging over the banister, the shoes and school bags and God knows whatever else left cluttering up the hall. The plates piling up in the kitchen, the wine bottles stacked around the sink, and yes, the beer cans left lying around in the den.

'We're fine,' I'd say, though clearly he thought that we weren't.

Perhaps, in some perverse way, I got pleasure from seeing the discomfort on his face as he sat there on his sofa, in his house that was no longer his home. If things were acceptable now that weren't acceptable before, what right had he to complain?

'I don't think Sam should be drinking,' he said to me one Sunday when he was here.

I didn't care what he thought. In fact, whatever he thought, I would automatically think the opposite. I took up my new stance, easy come, easy go.

I laughed at him. 'Don't you?' I said.

'No, I don't,' he said, all the more uptight because I wasn't. 'He's only just fifteen. He's only a child.' And then, ruining it all for himself, he said, 'He's got GCSEs next year.'

He looked at me, so intent with his righteousness, then, my erstwhile husband, and I looked at him. How familiar were his eyes. I had known him for almost twenty years. I had lived with him, dreamed with him, borne him his children. When his mother died, he cried in my arms. When his father remarried, the same. When Ella was a baby, he paced the house with her, hour after hour, night after night, holding her tiny, fretful body clamped tight against his chest.

And here he was now, an alien to his own family, so removed. What right had he to judge me, or Sam, or any of us? None, as far as I was concerned. He'd given up all rights the moment he betrayed me.

'Sometimes,' I said, 'you are such a hypocrite. Would you have Sam being a hypocrite too? Would you? Would you have him out drinking in a field somewhere, miles from home? Because that's what they do, you know, boys of that age.'

How easily I quoted Melanie to him, how convincingly. I did it, in part, to distance myself from David, and the soured memory of our lives together; from all that we'd shared and done and believed in. How could I carry on as before, half of what we'd been? I couldn't. I had to find myself a new way.

Yet David, for all that he'd left us, was still stuck in the old place.

'We moved here for the children,' he said, the sudden bitterness in his voice making him sound petty and mean. 'We moved here because you wanted better schools and a healthy, a wholesome environment for our children. We moved here for that. We gave up *everything*. A better life for the children, you said. But, tell me, how is this better?'

'It isn't my fault that you left us,' I said.

'I don't mean that,' he said, frustration tightening his face. 'I'm not talking about that.' He paused. He looked around him, casting his eyes about the place as if in doing so I would know what he was referring to. 'I'm talking about Sam, about our son,' he said. 'Drinking. How come that's OK with you? And who are these boys that seem to be forever in the house?'

'They're his friends,' I said. 'Would you rather he didn't have any?'

'I'd rather they weren't drinking alcohol,' he said. 'I'd rather he was working hard at school, playing football, doing normal 15-year-old things.'

'For God's sake,' I snapped. 'He has a social life. Lucky him.'

David shook his head, as though in disbelief. 'You used to worry endlessly about the schools in London and the wrong sort of peer pressure,' he said. 'Yet here you are, encouraging Sam to lead exactly the sort of life that you had us leave London to get away from. So what was it all for then, Jane?'

'I left London to get away from the constant, exhausting competitiveness,' I said. 'From all that "my kid's better than your kid" stuff that got rammed down my throat everyday.'

'We left London to get away from that school Sam was in,' he said, correcting me. 'But now I don't see that it would have been any different.'

'Of course it would have been. Things are so much more relaxed here.'

'You can say that again.' We were sitting in the living room, David on the sofa, leaning forward with his elbows on his knees, hands clasped. His left leg was juddering, caught on a nerve, or in irritation. The force of his resentment took me back somewhat. Wasn't I was the one who should be angry? Didn't I have the monopoly on all emotion, now?

'I want Sam to do well at school,' he said, stressing the words. 'Of course I want him to have friends but I don't want him hanging around drinking, at his age. Just because I'm not here . . . I still want what's best for him.'

And there it was; my hook. I caught it. I flung it back at him.

'Well you weren't thinking what was best for him when you decided to shack up with your Diana, were you?' I said.

David left, as ever, on a bad note. I could never let him go with any peace. My pride and my hurt wouldn't let me. He came, we all suffered, he went away again and we suffered more.

The irony was that Sam didn't actually drink very much. He'd have a can to fit in with his friends, but he'd make it last all evening. I think he'd have been happier with a coke. Maybe they'd all have been happy with cokes, but I bought them beer. I thought I was one step ahead, keeping down with the kids.

NINETEEN

My parents came to stay for a few days in the middle of August. So far, I'd managed to avoid telling them about David and me. One advantage of living further away was that it made it easier to pretend, and I'd dodged their questions on the phone. 'How is David?' my mum asked every time I spoke to her, and, more probingly, 'Is everything all right?'

'David's fine,' I'd say, because as far as I knew he was fine, physically at least. And as to everything being all right, I'd misunderstand her meaning, deliberately. 'Just busy,' I'd say. 'A bit tired, you know. Rushing the kids around.' That sort of thing.

But my parents are not fools, and their antennae were up. Sometimes, when my mum rang, one of the children would answer the phone. No doubt she quizzed them, though not directly of course. She was far too sensitive to ask them anything outright, but she'd have gathered enough fuel to build her suspicions.

They'd have to know eventually, but the thought of telling them brought with it such an air of formality, and of finality too. It made it real, and it made it their business, when I didn't want it to be their business. Also, and this really is the truth now, I was ashamed. My husband had gone off with another woman: what did that say about me? I couldn't bear the thought of anyone, let alone my parents, speculating, or judging me, or, worse than that, pitying me.

So I dreaded seeing them, because I dreaded telling them, and therefore I was off with them from the minute they arrived. I was defensive; I couldn't help myself. They pulled up in the car mid-afternoon on a hot, humid Tuesday, worn and tired from the journey, expecting me to greet them with my usual show of flowers in the hall and chilled drinks waiting in the garden, and the smell of a freshly baked cake. My lovely home all spic and span. Oh sure, I'd swept the floor and tidied up the kitchen, changed the sheets on my bed, where they would be sleeping, and thrown the spare duvet down for myself, in the den. But my house was suffused with an air of defiant gloom; it lay over everything, thick as dust. They would have noticed it as soon as they walked in.

Looking back, I see how cowardly I was, and really how cruel, leaving them to work it out for themselves. They went up to my room to settle themselves in, and there they discovered the absence of David's things. My parents travel light but even so I would always clear a space for them in my wardrobe, and tidy the clutter away from the top of my chest of drawers. But all of David's things were gone; what he hadn't taken with him, and what I couldn't bring myself to chuck out, I'd stuffed into boxes and hidden in the cupboard in the hall. My parents would have noticed the lack of *anything* of his hanging in the huge double wardrobe, or folded on the shelves above and below. I can picture them tentatively opening the drawers and seeing some of them filled with my various clothes and others left empty; I had not yet reached the stage where I was ready to expand into the extra space.

They were up there an awfully long time, and they were very quiet. I can imagine them sitting on my bed, forced to think the unthinkable, shocked, as the penny must finally have dropped, and I am not proud. I am not proud at all.

Yet with my parents I will always be a child, and I behaved like one. Too well I remember the teenage embarrassment of them wanting to know each time I'd got a new boyfriend, or had just broken up with one; of their over-concerned questions and over-personal intonations that they hoped I was being 'sensible'; the mortification of them realizing I was actually having sex. Well how much worse – how infinitely much worse – would it be to have to tell them that my marriage was over?

But was it over, totally, finally? I didn't want to believe it myself: how could I possibly present it that way to them? I couldn't. I didn't want to talk about it all. I wanted just to drift, and to be left to do so.

My father came down first, the advance patrol. It was always that way, in times of crises. He tracked me down in the kitchen, where I was waiting for him, as sulky and defensive as a 16-year-old girl. My mother, I knew, would be sitting on my bed, anxiously waiting another five minutes till she too would come down. My father was the calm one, the practical one, the one who took charge. He'd want answers, facts, and it was always deemed in our family that he would do better by tackling me alone. My mother brought too much emotion into it. Any drama, in our family, ended up being hers.

I was washing a lettuce at the kitchen sink, a task that demanded my total attention as this lettuce was from the garden, and riddled with slugs. My father came and leaned against the counter next to me. I kept my eyes focused on that lettuce.

'Everything all right, pet?' he said.

'So many bloody slugs,' I said, and turned the tap on harder.

My father stood there. He watched me. Ten, twenty, excruciating seconds passed. Where were the children when I wanted them, why weren't they clamouring about their grandparents as they used to, competing for attention, giving me my space? But Sam and Ella had slunk off to their own aloneness, wanting their space too now, making the effort for no one. That is how it was, these days.

'Your mother –' my dad said, and it was the same as always: your mother wondered, your mother was thinking, your mother was a little bit concerned – 'Your mother couldn't help noticing there are none of David's things in the bedroom.'

I said nothing. I scrubbed at that lettuce as if it was a rag.

'What's going on, pet?'

I could hear the floorboards creaking upstairs, the gentle thud of my mother's step on the stairs. She couldn't keep away any longer. Ridiculously, infuriatingly, I felt the sharp sting of tears. What is it with families? They strip you naked as the day you were born. They see everywhere; no secrets, no hiding away.

The lump in my throat swelled, hot and wet as a giant leech.

'Come on, pet. You can tell us.'

My mother entered the kitchen with a quiver of indrawn breath. 'What is it, Ray? What's going on?' she asked of my father, her voice feebly high, half sob, half plea.

'All right, Lynne,' he said. 'Everything's under control. Jane was about to tell me. Weren't you, Jane?'

I stared at my lettuce, at the water running off its leaves, an eternal, ferocious fountain. I willed myself away. I willed myself anywhere; anywhere, anything, but this. The sound of my mother's shaking breath sent the tears chugging down my cheeks, beyond my control.

'He's left me,' I said, staring down at my lettuce.

'What do you mean, he's left you?' my mother demanded and oh how that phrase could resonate down the years with just a minor change, here or there. 'What do you mean, you've lost your bag/coat/key?' Only this time, it was my husband I'd so carelessly mislaid.

'For somebody else,' I said, forcing out the words over a mouthful of stones.

My mother drew in her breath, then flung her arms around me, almost pulling me off balance. She cried into my neck, as if that made things any better, this outward pouring of distress.

'Oh no,' she wailed. 'Oh no. My poor Jane.'

They sat me at the table, fetched tissues – for my mother's benefit as much as mine – made me tea, and fussed, bombarding me with their questions and concern, and with their own hurt that I'd kept it from them. I cried, the way I always cried when forced to cry in the presence of my parents: till my nose was blocked and my eyes two tight and swollen slits, my head throbbing and my dignity utterly squashed. I hated being made to feel so vulnerable.

'Why didn't you tell us?' my mum kept saying, over and over. 'How could you keep it from us?'

'You should have told us, pet. We have a right to know.'

And how chastised I felt, sitting there at my own table. 'I didn't want to talk about it,' I said, though there was little chance of getting away with that now. 'To anyone.'

'I'm not just anyone! I'm your mother. You can talk to me.'

'I didn't want to involve you,' I said.

'But we are involved! He's our son-in-law!' Her voice rose on a wail and the hairs on the back of my neck shot up like little pinpricks. 'Oh my good grief, how could he do this to you?'

'Hush now, Lynne,' my dad said. 'We don't know what went on.'

'I want to know!'

'Of course you do. We both do.'

'Why would he go off with another woman when he's got his lovely family? Why would he do that?'

'I don't know, Lynne,' my father said. 'I don't know.' But then, as if he did know, as if it was blindingly obvious and simply anyone would know it, 'It doesn't do for a man to work such long hours, to be away from home so much, to be away from the family. It puts a strain on the marriage . . .'

They discussed me as if I wasn't there. I felt like a bystander in my own life. And it got worse as the week went on; they had planned to stay until Saturday, and leave after lunch, thus spending time with David, with all of us, as a family. But that had all changed now. Should they stay on until Sunday, and see David when he came? But could they trust themselves, given what he had done?

'He needs a piece of my mind,' my mother said. 'A jolly good talking-to.'

'We need to sit down and discuss things properly,' my father said. 'Sensibly.'

I said, 'I don't want to discuss anything.'

'And where's that attitude going to get you?' my mother demanded. 'What about the children? What's going to happen to them?'

'Nothing's going to happen to them,' I said.

'Children need stability,' she said. 'They need their father.'

'Well there's not much I can do about that,' I said.

'Of course there is! You and David need to talk about things. You need to sort things out.'

'Oh, Mum, please.'

'Your mother's right,' my dad said in the same tone that he'd have used to tell me my skirt was too short, or that I needed to be home by eleven, all those years ago. 'You need to make plans.'

Plans, plans. Conversations with my parents generally involved plans of one type or another; plans about what I wanted and what I wanted to do. Ever since I'd left college: my plans for my career, then my marriage, the arrival of my children. All my plans for Sam and Ella, and for David's career, and eventually our move out here to our new country life: always something, always onwards and upwards. My sunny existence; what pleasure it had brought them. It had all ground to a halt now. I'd no desire to make any more plans.

On previous visits they'd loved their little trips into the town, their walks to the village, just being here. I'd made it like a show piece: the chocolate-box country life. This time, I had doubly cheated them. No chocolate-box life and no happy marriage. Now, of course, with the benefit of time and distance I can see how selfishly I behaved, and how dismissive I was of their feelings and their sense of loss. But at the time I was too full of my own, and having my parents there and being forced to talk about it just made it worse. I didn't want to talk about it. Or think about it. Or make plans.

We struggled through to Saturday. The children bristled away from my parents, too aware of their sympathy. My father tidied up the garden, my mother fussed about the house. They wanted me to talk it through but I wouldn't. I didn't want to go over it again and again, reliving it all for them. They wanted to support me, but I pushed them away. It felt too much to me like they needed my support, and I couldn't give it. I had no answers, no great visions of what I was going to do now. I couldn't wait for them to just go, and leave me alone.

But I felt wretched then, watching them loading up their car on Saturday morning. They looked so defeated and sad. My mother hugged the children for far too long.

'My poor girl,' she said to Ella, who she clasped in her arms like a rag doll. 'You can always talk to Granny, you know. I'm just a phone call away.'

And to Sam, who stood rigid as a skittle when it was his turn to be hugged, 'Be a brave boy. Look after your mum.'

'For God's sake, Mum,' I snapped. 'No one's died.'

'No,' she said. 'Right.' She held back from embracing me, clearly hurt. But she did, bizarrely, say, 'Does David's father know?'

'I don't know,' I said. I see David's father once a year at most and we rarely speak in between. He and David are not exactly close; my mum knows this.

'And his sister?'

'I don't know,' I repeated. 'I certainly haven't told her. That's up to David, surely.'

'You can't keep a thing like this secret,' she said. 'Other people are affected too.'

'Then what would you have me do?' I said. 'Put out a general announcement?'

She clamped shut her mouth, a thin miserable line. Her eyes, which avoided mine, were glistening with tears.

'Jane!' my father said.

And I said, 'I'm sorry, OK?'

Just past my mum, Sam was already creeping backwards to the house, step by miniature step, obviously hoping no one would notice. Ella, on the other hand, listened to every word, intrigued.

'Well,' my mother said stiffly. 'Love to you all.' And she got into the car, wiping at her eyes.

My dad quickly squeezed me, and kissed my cheek. 'Look after yourself,' he said. 'And the kids.'

Feeling guilty now, I said, 'Are you sure you won't stay for lunch?'

'Best to get back before the traffic,' he said. He looked as if he was about to say something else then, but thought better of it. How old he looked, suddenly, my dad. Disappointment and uncertainty do that to people. I've noticed that. They age you even more.

I watched them as they drove away, pulling the car so slowly into the lane.

Ella, watching also, said, 'Granny was upset.'

'We're all upset,' I said.

'Yes but grandparents aren't supposed to be upset. They're supposed to be happy all the time.'

'Oh, Ella,' I said. 'No one can be happy all the time.'

We started walking back into the house, and she said, 'Is Daddy still coming tomorrow?'

'Yes,' I said. 'As far as I know.'

And I thought that was that, the question answered. But once inside the house, and just before she disappeared upstairs, she said, 'I wish Daddy still lived here. I do. And I know Granny wishes it too. And Sam.'

And then she ran up to her room, slamming the door behind her.

*

I felt as if I was being suffocated. I walked through my house, hot, clammy, my chest an explosion of tears. I didn't know what to do with myself. I could feel my heartbeat, pounding in my head. My feet stuck to the tiles of the floor, I was so hot. I sat down at the kitchen table and cried like a kettle boiling over. There was no one to comfort me, no one to care. The children, as ever, were in their rooms, doors shut, shutting me out. I'd wanted my parents to go but now that they had I felt so glaringly alone. I pictured them, slowly winding their way through the country lanes in their beige Rover, their faces drawn and rejected. I could see them on the motorway, joining the crawl of the slow lane, discussing me for all the hours it would take them to get home. I could feel the scale of their disappointment. I had torn the security of their expectations for me away from them. I had been horrible. And now they were gone.

I looked around my kitchen at the trappings of my life and I hated everything. The rustically painted blue cupboard doors, the overblown sideboard stacked with crockery and these days God knows what other crap, the AGA, and all the other either helpful or just plain pretentious symbols of the country idyll. What was the point of any of it? Who was I trying to kid? Who was still there to kid? The life I'd so wanted was now stifling me, slapping itself in my face, rubbing my nose in it as my mother would say.

An image of David ripped through my head, sudden, unwanted. I could see him as clearly as if he was there, his handsome face so relaxed, so free of us. I thought of him in London, enjoying all the delights of the city on this fine summer's day, with the other woman, so unencumbered.

I got up from the table. I opened a bottle of wine, and within the next fifteen minutes or so I had drunk it. Do you know how quiet it is in the country? It was a Saturday, for God's sake; a day for shopping and getting out and about, for seeing friends, going to sports matches, cafés, the cinema, for enjoying your precious, hard-earned weekend in your precious and oh-so-short life. I sat at my table, spent from tears and alcohol, and my world was filled with utter silence.

Then the phone rang, cutting into my misery. I ignored it at first because I was too suddenly drunk and too numb to do otherwise. But it rang and it rang. Eventually I pushed back my chair and stumbled over to the dresser to answer it.

'Hello,' I said, the demands of the real world pulling me up, sharp.

It was Melanie, though it took a while for me to know it. It took her a while to speak. I imagine she was taking in the many layers of my hello. I held the phone against my ear and the silence batted in my head. And then she spoke, like a saviour, my only friend in all the world.

'I'm coming over,' she said.

She brought Max and Ella with her, two bottles of wine, a packet of biscuits and some sausages.

'Lunch,' she said. 'Bet you haven't had any.'

Lunch turned out to be dinner by the time we got round to making it, finding a few old potatoes to bake in the Aga along with the sausages, a tin of baked beans and some pasta that we mixed with a jar of pesto from the back of the cupboard. We'd drunk one of the bottles of wine by then and I'd moved on from drunkenness into that thin altered state in which you can drink and drink and never feel the escape again. I functioned robotically, doling out food for the kids, shoving some into myself. We sat out at the table on the patio, Melanie and me, sat there as the sun went down, talking, drinking, and in my case, intermittently crying.

'Don't let him do this to you,' Melanie said. 'You've got to be strong.'

But I didn't feel strong. I felt trampled, utterly ground into the dirt.

The girls came out for a while, hanging around us as girls do when there's an adult drama to behold; they played on the swing, surreptitiously listening and watching, until they got bored and wandered off to climb up the hill. We could see them from where we sat, two little stick figures silhouetted against the dusk. The boys were in the house; through the open windows came the fairground crackle and blare of some Xbox game or other, and the tinny guitaring of Sam's latest CD, played over and over.

At some point, when it was almost dark, Max came out and joined us. He'd got himself a beer from the fridge, and he sat himself down at the table with us to drink it, quite at ease in our company in a way in which Sam could never be.

'What's Sam doing?' I asked.

'Sulking probably,' he said with a grin. 'I just thrashed him at Halo.'

'Go and get the girls down, will you, Max?' Melanie said.

'Yeah, yeah,' he said. 'In a minute.'

He expected us to carry on talking while he was there, and Melanie did so, including him in our conversation as if it was the most natural thing in the world. I wished my kids were like that; that they'd sit down and join in instead of being so separate. I especially wished Sam was like that. But it was just one irony in a long list of cruel ironies that the more I craved Sam's company, the less he wanted mine.

'Jane needs to get out more now, doesn't she, Max?' Melanie

said. 'She doesn't want to be stuck out here moping on her own.'

'That's right,' Max said.

'Need the loo,' Melanie said, and she went off inside.

When she was gone Max leant over and rubbed my arm.

'You'll be all right, Jane,' he said.

The contact startled me, the gesture itself. Sam would never do anything like that. Sam would never sympathize or empathize with me, or offer me comfort. Sam would not even talk to me. I looked at Max and he grinned at me, not the least embarrassed.

When Melanie came back out she said, 'You know what you need? You need a holiday.'

'Oh sure,' I said shakily. 'I can really manage that.'

'Of course you can. We'll all go. We'll go camping.'

'Camping?' I said, my head so groggy, so slow to follow.

'Yes,' she said. 'Next week. Last week of the holidays.'

'Cool,' Max said.

'We'll have a right laugh,' Melanie said.

'But we haven't booked anywhere,' I said, and Melanie and Max both looked at me like the out-of-Londoner that I was.

'We don't need to *book*,' Melanie said. 'We'll just pitch up. We'll drive down to Dorset. '

'We haven't even got a tent,' I said.

'Never mind that,' Melanie said. 'We've got a couple, haven't we, Max? Three if we take Jake's. Let's just pack up tomorrow and go.'

'David's coming tomorrow,' I said.

'Well can't you tell him not to? Can't you tell him you're going on holiday?'

'I don't know. The children want to see him.'

'The children want to see him?' Melanie said, her voice too sharp.

'Yes,' I said. 'I can't just cancel him.'

'You could if you wanted to.'

'I can't,' I said.

'OK then,' she said tightly.

'Right,' Max said. 'Think I'll go and fetch the girls down.'

'You do that,' Melanie said.

Now *she* was annoyed with me. I felt like I was drowning. Nothing was solid. Nothing was sure.

'Look,' I said. 'I do want to go camping. It's a great idea. Just not tomorrow.'

'Fine,' Melanie said. 'Then we'll go on Monday.'

Melanie, Max and Ella all stayed over that night. Melanie slept next to me on top of my bed in an old T-shirt of mine. It was oppressively hot, even with the windows wide open. I'd had far too much to drink but still I couldn't sleep. The wine had made my heart race and I felt too tense, touched with irrational anxiety. I'd downed two large glasses of water before coming upstairs, but my whole body was still horribly dehydrated, my insides pinched and dry.

Beside me, Melanie slept easily, her breath coming in short, faint snores. She'd collapsed back onto the bed and fallen asleep almost instantly, untroubled by all the issues that bothered me. I have never been able to just crash down anywhere, sleeping wherever and alongside whoever; not even back in my student days. I guard my privacy too tightly. And although this was my bed it didn't feel like it, with Melanie there, and with the scent of my parents still clinging to the sheets. I could smell the stuff my mother used on her hair on my pillow, and around me the familiar man-smell of my dad. And I felt hollowed out with loneliness.

I missed David. I missed the smell of him and the sound of him; I missed the security of the known. Memories of our time together before we moved here haunted me, and how very fine it all seemed now in retrospect, our shared life in our little house in our little street in London, especially those years back when Sam was small. We got by. We were happy then, before the demands for a better life started adding up. I'd been so quick to reject it all but now look at all that I'd lost. I'd been so sure of what I wanted when we moved here, but now I'd have given anything to wind the clock back. Yet who could I ever confess that to? Not my parents, whom I'd sent so miserably packing. I was far too proud. And not those friends back in London I'd too quickly lost touch with; how they would gloat now, if they knew about David and me. The last time I'd seen Karen I'd practically rammed it down her throat how blissfully happy we were out here; how could I tell her it had all gone so wrong?

But nor could I tell Melanie. It was a very particular picture I painted for Melanie but it was the picture that she wanted to see. David was all evil in her eyes; I was better off without him. She rallied me, supported me and she kept me going. Without Melanie my loneliness would have swallowed me whole. But I couldn't tell her that I missed David. Nor that I wished we'd never left London now. Oh no. She wouldn't have been quite so understanding then; I sensed that well enough.

TWENTY

Melanie and her kids were still here when David turned up on Sunday. She and I were hunting through the house for anything that might be useful to take with us, and stuffing it into my car. We are a family ill-equipped for camping, having only ever stayed in those ready-erected home-from-home tents on purpose-built sites in France, and that was just a few times, years ago when the kids were small. We'd a couple of sleeping bags, a torch, and some picnic plates and that was about it. Oh, and the infuriatingly hard-to-put-together camp beds that the kids slept on when Nicola and her family occasionally came to stay.

'Jesus,' Melanie said when she saw me lugging them down the stairs, their various poles sticking out of their too-tight sacks. 'What do you want them for?'

'I'm not sleeping on the ground,' I said.

'Our tent's going to be like the fucking Hilton,' she muttered, and Max, who'd just wandered out of the kitchen eating a piece of toast, smirked.

I wished I could do it better, the whole spontaneity thing. But I'd a thumping hangover, and I was just too wretched to do a convincing job of pretending otherwise.

'I'll just grab the pillows off our beds in the morning,' I said. 'And my duvet.'

'If you must,' Melanie said. 'Or I could lend you some sleeping bags.'

'Oh, OK. Thanks.' I'd rather have had my duvet, but perhaps sleeping bags would be better. 'What about food?' I said, trying to summon a little more enthusiasm.

'We can stop off on the way,' she said. 'Pick up one of those little barbecues.'

'I've got a cold bag somewhere,' I said.

And she said, 'Excellent.'

I felt like a child, trying to please her. I told myself I was doing this for my children, but in truth I was doing it because Melanie had said I should do it, because she had said it would be fun, and I was too weak, vulnerable and lonely to ever disagree with Melanie.

'Not much of a camper, is she, your mum?' Melanie said to Sam when he too came shuffling out of the kitchen, Max's pale and latent shadow. 'We'll have to show her how to have a good time, won't we, eh?'

And Sam smiled, nervously.

'Guess what, kids,' I'd bellowed at them late last night, the drink and its deceitful, miserable effects distorting my world and everything in it. 'We're going camping!'

Were they thrilled? Ella had seemed happy enough, but Sam, he looked just as I felt. Pinned against a wall. 'You will have a good time!' I'd thrust it upon him just as Melanie had thrust it upon me.

When I heard David's car drawing up outside I felt stupidly uneasy, with Melanie still there. I'd wanted her to be gone when he arrived. Like Sam, I found it too difficult to mix such opposite sides of my life.

'That's everything for now, I suppose,' I said, hoping she'd take it as a hint to leave. 'If I think of anything else I'll just stick it in the car.'

David's feet were on the gravel, his key in the door.

'He still has a key?' Melanie said, staring at me in disbelief. 'I'd have changed the fucking locks.'

And she ignored him when he walked in.

'Oh. Hello,' he said, clearly not thrilled to see her either.

'I'll sort out the tents,' she said to me, blanking him totally. 'Get over to mine early and I'll stick one in your car. You need to go back to sleep,' she said, putting her hand on my arm proprietarily. Then she laughed, loudly, flashing her strong, white teeth. 'We're going to have such a laugh.'

'Going somewhere?' David asked.

'Sure are,' Melanie said without looking at him.

Our hall was too crowded with the three of us. Awkwardly, David squeezed his way past us and wandered first into the kitchen and then the living room, in search of his children. My senses followed him. Max and Sam must have gone back into the den. Soon I heard David's voice. 'Hello, Sam, how are you?' So hopeful, so trying to be normal. I could not hear Sam's reply.

'Right, then,' Melanie said at last. 'I'll see you tomorrow.' And she yelled, 'Max! Abbie! Think it's time we went home!'

'I'm not chasing you away,' I said quickly, and she gave me the strangest look, part pity, part challenge.

'Just you be strong,' she said. And not even bothering to keep her voice down, 'Stand up to him.'

It was another ten minutes before they finally left. I went straight into my empty kitchen and sat down at the table, exhausted, expecting to be left alone. But almost straight away, David came in.

'She's as charming as ever,' he said.

'She's my friend,' I said. 'She's just protective.'

'What does she think I'm going to do?' he said. 'Beat you up or something?'

I rested my head in my hands and mumbled through my fingers, 'Did you want something? Only I have got a headache.'

He pulled out a chair and sat down. I wished he wouldn't. I wished he would leave me alone.

'We need to talk,' he said.

I think I must have groaned. I could feel him looking at me, and what did he see, I wonder, as I sat there slumped in just an old oversized, baggy T-shirt that I tried to pass off as a dress, and with my hair all wild and everywhere? I hadn't washed since yesterday morning, and even I could smell the wine from all those empty bottles cluttered by the door.

'Jane,' he said firmly, as if calling me into consciousness.

Groggily I raised my head. 'What?'

'We need to talk.'

'So you said.'

He was studying me intently, and frowning. Quickly, I looked away from the expression in his eyes.

'I gather you're going camping,' he said.

'Is that what you want to talk about? Do you have a problem with that?'

'No,' he said. 'Of course not.'

'What, then?'

This time, when I looked at him, I saw the evidence of stress in the tightness of his face and the pallor of his skin. There were lines where I didn't remember seeing lines before; he looked older. It did occur to me that a man enjoying the fruits of a new love ought to look a little happier – all that sex, all that freedom. A man having his cake and eating it.

'We need to talk about money,' he said. 'We need to sort things out.'

'Money?' I said. Money was the last thing I felt like talking about.

'Yes,' he said. He had one hand resting on the table in front of him, though resting is perhaps not the right word. His fingers were curled over into a semi-fist, and he was digging away at the skin at the side of his thumbnail with the nail of his forefinger. 'We need to sort things out . . . make a plan.'

'Now you're sounding like my parents,' I said.

He swallowed. This certainly wasn't easy for him. 'My expenses have increased,' he said carefully, and I laughed a short, harsh laugh. 'I need to know what you're spending,' he said, two faint blotches of colour rising high on his cheeks as if his face had been slapped. 'I feel like I'm losing control of my finances.' Again I laughed, nastily, and he said, 'For God's sake, Jane, we've got to work out what we both need. I can't afford things as they are.'

'What are you going to do?' I said, my voice too shrill, too loud. 'Take my credit card away? Make the children go around in rags?'

'No, of course not.' He was driving that nail into his thumb now, clinging to his control. 'But I need to budget.'

'You can hardly accuse me of spending too much money,' I said. 'I'm not exactly the last of the great shoppers. I'm not getting my hair done every week.' I stuck my hands into the mess on my head, my fingers catching in the tangles, lifting it up and making me look, no doubt, more of a wreck than ever.

'I know,' he said.

'Other women would have cleaned you out by now.'

'Jane,' he said. 'Please. '

'Perhaps it's just the cost of all those romantic dinners. Perhaps it's expensive having a lover. Perhaps you should have thought of that.'

'Jane, I am still paying the mortgage, as well as living in London—'

'Is she charging you rent now? Are your services not enough?'

The colour in his cheeks deepened. For a long moment he said nothing and my head echoed with the sound of my own voice, goading, mean, and cheap. What a bitch I am when I'm hurting. The joke is I didn't care one dot about money. I could live in rags quite happily, I mean when did I last buy anything new? Perhaps if I had, he wouldn't have left me. Perhaps if I'd primped and groomed and put on a better show.

It was the severing I couldn't bear. The disconnection. He was throwing out my anchor, and then what? I saw my name scrubbed off the joint account; scrubbed off everything.

The tears were burning in my eyes.

'Jane,' he said at last. 'There is not enough money. We need to come to an arrangement.'

I swear, I could hear it then; the actual breaking of my heart. He must have heard it too, because he looked miserable as hell. The fabric of a marriage tears like the toughest of material; you have to really grab hold hard and rip, and he had, and he knew that he had. All of those photos stashed in the sideboard of the two of us and the kids when they were tiny; all those piles and piles of photos of little Sam and little Ella with us, the adoring parents. All our dreams of the future, and the sweet, binding haze of the past. All we had done, and built together and lived for . . . it meant nothing. I looked in his eyes and I saw it. He had cast us into freefall.

We didn't come to an arrangement, David and I, we didn't make plans. I was too hysterical; too loud in my objections. And Sam and Ella were too close by, listening. 'Stop fighting, please, stop fighting,' Ella sobbed from the hallway. Sam kicked a ball against the wall of his room methodically and angrily; thud, thud, thud. You could hear it throughout the house. David left on Sunday evening with nothing resolved, leaving behind him just the damage he had done; the ripped-up, agonizing shreds.

And so Sam, Ella and I drove over to Melanie's house on Monday morning with whatever we'd remembered packed into the car and whatever we'd forgotten, not; our hearts just so not in it. It felt just like something else to be got through. We didn't want even to be together, never mind together with anyone else.

I forced a smile on to my face for Melanie's benefit. I put on a bright, chirpy voice when I spoke to her that had Sam tutting beside me in disgust; I laughed a fun laugh that had him tutting even more. I made an effort; what else could I do?

Melanie was in fine spirits. The boot of her little car was crammed to the hilt with God knows what; every space filled with something useful, be it a cup or a loo roll or a stray pair of jeans. The red plastic bowl from her kitchen sink was stuck on top of a load of other stuff and wedged down so hard it was starting to split. Max and Abbie were strapping a tent onto the car roof, threading a length of rope through the open car windows, and up and over and round. It was not, exactly, secure. The other tent I stuck across the footwell in the back of my car, for Sam and Ella to complain about for the whole journey. There was no third tent; Jake had left it at Kelly's parents'. We were going to be very cosy.

'All set?' said Melanie as she forced shut the boot of her car. 'You lot certainly look like you need a holiday.'

We drove southwards in a convoy, Melanie in front, me behind her with my eye on that tent. I tried to keep a safe distance in case it came shooting off her roof and straight through my windscreen, but every time I pulled back she did too, honking her horn or flashing her lights; several times Max wound down his window and leant right out to yell at us, the wind whipping back his hair and his words.

'What's the matter?' Melanie kept texting on her phone, car veering from side to side as she did so. 'What do you keep slowing down for? Won't be there till next week at this rate.'

I didn't know where we were going. Dorset, she'd said, vaguely, but where in Dorset? Once, years ago before we were married, David and I spent a weekend in Lyme Regis. I remembered it well; the little watermill and the pretty houses, the hotel overlooking the sea. He bought me a pair of earrings, silver drops with jade stones in the middle. I still have them, somewhere.

'How far is it?' Ella asked from the back but I hadn't a clue. When David and I had gone to Dorset we'd driven straight down the A303 from London. It seemed an awful lot further from where I lived now, travelling along unfamiliar roads. Several times we stopped, for the loo, for food, to tie that tent back down on Melanie's car. I'd assumed Melanie knew where we were going; between us we'd no map. It turned out to be guess-work: that way was Dorset, and that way the sea. For miles we wove down winding roads searching for a campsite, glimpsing the sea in the distance and then losing it again. It was late afternoon before we finally found somewhere; much later still when we'd put up the tents.

I am struggling here. I would like to say what a laugh it was, putting up those tents, trying to work out which pole went where, realizing we'd no hammer with which to bang in the hooks. Sending the kids to buy chips from the hut at the campsite entrance, getting steadily pissed on the cheap wine we'd stopped off to buy. Rigging one tent up eventually, with Max smashing the hooks into the ground with a rock, and laughing at Sam's attempts to do the same and banging his thumb instead, then finding out that the other tent, the smaller one, had a whopping great tear in the side of it, that we had to cover all week with a towel. Oh yes, how funny it was every time the girls poked their heads out of that hole like it was a window, saying hello in silly voices, especially later on in the week, when it rained. And what fun too when the wind blew in off the sea at night, straight through those worn inadequate sleeping bags. Melanie and I, we drank and drank. We had to, just to keep warm.

Perhaps it would have been fun, in a different time, a different place; if I had been different. But that camping trip sticks in my memory, a painful, shameful blot.

The first night I cried just a little, as you do after too much wine. The boys were just up the field, kicking a ball at each other in that slightly goading, aggressive way that seemed to be the way with boys, and the girls had gone off to the little playground next to the shop. Melanie wanted to know what had happened yesterday with David and I told her, about how things were starting to hurt him, now that he was feeling it in his wallet.

'You mustn't be the one to pay,' she said, and I remember nodding, agreeing wholeheartedly through the great fog in my head.

I hardly slept at all on the cold, hard ground. We persuaded the boys to take the little tent with the hole in its side, which left the rest of us to squeeze into the other one. Our tent wasn't much bigger than the boys', but at least it divided into two, so the girls could go in one side and Melanie and I in the other. There was no room for my camp beds though, not by the time I'd struggled to put their legs on. Melanie and I ended up sleeping on just the top parts of the camp beds, the hammock part if you like, which was just a layer of heavy canvas, and the kids had her motley collection of old mats to lie on. I don't know which was most uncomfortable. And the girls chattered way into the early hours, no matter how many times I hissed at them to be quiet, and far, far too early the combined assault of birdsong, the cold, and my stiff, sore body forced me awake to a pounding headache.

All the next day Melanie and I sat outside our tent in her wonky old deckchairs. Now and again the kids appeared wanting food, and we sent them off to the takeaway or the shop. At some point I remember Sam coming back and loitering by the tent, doing his best not to look too tired, or bored, or lonely. He sat on the grass, pretending to be busy with his phone.

'Where's Max, Sam?' Melanie asked him.

'Oh, he's gone off for a walk with some other boys,' Sam said nonchalantly. 'To find the beach, I think.'

'They'll have a long walk then!' Melanie laughed.

And I said, 'Didn't you want to go with them, then?'

He shrugged, avoiding my eye. Carefully, he said, 'I might have done.'

And my heart sank. I knew exactly what had happened. Max had found some other cooler and therefore more interesting boys to hang around with and dropped my Sam like a hot brick. It was the story of Sam's life. If we'd been at home I'd probably have made some attempt at comforting him. I'd have said, 'Never mind, Sam,' or, 'Don't let them push you out' – I'd have given him a safe refuge, at least. But we weren't at home, we were with Melanie. I'm ashamed to admit that my overriding concern was just that Sam shouldn't spoil things, that he shouldn't make things unbearably awkward, by not getting on with Max.

'Well go and catch them up,' Melanie said. 'Surely you don't want to sit around here with us?' And when Sam mumbled his excuses about wanting a rest and not knowing which way they'd gone, his face painfully pink, she laughed and said, 'God, you are a funny one, Sam.'

That night I drank to escape, to set myself free. And then I drank a whole lot more. You get used to it after a while; you need more. And I did want to enjoy myself. After all, wasn't that why I was there?

'Your mum needs to relax,' Melanie said to my kids, to Sam in particular, who watched me all evening, never letting his eyes off me for a second, never giving me any space. 'She's had it bloody hard. You want to cut her some slack.'

We barely left the campsite. We were actually quite a distance from the beach. Once, we all made it down there, late one afternoon when the tide was in and we had a mere strip of shingle to perch ourselves on. Other than that we didn't bother. We were too tired by day from the lack of sleep at night to want to do anything much. Besides, we had the shop at the front of the campsite, and that takeaway, and fields for miles for the kids to play in; we had everything we needed. And the weather was fairly good, the first few days, if somewhat cold at night. The kids roamed wild, forced to entertain themselves without computers or TVs. That was what camping was all about, Melanie said. Just relaxing. Just letting go.

On Thursday the weather changed. The wind picked up, bringing in the clouds from the sea and with them the threat of rain. In the evening we huddled around our tents, with nothing more than the remains of our throw-away barbecue to warm ourselves by. The girls brought out their sleeping bags and wrapped them around their shoulders; soon they retreated into the boys' tent, whispering, giggling, sticking their heads out of that stupid tear of a window to repeatedly squeal hello. The boys had had a few beers and were now hanging about, listless. Max lay sprawled out on his side on the grass, seemingly oblivious to the drizzle driving in and coating us all with its slow, creeping dampness. He reminded me of a lion, so apparently relaxed, yet also so alert, listening, watching. He was listening to Melanie and me. His expression changed as we talked, now that smile, now that raised eyebrow of agreement as he followed our conversation. My Sam sat cross-legged in the entrance of his tent, part in, part out. He tugged at the grass, pulling it out with agitated hands, getting angry with the girls every time one of them squealed too loudly behind him, or accidently kicked him, or just generally crowded into his space.

'For God's sake, Sam,' Melanie said. 'Why don't you just move?'

And he scowled, and shuffled over a little, to the side. He was listening to us too, though I paid no heed to that at the time.

Melanie poured some more wine into our cups.

'Your trouble,' she said to me, 'is that you can't move on. And you're on edge all the time. Worrying about your kids. Worrying about everything. He's got you right under his thumb, even now.'

He being David, of course. I sipped at my drink, too cold and too numb to argue. Besides, why would I argue? What she said was true enough.

'And it's wrong,' she said, uncurling one finger from her cup and jabbing it at me. 'Do you think *he* worries about his kids? Do you think he even thinks about them while he's off shagging his mistress? No. Because he doesn't need to. You're doing it all for him.'

'Helloo!' Ella cried, sticking her head out of the tent.

'Shut up!' said Sam.

Max smirked and neatly rolled himself over, moving himself closer to Melanie and me.

'You want to loosen up a bit,' Melanie said.

'I am,' I said. 'What more can I do?'

'Jesus,' Melanie muttered under her breath, and louder, 'Don't make it so easy for him.'

'I'm not.'

'You *are*.'

Oh what it is to be criticized when you are already so low. To be picked over like a chicken carcass, your character dissected bit by little bit, all in the name of friendship. I stared at the middle distance, tears stinging my eyes. How bleak, how miserable, how utterly grey the English landscape can be at dusk with the rain driving in. And this was supposed to be fun.

'Look at you now,' Melanie said. 'You're all pent-up. Your husband is out having a wild time thinking about no one but himself . . . but you . . . you've no idea how to enjoy yourself.'

Accidently, I caught Max's eye. And oh what big eyes, so wide with sympathy. I was uncomfortable talking like this with the boys listening, though for Melanie there were no such boundaries. Take me as you find me, she'd say, and that dictate applied to her kids too.

'What you want,' Melanie said, 'is to get yourself a new man.'

Max laughed a gentle little ho-ho-ho, and Sam's entire body jolted as if he'd sat on a nail. He twisted away from us, not wanting to hear any more, then instantly twisted straight back again, unable to stop himself listening in.

'The last thing I want,' I said, 'is another man.'

'But why not?' Melanie said. 'It would do you good.'

'It would not,' I said.

'Yes it would. And besides which, it would show him.'

'Show who?' asked Ella, sticking her head out of that tent.

'No one,' hissed Sam.

'Show him you're having fun for a change,' Melanie said. 'See how he likes it then.'

'I am having fun,' I said.

Max rolled onto his back, chuckling to himself, and Melanie said, 'Oh please.'

We'd finished that bottle of wine, and she heaved herself

out of her deckchair to reach inside our tent for another, and opened it, and filled up our mugs. 'I swear,' she said, 'you are going to have a good time if it kills me.'

She balanced her cup down on the grass next to the wine bottle and disappeared into the tent, and started poking around in the little holdall in which she'd brought her few clothes. She muttered to herself, rummaging through knickers and socks and T-shirts. Then, 'Ah! Here we are,' she said. And out she came again, grinning, and holding something hidden in her hand.

Max clearly knew what it was. 'Aw, mum,' he said, a little too gleefully.

'Courtesy of Colin,' Melanie said, unfolding her fingers to reveal a knotted-up plastic sandwich bag, filled with what could easily have been chopped herbs. 'Thought we might be needing it.'

Max was laughing properly now, a kind of *what-is-my-mum-like*? laugh, as he lay on his back, staring up at the absence of stars. Sam on the other hand sat there rigid as a stick, his face dark with fury, tangibly emanating . . . what? Hatred? Then hatred of whom . . . of me? I looked at him and I looked at Max, or rather I looked at Max and how he was with his mother, and I felt so overwhelmed with sadness and with envy. Why couldn't Sam be like that with me, so at ease, so accepting? The affection between Melanie and Max was palpable, yet she didn't spend her life fretting over him, worrying for him, moving halfway across the bloody country for him. Oh no, Melanie's take me as you find me mantra stretched both ways. She was totally uncritical of her kids, and, it seemed, they of her. Apparently, she had got it right. Whereas it seemed I had got it all so wrong.

She sat hunched over in her deckchair, balancing a Rizla

paper on her knees, doing her best to shelter it from the wind, and rolling us up a nice fat joint as if it was the most natural thing in the world. 'Don't worry,' she said, suddenly turning to look at me and smile reassuringly, 'it's home-grown. Perfectly harmless,' as if remembering what kind of a person I was.

Oh me, me. I so didn't want to be me.

'There we are,' Melanie said. 'Done.' She lit up, and took a long slow drag. 'Lovely,' she said, and handed the joint to me.

'Mum!' Sam hissed.

'Oh be quiet, Sam,' Melanie said. 'You can't tell me you boys don't like a little smoke now and again.'

And Max laughed, and rolled a little closer to us, big brown eyes like a puppy's, awaiting his turn.

And do you know how exciting it was, how thrilling, to be doing something really bad? This wasn't about Sam, or Ella, or David or the confines of my ordinary life. This was just about me, trying to let go. Being only me again, not mother, not wife. So I ignored Sam sitting there glaring at me, and I took a puff on that joint. It was no big deal to Melanie; it need be no big deal to me.

And oh how we laughed the next time the girls popped their heads out of their tent to see what was going on, and we had to hide what we were smoking from them because they were too young. How funny it all seemed, then. And how funny Sam was too, all bug-eyed with outrage, scolding me like he was the parent.

'You want to leave your mum alone,' Melanie said languidly, waving the joint at him. 'She's been the good little wifey for far too long. It's time for her to let her hair down.'

Let my hair down I did. I had not smoked dope since I

was a student. Combined with the wine, and my poor state of mind, it slammed me.

Vaguely I remember the boom-boom in my head as my eyes tried to focus, the chair that I sat in and the tent, the drizzle in my face and my kids' distorted bodies whooshing in and whooshing out again. I remember Sam's face up close to mine, his mouth moving, popping like a fish's, yelling senselessly. And Max laughing that high-pitched crack of a laugh, saying, 'Sam you're so square, you're like a fucking old man.'

And Melanie, God damn her to hell and God damn me too, saying in that jokey-jokey way of hers, 'Well you know he is just like his dad . . . '

Sam threw up his arms and stormed away from me. I couldn't have stopped him if I'd tried. I was stuck in that old deckchair, limbs boneless and heavy, beyond use. And there was Ella now, crying about nothing in particular, her face frightened, as if this was some kind of a row, an upset. In my heart I screeched for them both, but also, oh, how I longed to be free.

I was sick. I know that. The little pile of it was still there in the morning, at the side of the tent. And at some point in the night it started raining, properly, soaking its way through that rotten old canvas as quickly as if through a sheet. Water dripped on my face, rousing me. And squeezed in between Melanie and me was Ella, squashed up close to me and shivering with the cold, her hand on my arm. She was whimpering in her sleep.

TWENTY-ONE

The rain that started in the night carried on into the next day, heavy, relentless. Our stuff was soaked, as were we. We'd no choice but to pack up and leave, and thank God for that. Melanie and Max thought the events of the previous night were hilarious, but I didn't, and neither did Sam nor the girls. Sam would not speak to me; he would not even look at me as he tried to squeeze the water out of his sodden sleeping bag before rolling it up and miserably dismantling the tent poles. The girls whispered to each other as they pulled the pegs out of the ground, and repeatedly stared at that pile of sick with wide-eyed horror, fascinated by its slow spread and disintegration in the rain.

My shame was absolute. I had the hangover to end all hangovers and felt like my head was splitting in two, but no physical suffering could alleviate how bad I felt in my heart. Fixed behind my eyes was the image of Sam, stamping his feet, shaking his hands at me, pleading with me to just stop. But we three, Melanie, Max and I, had just laughed at him. And surely that is the lowest of the low.

Sam did not speak all the way home. He sat in the back, staring out the window, mouth locked shut with fury. Ella, who was tired and tearful and didn't understand what was going on, whined the whole way. I drove that car feeling like shit. I gripped the steering wheel with shaking hands, straining my eyes through the rain, the steamed-up windscreen and the hell inside my head. No doubt I should not have driven at all.

Sam's silence didn't end when we got home. He kept it up for a good few days. We were home on the Friday but had expected to be camping till Sunday, and so I'd put David off coming – I had that small grace at least. He phoned though, to speak to the children. I loitered within earshot, dreading what they would say when he asked if they'd had a good time, as he would, of course. Yet each of them replied in the same way, as they did to all his questions on the phone. Just, 'Yes', and 'Fine', and occasionally, 'OK'. These conversations crucified me, as they did the children, and no doubt David too. Sam and Ella hated being questioned, and they responded to David as if to a teacher at school or a stranger. But how else was he to know what was going on in their lives, to show an interest? I listened in, and I recognized the similarity to how I had responded to him when he used to phone me from work, asking how I was, how the children were. Resentment had driven me monosyllabic, too. I had held back, deliberately, and Sam and Ella now did the same. Never believe that stupid saying about distance making the heart grow fonder. It doesn't. It just takes the person you love away.

But how glad I was, right then, for my children's unwillingness to talk.

They were starting back at school the coming Wednesday, Ella moving up, now, to Renfree Park. There were things to buy and organize and sort; I threw myself into the tasks. I did my best to be a good mother again, seeing that clothes were labelled and folded into piles. I wrote notable dates on the calendar and polished shoes; I fussed about. I tried to make up for my failings by being subservient, hoping they would forget, hoping I would please them despite the awful memories.

Yet still Sam would not speak to me.

I tried to talk to him, often – too often. I tapped on his bedroom door and walked in, uninvited and unwanted. 'Understand what it is to be me,' I said, 'to feel as I do, to have to go through what I have been going through.'

He didn't, of course. He didn't want to. Nor did he want me barging into his room, railing at him. To him I was just his mother; I began and ended there.

The memory of our camping trip entertained Melanie and Max for weeks. 'Oh what a laugh we had,' they'd say. 'Didn't we, Jane? Didn't we have a laugh?'

I'd met with their approval, at least.

A new standard had been set in my house now. Boundaries can only be breached when boundaries exist. By getting stoned and behaving as I had in front of my kids and their friends, I'd shown that I had none. Anything went, now, in my house. Oh sure, Max would do me the honour of not lighting up indoors and he was discreet around Ella, but who was I to complain now if he and perhaps Will and Tommy nipped out the back for a smoke when they were round? Especially as they always took care to offer me a toke, although I did, please note, always refuse. Oh no, I'd joke, not after last time.

In my effort to please Sam again, I courted his friends. I

was nice to them, thinking that then they would be nice to him, and so he in turn to me. If Sam was popular, Sam would be happy. That was what I told myself, and that is what, in my desperation, I believed.

TWENTY-TWO

'We need to sell the house.'

How gently David said those terrible words. I knew it would come to this, sooner or later. But I didn't want to face it. I didn't want to see ahead because there lay only emptiness, an unbearable end.

'No,' I said.

'Jane, we have to. I'm sorry.'

Again I said, 'No.'

We were sitting in the living room, late on a Sunday afternoon, David at one end of the sofa, me at the other, both of us perched forward on the cushions. He leaned towards me slightly as he spoke, as if in empathy, as if in concern; in truth just to soften his words. He had taken the children out earlier to gather the last of the blackberries and now they were dispatched to their rooms to finish homework so that he and I could have *time to talk*. The silence in the house was ominous.

Slowly, he said, 'I need to get a place near work, just a flat, just something small . . . but I can't afford it as well as this place.'

How reminiscent of previous conversations; and of last winter when he sat glued to his computer searching through

London flats for sale and rent; all those grotty, forbidding little dives that drove him to shack up with Diana. How strangely life just goes round and round, mirroring itself.

'You want to sell my home,' I said, 'our children's home, so that you can get yourself a nice little London flat? Why can't you just stay where you are? Is her place not big enough?'

Carefully, he said, 'I'm not . . . it's not like that between us any more. It hasn't been for a while. We're friends' – he added this last quickly, as if he needed to make the point – 'but we're not . . . together.'

I stared at him, dumbfounded.

'There is nothing between us now,' he said, as if he thought I had not understood. 'Diana's been very good letting me stay so long, but I need to find a place of my own.'

'You mean you broke up our marriage for nothing?' I should have been pleased. I should have been delighted that things hadn't worked out with Diana; I should have been sitting there gloating. But emotion is a funny thing. Instead of all the things I would have thought that I would feel I was struck by an icy outrage. It started in my heart and spread outwards, tingling into my fingertips. I felt cheated, and then cheated again. 'You put me, and our children, through all this for nothing?' I said.

Part of me wanted him to plead to come back to me now, so that I could have the pleasure of refusing him, if nothing else. But he didn't. 'Diana was the result,' he said. 'Not the cause.' And oh how that hurt. 'This whole thing' – he threw his hands out expansively – 'has been a disaster.'

'So you want to sell up and be done.'

'Don't you?'

'No,' I said. 'I do not.' I threw myself back into the sofa, as if pinning myself to the house.

'Jane, I cannot afford two homes,' he said, keeping his voice down, though I was not so careful.

'Then stay where you are. Stay with Diana.'

'I can't do that.' He was struggling now, to stay so calm. 'We have no choice. I cannot keep paying the mortgage.'

'You're blackmailing me.'

He flushed, two dark streaks on his otherwise pale face. 'I'm not,' he said.

'Yes you are. You're forcing me and our children out of our home.'

'For God's sake, Jane. I have to live somewhere too. This isn't sustainable.'

I remember sobbing then; this weird choking sound catching in my throat. It was the absolute finality of it; the dismantling of all my dreams. Clear as a picture I could see the day we first moved here; the exact moment when we pulled up outside in the sunshine, and the children ran, whooping, from the car. 'We can't just move,' I said. 'What about the children? This is our home.'

'I'm sorry, Jane,' he said. 'I'm sure you'll find somewhere nearby, if that's what you want. I'll help you all I can.'

'I don't want your help!'

'I'll help you tell the children, I mean; we'll tell them together.'

'I don't want to tell them. I don't want to move!'

'Jane,' he said, spreading his hands out to me, hands full of nothing but air. 'What else can we do?'

We have no choice, he said. *No choice*. That was the way things were, in his eyes. He had gone, and moved on from us, with or without his Diana.

He did not want to come back. Not to me, not to this place.

We didn't need to tell the children. They'd heard most of it through the door. That night, when David had gone, they skulked around me, loitering as I made supper.

'Are we moving?' Sam asked, doing his best to make his voice sound bored.

'Not at the moment,' I said briskly, tipping spaghetti into a pan.

'Will we go back to London?' Ella asked, adding quickly, 'If we move.' And then, as if she'd realized what it would mean, 'But I'm friends with Abbie now.'

'We're not moving though are we, Mum?' Sam said. 'You just said so.'

Then Ella said, 'But what about Dad? Could we live with him again if we moved?'

'God,' Sam said. 'You are so stupid.'

Now that Ella was at secondary school, there was no more meeting up with other women at the school gates. I drove Ella and Sam to school, sat in the traffic through town, and literally let them out of the car wherever I could find a spot near the school to pull over for a second. And then I drove on. And of course it was unthinkable that I should approach the gates in person at home-time; oh no, I had to loiter in the car with the engine running, parked up on the kerb somewhere nearby, along with umpteen other useful but never-to-be-acknowledged mothers. Unless I met them both back at Melanie's. She was the only adult I spoke to most days. Who would believe that friends were once a commodity I had seen fit to fritter and waste, so plentiful was the supply? Now I had but one friend, and lacked the sociability to make any others. I had become unappealing even to myself, and it was easier to hide away.

For a long time I'd thought about phoning Karen, my friend from back in London. We had known each other since Sam was a baby; we'd met at a post-natal coffee morning and been friends ever since. Her son Joseph and my Sam had grown up together, gone through school together. I felt regret now that I had so easily let her go, but I'd been too full of my move here, and my belief that a new school and a whole new environment was the right thing for my Sam, for all of us. The loss of a few old friends had seemed a price worth paying when I was flushed with the thrill of our new country life. Friends were two a penny back then, and I was naive enough to believe that those we left behind would somehow still be with us; that they'd be as thrilled with our move as we were, that they would never tire of slapping up the motorway through the Friday night traffic to visit us and admire our so-much-better life.

I had not spoken to Karen for well over a year. We'd exchanged Christmas cards, that was all. But I'd thought about phoning her often, and one wet morning in a moment of excruciating loneliness, I did.

Ridiculously, my heart was pounding as I dialled her number. I thought she might be out and half hoped that she would be; then I could leave her a message and give her the option of calling me. But how cowardly, how silly that was. Surely, old friends can always pick up the reins. Old friends will always be there.

She answered on the third ring. 'Hello?' she said.

'Karen,' I said. 'Hi. It's Jane.'

'Jane,' she said in surprise.

'Hi,' I said again. 'How are you?'

'I'm fine,' she said. 'How are you?'

'Fine,' I said, and quickly, 'We haven't spoken for ages.'

'No,' she said. 'Well, we're all busy, I suppose . . .'

And so we carried on. Superficial, stilted chit-chat. The awkwardness was palpable. I held the phone in one hand and slipped my other hand inside my sweatshirt and pinched at the soft skin of my stomach with my fingernails. Finally I braced myself to say, 'Actually, things haven't been that good lately. Between David and me.'

She said nothing.

I forced myself to continue. 'He was seeing someone else. Can you believe it? I found out after we'd been away for the weekend. Some colleague from work. Karen, it's been awful.'

Still she said nothing, but I could hear her breathing.

'He's staying in London now,' I said.

And she said, 'I know.'

'*You know*?'

'Yes, he – he told Ed. I think they met up for a drink a couple of times.'

'Oh,' I said.

After a moment she said, 'I was really sorry to hear about it.' Though not, apparently, sorry enough to have phoned me. 'Look,' she said. 'I was just on my way out. I can't really talk now. I'll call you back, soon.'

She wouldn't though; we both knew that. I cannot tell you how betrayed I felt. David and Ed had only ever met because of us; she and I were the real friends. That's what I'd thought. The hurt of it stuck in my throat.

The happiness had gone from our house, snuffed out like the flame of a candle. I drove Sam and Ella to school on damp, gloomy mornings and killed the hours in between until it was time to collect them again. I wandered around the town, making the most of any errands. So far, I'd avoided actually going into the one and only estate agents in town, though David had of course; David had driven up one Saturday and arranged the valuation. I had signed the agreement, numb, thinking still this wasn't real. Still there was time for us to stop, and go back to before. But one morning I looked in the estate agent's window, and there it was: our house, photographed with the autumn sunlight glinting off the windows. There was my car in the drive, and the front wheel of Sam's bicycle peeping out from around the side. Ella's riding boots were propped beside the front door. I stared at that picture of my home, feeling as if the strings of my heart had been cut.

'You want to get yourself a lawyer,' Melanie said when I talked to her about it, and no doubt she was right. But that way lay the end, and for me that end might well be a tiny ex-council place in one of the less desirable villages around here, the kind of place that people like David and I always bypassed in our search for the country proper. A place where dogs barked all day and kids roared around in uninsured cars for kicks. Our house was so heavily mortgaged that with my small portion such a place would be all I could afford. The prospect was unthinkable, a hideous, flipside nightmare to my whole country dream. Yet neither could I go back to London. I could not uproot the children and make them change schools again. And besides, what would I ever afford in London? I pictured David and me in identical, soulless flats in matching tower blocks – perhaps even the *same* block, high, high above the ground with the traffic roaring below. Oh sure, I painted a pretty bleak picture for myself, and maybe things wouldn't be quite that bad, but I had moved here for a better life; for me, for my family. How could I admit it had failed?

My volunteering at the primary school had come to an end now that Ella had left and I needed to get a proper job, and one that paid well, but what? And where? Opportunities around here were few, and whatever I did it had to be local; the children needed me as a means of transport if nothing else. Of the other women I knew those who worked did so either seasonally or part-time, and got paid a pittance.

'Come and work at the school canteen with me,' Melanie said, and then, just in case I hadn't got her point, 'It was never in my career plan to be a dinner lady either.'

I scanned the paper, hoping something would come up.

At home, I listened to my children's endless complaints about school, and homework, and our inadequately stocked fridge, if I listened to them at all. They bickered so much more than they used to, now that they were at the same school. Sam was sweet on a girl called Lydia; I knew this because Ella teased him mercilessly. She and her friends spied on him at break-time, following him about, giggling if he caught them.

'She's so annoying,' Sam complained to me. 'Tell her to stop.'

'Oh, Sam, she's just being a girl,' I said. 'Just ignore her.'

'Lydia, Lydia,' Ella sang under her breath and Sam flushed scarlet.

'Mum, tell her!'

'Ella, stop it,' I said.

'Lydia's got lovely long blonde hair,' Ella said, drawing an imaginary mane down her shoulders with her fingers. 'Abbie said Max said Sam can't take his big blue eyes off her.' She batted her own eyelashes, tauntingly. And every time Sam went out, she asked, 'Will Lydia be there?'

Still, at least Sam had something to distract from the misery of home. Lucky him.

I watched the leaves falling from the trees; so many leaves, forever drifting on the breeze. Once, I looked out of my living-room window at the hideous For Sale sign that had been slapped up outside our house just as a gust of wind snatched those leaves up again and whirled them around, a mesmerizing tornado of red and gold and brown. I always loved the autumn here, on bright days; the colours, the freshness of the air and the lovely prospect of the planning for Christmas. Not so now. Winter loomed ahead; I could not bear even to think about it.

TWENTY-THREE

One Saturday in early October David drove up early so that he could fix the trellis that had come loose at the front, and sort out the garden; we had to keep the place tidy now, we had to keep it presentable. Who knew when some prospective buyer might come wandering by, some other family wanting to escape the city for the good life, perhaps? While he was here he drove into town to visit the estate agent's. To check on progress, he said, to try and get things moving.

He tried to make out he was helping me and came back with a handful of details of other random and no doubt totally inappropriate properties around here. That he had so quickly selected a number of places he deemed suitable for me and his children to live in, and that he had therefore already stuck a price limit on those places, infuriated me. It made me feel as if he thought anything would do. He placed the details down on the kitchen table and there they lay, fit for composting, nothing more. I would not touch them. I would not play along.

'At least look at them, won't you?' he said. 'We have to start somewhere.'

I ignored him, and he sighed.

'Look,' he said, 'the guy fixed up a viewing while I was

there. They're coming round on Monday at about four. I told him you'd let him know if that time's not convenient.'

'Of course it's not convenient,' I said. 'I'll be picking the kids up from school.'

David flushed, ashamed at himself for being so stupid, I presume, as well as with irritation at me. 'Phone them and change it to a time that is convenient,' he said. 'Or we'll have to let the agent have a key.'

'No time is convenient,' I said. 'And they're not having a key.'

'Do you have to be so stubborn?' he said. 'This really isn't fair on me.'

'On *you*?' Heat rushed into my head, roaring in my ears. 'It isn't fair on you?'

'I need a place to live too,' he said.

'I don't care if you live on a fucking park bench after what you have done to me,' I yelled at him. 'You are not fair!'

Max came round that night, after David had gone back to London. Jake dropped him off in Melanie's car. Abbie was supposed to be coming too but she'd gone down with a throat infection, ruining Melanie's plan for the evening. Actually I was quite glad; I had to make more of an effort when both the girls were there. I had to be more attentive and more fun, and provide nice things to eat. And no way could I be fun tonight.

I could not stop crying.

Max had brought a couple of films round on DVD; the boys would be closeted in the den all evening, Ella too. I sat in my kitchen and I looked out at the black, black sky beyond my window. The darkness was infinite; you could be in a hole looking out there, you could be buried alive. No stars tonight, no streetlights ever.

The kitchen door opened, and Max came in. Automatically I stood up, and went to busy myself at the sink. I didn't want anyone to see me crying.

'Jane?' he said.

I found a cup to wash up, and turned on the tap.

'You OK?'

My eyes were heavy with tears. I felt so incredibly tired.

He walked towards me, and laid his hand on my shoulder. And God forgive me but he was big and he was warm and he was solid, and I was just so desperate for comfort, any comfort. I turned into his arms and he held me against his chest, so close that I could feel his heart beating rapidly beneath my ear.

'Ssh,' he said, as I cried into his T-shirt. Clumsily, he stroked his hand up and down my back. 'Ssh, now. It'll be all right.'

A moment's peace, that was all; a moment's understanding. A little human warmth. I wished to God it was my own son comforting me, but he was ensconced in the den, glued to the TV, oblivious to me, entirely blind to my feelings.

Later, when I had washed my face and recovered myself, I stuck a couple of bags of popcorn into the microwave, and loaded up a tray: popcorn, cookies, lemonade for Ella, beer for the boys and wine for me. I carried the tray through the living room to the den. I could hear the shatter and scream of some hideous action adventure; they had the volume up far too loud as usual. I hooked the door handle down with one hand, careful not to upset the tray, and kicked open the door.

'Hi,' I said over the roar of gunfire, 'refreshments.'

Sam ignored me; he was lying on the floor, sprawled across cushions. Ella, who was on the floor next to him in her pyjamas now, ready for bed, jumped up to grab the popcorn and sent the tray wobbling in my hands.

'Woah!' said Max. 'Careful.' He got up from the sofa where he had been stretched out full length, legs hanging over the arm, and helped me set down the tray on the floor.

'Thanks, Jane,' he said, taking a beer.

'Ssh,' Sam said. 'Be quiet.'

I sat on the sofa next to Max. He moved over to make room for me and I sat on my side with my legs curled up, leaning on the arm of the sofa, one hand holding my glass. My feet were bare and cold; I tucked them under Max's legs to warm them. I watched the film seeing none of it. I wanted just the comfort of being near to those that I loved: my children. Max, too, seemed much like another son to me. It is quite a strange thing for your son's friend to see you cry. The way he had responded struck me as very tender, very sweet. I drank my wine, and I sank into my tiredness, curled up on that sofa.

'Look!' Ella squealed, sitting up and pointing at the TV. 'That girl looks like Lydia, doesn't she?' She turned to Max for verification, sticking out her arm, pointing her finger.

'Shut up, Ella,' Sam said and kicked her.

'Ow!' yelled Ella. 'But she does, doesn't she, Max? She's got hair just like Lydia.'

Beside me Max laughed, that gentle ho-ho-ho.

Sam was furious. Again he kicked Ella and again she squealed, and then she upset the popcorn, all over the floor.

'Mum,' Sam whined. 'Tell her to go away. Why is she even in here? Send her to bed!'

'You're missing the film,' I said. 'And look, there's popcorn everywhere.'

'Well *do* something,' Sam said to me.

'Just ignore her, Sam,' I said.

And Ella, who was nearly in tears now, said, 'I was only saying. And she does look like Lydia.'

Beside me, Max said, 'She does a bit.'

And Sam swore under his breath, and moved as far away from Ella as he could get in that somewhat restricted space.

'Does your sister drive you nuts?' I said to Max.

He smiled at me lazily. 'Sometimes,' he said.

We watched two films, back to back. It was an awfully long time to be sitting there. I dozed, resting my head on the arm of the sofa. Then finally Ella decided to go off up to bed, and I stretched, rousing myself.

'Night, sweetie,' I said.

'I'm going to bed, too,' Sam said, clearly still offended by that earlier little incident, and off he went too, leaving just Max and me.

'You'll be all right down here?' I said to Max. 'You know how to get the bed out, don't you?'

'I'll be fine,' he said, totally at home.

'Right, then.'

'I might just watch a bit more TV,' he said.

'OK,' I said. 'Turn out the lights when you've finished, would you? Sleep well.'

'You too,' he said.

Ella took forever to clean her teeth. Sam was outside on the landing. I could hear him banging on the bathroom door.

'Hurry up,' he yelled.

But Ella would not hurry. It seemed an age until they were

both done, and finally in bed. I sat on my bed, waiting for the bathroom to be free. My bedroom curtains were open, as I liked them that way. There was no need to draw them for privacy here; there was no one to look in, no one to see. I had privacy in abundance whether I wanted it or not. And the blackness of the sky never failed to astound me on moonless nights such as this. In London the sky was always burning from underneath, suffused with an orange glow from all those buildings and streetlights. I had never really known dark until I moved out here. I listened to my children going to bed. I listened to the silence descend.

When the house had been quiet for quite some time I undressed, put my bathrobe on over my nightshirt and went to the bathroom myself. There I cleaned my teeth, and splashed water on my face. It was a sad expression that met me in the mirror; those shadowed eyes, that pale face. These days I avoided looking at my reflection for any longer than I had to, because therein lay the reminder of what I used to be, and more poignantly, of what I had lost. Quickly, I rubbed moisturiser into the dry skin on my cheeks, concentrating on tasks to be done.

There was still a light on downstairs when I came out of the bathroom and went back to my room, but I thought nothing of it. Yet I am struggling now, writing this. I am trying to reconcile my actions then with how I feel now. I am looking back, tracing the very ordinariness and tiredness of my movements that night. My head ached. I drew the curtains against my bedroom window lest the morning light should wake me; I wanted to sleep in. And I turned my bedside light on and then the main light off, and hung my dressing gown on the hook on the back of the door. I walked back around to my side of the bed – oh, yes, I still slept on my side – and was about to get in when there was a tap at my door. At first I thought I'd misheard but that tap came again. Had it been Sam or Ella they'd have come straight in, so I knew it was Max. And sure I was a little startled but I assumed he must have a problem folding out the sofa bed or something; some minor concern from downstairs.

'Just a minute,' I said, quietly, so as not to wake anyone else. I was midway to the door to get my dressing gown when in he came, right in to my room. I was wearing just an old thigh-length T-shirt, but still, he'd seen me dressed much like that before, when we were camping, for instance; I did not think it odd. Not straight away. He closed the door behind him, and even then I did not really think anything of it. I just waited for him to tell me what he wanted. He was smiling, and I felt no need for alarm.

He walked towards me in slow, careful steps. I was aware then, of the size of him, of how of very much bigger than me he was. Much, much bigger than my Sam, in both height and in width.

'What is it, Max?' I said.

He stood right in front of me, filling the room. My heart started beating a little harder then and I folded my arms across my chest, covering myself.

'You OK now Jane?' he said.

'Yes, yes,' I said. 'I'm fine now. Thanks.'

And still I waited for him to tell me why he was there. He put his hands on my arms, one each side. Suddenly I felt very uncomfortable about that closed door, and my children on the other side of it. Yet how silly; this was only Max.

'You sure you're OK?' he said.

'I'm fine,' I said again. And then it struck me: 'Is that why you're here?'

'You were upset earlier,' he said.

'I know,' I said. 'But I'm all right now, thanks.'

I expected him to let me go and for that to be that. How sweet, I would say to myself when he'd gone back downstairs. How kind of him to worry about me.

But he didn't let me go. He was staring at me intently; much too intently. Uneasy now, I laughed and tried to pull away. But his hands were strong. I was not sure if it was a caress or restraint with which he held me, but to think the latter seemed absurd; this was *Max*. He pulled me closer to him and I resisted, taut within his grip; his chest buffeted against mine.

'I think David's mad to let you go,' he said. 'I think he's a fucking idiot.'

And all I could think of was Sam and Ella sleeping in their beds, and of how awful it would be should they hear this.

'Max,' I whispered, 'let me go,' but he slammed me to him, sticking his mouth on mine. Revulsion heaved inside me. His mouth was wet, suffocating. I tried to push him away but he caught me harder – I could barely breathe, but when I did I could smell him, the close-up boy-smell of his body. He groaned into my mouth and I twisted against him, still thinking we could recover this; still thinking we could laugh it off as if it had never happened and be done.

He pushed me onto the bed. With nothing to grab onto – and I wasn't going to grab onto *him* – I fell straight backwards. I could have screamed then, I should have screamed, but who would have heard me? Sam? Ella? The scream stayed in my throat, silenced. He came down on top of me, forcing one leg between mine, his hands all over my chest. I was pinned there, trapped. His eyes were blank, fogged out; he can't have even known what he was doing. He had one hand on my chest holding me down and the other hand ripping open his jeans. I froze like a rabbit and he *rammed* himself into me; it was done in seconds. The shock of it left me reeling; I could not believe it had happened at all.

Moments later he moved himself away from me, resting on one elbow. He actually smiled down at me, and drew one finger around the side of my face, pushing back my hair. And then he pulled down my night shirt, zipped up his jeans, crept out of my room, and was gone.

TWENTY-FOUR

I lay there for a very long time.

I lay on my back as he'd left me, squashed into the mattress, my legs dangling over the end of the bed. To move was to acknowledge what had happened, and I could not do that. I could not move. My heart was banging against my ribs. I counted the beats, trying to slow them. Counted, to try to stop me thinking about anything else, to stop me acknowledging what had happened.

Then I heard a door open just along the landing. Ella's door; I knew by the creak, and my heartbeat raced up again, thundering in my ears. I heard the squeak of the floorboards and the click of the bathroom light; I turned my head and saw the momentary glow of light through the gap under my door before she closed the bathroom door behind her. She would see the glow of my light through that same gap, if she looked. She might have seen it already; she might come in, saying, 'Mummy, why are you still up?'

I forced myself to move. My body felt flattened, all my joints stiffened up. My chest hurt where he had leant on me, holding me down. Quickly, I sat up and the blood roared in my head. I stuck out an arm to turn off my lamp, and I knocked it right off the bedside table and had to scramble for it on the floor. I hoped to God Ella did not hear. Then I lay down on my bed, pulling the duvet over me, as if I was asleep. I lay still as a corpse in the dark, my heartbeat pounding, listening to Ella flushing the toilet, then running the taps. I heard the bathroom door open, and again the click of the light. I dared not breathe. Go back to bed, I willed in my head. Please, go back to bed. She was out there, hesitating; I could sense it. Then I heard her feet on the floorboards, the creaking of her own bedroom door.

I had not heard Max, creeping up the stairs. I did not hear the boards creak under his weight. But then I had not been listening out for him; I had been lost in my own thoughts, thinking I was safe, thinking we all were. I had actually felt reassured by his presence downstairs – another man in the house and all that. Sam might have heard him, though, or Ella. They could very well have heard him making his way up the stairs; they might even have heard us talking. The thought chilled me; it absolutely appalled me. Never mind what he had done to me, but that he had done it in my house with my children there; with 11-year-old Ella lying in her bed just across the landing – it was unthinkable, incomprehensible, barbaric. I lay there, rigid with fury, staring at the dark. I could feel his . . . *stuff* . . . running out of me so foul, so entirely repulsive and disgusting. I could smell him still, in my room, on my face. His saliva had dried on the skin around my mouth, powdery and tight.

I waited till the house was silent again, truly silent. I listened so hard I could almost hear my children sleeping behind their closed doors. There was the odd creaking of the beams and the wind outside, nothing more. And then I ripped off my nightshirt, put on my dressing gown, and went to the bathroom to wash myself. I squatted in the bath and scrubbed at myself, using the hand shower, scrubbed and scrubbed till my skin was raw, till I hurt. But I could not feel clean. The pipes hissed and clanked and I crouched low in the bath; I turned the taps down to try to lessen the noise but it was no good, I could not wash under just a trickle. I was crying too, a sort of groaning in the back of my throat; I didn't realize till someone knocked on the door and then I froze.

It was Ella, come back again.

'Mum?' she said through the door.

I turned off the taps. I squatted there, my heart pounding.

'What do you want?' I hissed.

'The toilet,' she said sleepily.

'But you've just been,' I snapped.

'No I haven't,' she said, injured. 'That was hours ago.'

'Just a minute,' I said. The room was thick with steam. Quickly I climbed out of the bath and dried myself. I wiped the towel over the mirror to clear it, put on my bathrobe and willed myself to look normal.

'Mum,' Ella whined.

I opened the door and she padded in straight past me, eyes squinting in the light. I closed the door for her on my way out and whispered, 'Go straight back to bed, won't you?'

She didn't reply.

I went back to my room and turned off the light. And I stood by my door, waiting till I heard Ella finish in the bathroom and go back to bed. It seemed she hadn't noticed anything out of the ordinary in her half-asleep state, thank God. But she could have done. So easily, she could have done.

I got back into bed, but I would not sleep. I could not sleep, with Max downstairs. I lay rigid, every cell in my body alert. What if he came back up? What would I do then? I stared through the dark at my door. I strained my ears, listening.

And then the recriminations and the doubts came storming through my head. What had I done to make Max think I would want him to come to my room? Because I must have done something – a 15-year-old kid does not act without some kind of go-ahead, surely. Did I lead him on in some way? I couldn't have done. I certainly never meant to. Yet I thought of how I tucked my toes under his legs on the sofa earlier, of how I let him comfort me in the kitchen, and of how grateful I had been for that comfort. But surely he did not take that as encouragement? We were easy together, that's how it seemed to me. He was my son's friend and my friend's son. Part of the family, you could say. And a child. Is it really true that you cannot be at ease with a child without them thinking they can do such a thing?

Repulsion rose inside me, acid in my throat. I clenched my fists under the duvet, driving my nails into my palms.

Should I have read the signs somehow? Were there any signs? I thought of him, always listening in on conversations between Melanie and me. I thought of his advice so maturely given: 'You'll be all right, Jane.' Again I thought of him holding me in his arms downstairs, earlier, in the kitchen. Being, I thought, so very kind to me.

It never occurred to me that he might think it more than that.

But he'd come upstairs to see how I was, and he had thought he would be welcome. He'd thought there was a chance at least; in his arrogance he had thought it worth a shot. And backing down does not come naturally to people like Max – oh no, people like Max and Melanie are always right, they always see things through.

Max was still there in the morning, and would be till Jake came to fetch him on his way back from Kelly's. Melanie wasn't coming for him, thank God; at least I didn't have to face her.

He was down in the kitchen with Sam. They were talking; I listened through the open crack of my bedroom door, trying to catch what they were saying.

'You've got to line them up first then you take all three,' Max was saying in his usual, know-it-all manner.

'Yes, but you can do one at a time,' said Sam.

'No, no, mate. That's where you're wrong. You've got to have all three . . .'

He wouldn't tell Sam what he had done, surely. He wouldn't tell anyone, would he?

They were making breakfast. I could smell toast and I could hear both boys, opening and closing cupboard doors. I pictured Max's hands on my plates and my cutlery, I saw him opening the fridge and helping himself to butter and jam. His filthy fingers, touching everything. I didn't want him sitting at my table, eating my food. I didn't want him in my house, now or ever again.

'Mum?' Ella called, bounding up the stairs. She'd gone down early to watch TV. Now she came into my room, still in her Pink Pig pyjamas, her hair all messy, her bright blue eyes so shiny and keen. 'Can I go to the stables later?' she said. 'Can I, as Daddy's not coming today?'

I could not bear that she had been downstairs unprotected from him.

'I don't know Ella. I've got a headache. I can't think now.'

'Oh please,' she said. 'I hardly ever get to go on Sundays.'

'I don't know.' I wanted to hear what Max and Sam were saying, and I couldn't with Ella bleating in my ear. But I looked at her crestfallen face and I felt even more wretched. 'Look, I'll see,' I said. 'But please, just go and get dressed now.'

I watched him leave from my window. I swear, I had counted every second till Jake finally arrived, screeching Melanie's car to a stop outside our house, and slamming the door as he got out. He swaggered to our front door, and Max, when Jake had knocked for him, swaggered out. I watched them with loathing, and I felt the wool brutally ripped from my eyes. How did I ever think there was anything to be admired in that family? How did I ever mistake their arrogance for confidence; their indifference for laid-back charm?

I never wanted to see Max, or Melanie, or any of them again.

TWENTY-FIVE

On Monday afternoon I sat parked up in my car just past the school in the rain, waiting for Sam and Ella. I'd got there early but still the only space was on the road facing towards Melanie's. I sat there with the engine running to try to stop the windows steaming up, and with the front and back wipers going full pelt. And I watched for my kids in the rear-view mirror. I wanted them to be quick. I wanted to get them in the car and be gone.

Then Max came strolling through the gates in a crowd, five or six of them, all boys; his little pack with their ties undone, shoving at each other, taking up space so that other kids instinctively got out of their way. Will was among the group, and Tommy, and coming up behind them a clutch of girls; I recognized some of them, too, including Lydia, the girl Sam liked. But there was no sign of my Sam. I watched Max; I could not help myself. I felt the strange pull of loathing. I watched him getting closer to my car. I watched his face with its constant, semi-mocking sneer, and the way he interacted with his peers; those leadership qualities I had so admired. Oh yes, he was a leader all right. He was the boss.

I knew he'd seen me; he'd have recognized my car, and I was right there in his path. I slunk down in my seat when he got nearer; until he'd gone past. But then he turned round, and he smiled at me. A complete smile; that's the only way I can describe it. No shame, no regret, just satisfaction at the way things were. Oh yes, everything was fine in Max's world.

What did he think, that I'd be OK with what had happened? That if I hadn't wanted it then, I would, in retrospect, want it now? What's a little force when a little force is all that's needed?

He took his time with that smile; for a moment, to my horror, he separated from the crowd. I can only think that he could not properly see me; that he could see, perhaps, the outline of me, the positioning of my face, but not the expression on it. Not my eyes.

Again and again I asked myself how I did not see it coming, somehow; and, worse still, how did I not stop him? I went over and over it, tormenting myself. There was no escape, especially at night. I could not shut it out of my head. I could not sleep, had not slept since it happened. I lay in my bed at night, tense, alert to every sound; so many threats in the silence. The clunk of a radiator cooling; the creaking of settling wood. Outside the far cry of some night animal; closer, the scratching below my window of . . . what? A squirrel; a rat? A fox perhaps, prowling.

How did I not hear Max's tread on the stairs that night when I could hear it now, again and again? When every single noise now sounded like him; even the wind in the trees was a warning.

We were so alone out here, Sam, Ella and me.

Melanie called me on my mobile but I didn't answer. I didn't answer the home phone either when it rang, in case it was her. I hid myself away at home with no one but myself for company, and nothing to do but go over and over in my head what had happened. I replayed it constantly; Max's hand on my chest, holding me down; the smell of his body. The utter violation of it sickened me. I could not squash the memory; I could not dampen it down.

I made endless excuses to my children about why we could not see Melanie and her kids; we had viewers coming round to see the house, I had a headache, Ella was going down with a sore throat. Feeble excuses; they would not work forever.

Of course Sam and Ella still saw Max and Abbie every day at school. It killed me to think of them being around Max, of having anything to do with him. But what could I do about it? I could not keep them away from him. If I did so I would have to tell them why.

On Thursday evening when she was eating her pasta Ella said, 'I'm going round Abbie's after school tomorrow. I haven't been round there at all, all week. She said I could stay over.'

'You can't stay over,' I said, too quickly.

And she said, 'Why not?'

I looked at her, at her eyes so determined and, it seemed to me, so suspicious too. 'You've got riding on Saturday morning,' I said.

'So?'

'So you need to be here.'

'No I don't. You could pick me up on Saturday morning and take me to the stables from there.'

'Ella,' I said, 'I am not your chauffeur.'

'You've done it before,' she said.

'And I don't want to do it again.'

She glared at me, the colour hot in her cheeks. 'Abbie's

right,' she said, throwing down her fork. 'Abbie said her mum said you've gone all stuck up and don't want to know her now we're moving back to *Lon*don.'

And she slammed back her chair and flounced out of the room.

Sam, who was still eating, looked up now. 'Are we moving back to London?' he said.

'No,' I said.

'Then why did she say that?'

'I don't know. And I don't know where we're moving to.'

He carried on slowly eating, and frowning, and I sat there, feeling myself trapped in this web of my own stupid making.

'Is Max coming round here on Friday?' he said after a while, because remember it was always up to me to arrange these things, to invite Sam's friends round. It was always me that invited Max.

'Probably not,' I said, the words so bitter in my mouth.

Reluctantly, I suggested that he go round Max's after school with Ella, just for a few hours. I suggested it, only so that Ella wouldn't be there on her own. I could not bear the thought of her being near Max, yet nor could I think of a believable reason to stop her going round there. How could I keep her away from Abbie?

'I'll pick you both up later,' I said, though God knew how I would. God knew how I would walk in to Melanie's house, and chat, and act as if everything was normal.

On Friday evening, when my children were both round at Melanie's, I sat out here in my house miles from anywhere, unable to think properly, unable to do anything but stare out of the window at the dark. I could not even have a drink because I had to drive later to pick up Sam and Ella. I counted the hours, literally; I sat at the kitchen table and watched the clock and counted the hours.

I hated the thought of Sam and Ella being in that house with Max, and I hated myself for letting them go there. It was wrong of me, stupid of me, but what else could I do?

And God help me, but I deserve an Oscar, I deserve every award going for the performance I put on collecting my kids from Melanie's. I drove over there in the dark steeling myself.

Melanie answered the door to me, so cool towards me, so clearly pissed off with my remoteness this last week.

'Hi,' I said.

I could barely bring myself to look at her. Any affection I'd ever felt for her was dead in the ground. I could see only her failings as a parent, magnifying my own.

But I walked into that room, and I stood there, my weight on one leg, my arms casually folded in front of my waist, car keys dangling. The smile that I'd slapped on my face dug in at the corners, as if pins were holding it. Sam and Ella weren't ready, they never were. They were upstairs with Abbie and Max; I could hear them all, their feet hammering on the floor above, the clashing racket of separate CDs.

Normally Melanie would invite me in for a drink. But this time, she said, 'You been busy?'

'Oh yes,' I said. 'You know . . .'

'Oh I know,' she said sarcastically. 'Takes a lot of time up, moving.' She turned to the stairs. 'Kids!' she yelled over the din of the music.

We stood there, waiting for a response.

'Kids!' she yelled again, louder. 'Turn that off, won't you? Jane's here.'

Max came down first, with Sam following after. I could

not look at Max, but I could feel him watching me, the smirk on his face turning sullen.

'Ella!' I called up the stairs. 'Ella, we need to go.'

He was looking at me. He didn't stop looking at me.

'So have you sold your house yet?' Melanie said.

'No,' I said. 'Not yet.'

'Mm,' she said.

'Ella!' I called again. Without looking at Melanie I said, 'Thank you for having them.'

'You're welcome,' she said, so polite, so off.

I was shaking when I got back in the car. I drove too fast, gripping that steering wheel so hard I had bruises on my fingers the next day. I never wanted to see any of them again, but how could I avoid them, when my kids were friends with Melanie's kids? When I had worked so hard for it to be that way? How could I disentangle us now?

Sam and Ella were both in the back of the car, both tired, both quiet, busy with their own thoughts. I looked at them in the mirror; I looked at Sam. What had he and Max talked about? Boys never talked about anything, did they? Just Xbox, games, football.

They wouldn't talk about me, surely?

Would Max hint at what he'd done, though? Would he say . . . *what*? Your mum's fit? Your mum's . . . I could not imagine it. I slammed my foot down to hard on the accelerator and in the back Ella lurched in her seat.

'Mu-um,' she complained.

And I said, 'Sorry.'

What had happened was bad enough, but it would be far, far worse if Max should ever tell anyone. Because how would I live with it then? How would I carry on? I looked at them again, at Sam and Ella; my children. And they were just children; innocent, oblivious. I loved them so much that it hurt my heart. They could never know about Max and me, never. The thought of it appalled me.

I had to speak to Max. I had to be sure he would never tell.

TWENTY-SIX

I needed to catch Max alone. It would be no good after school; he always came out in a crowd. And no way could I speak to him at his house, not with Melanie there. So it would have to be in the morning.

Each day I got up extra early. I chased the children along; I allowed plenty of time for starting the car. And so I dropped them at school earlier, and then I turned the car round and pulled up wherever I could to wait for Max. I sat in my car as so many kids dressed in grey and blue wandered past and watched out for him. It did not occur to me that anyone would think it odd should they see me; I could only think of what I had to do. The first couple of mornings that I did this Max walked past me, but he wasn't alone, and if he saw my car he did not acknowledge it. On Wednesday I parked further down the road, nearer to the main turning into the town centre. He was late that morning and at first I thought I'd missed him, but then I saw him, hurrying up the road on his own.

I got out of my car. 'Max,' I said.

He hadn't seen me, and now he looked up, and slowed his step. I watched the surprise on his face turn guarded, and he stopped in front of me, slinging his bag up higher on his back.

'We need to talk,' I said, my voice wooden and awkward. And I forced myself to keep looking at him. He's just a boy, I told myself. He's fifteen.

'OK,' he said, and very slightly he raised one eyebrow, and one corner of his mouth, in a look of studied cool. I bet he had been practising it in the mirror. I bet he had been practising it for years.

'What happened,' I said, struggling to keep my voice steady, 'was wrong. You were wrong.'

That half-smile slipped off his face. 'You're saying I was wrong?'

'Yes,' I said. 'You had no right to do what you did.'

'And there was me thinking it took two,' he said.

My heart was pounding. I could feel the sweat trickling down my back. 'I did not want you to do what you did,' I said. 'And it will not happen again.'

He stared at me now, eyes narrowed, looking every bit the petulant teenager.

I swallowed hard. 'And I want you to promise me that you will tell no one.'

Slowly, he nodded his head. 'Ah,' he said. 'So that's what this is about. You're worried about your precious reputation.'

He smiled then, but it wasn't a nice smile. And before I could say anything else he gave the bag on his back a shove and sauntered off down the street.

The following Friday Sam was invited to a party at a house just the other side of town. Normally, on such an occasion, he would stay over at Max's. Normally, I would not have given it a second thought.

This time, I said, 'I'll come and pick you up, if you like.'

Yet even as I offered I was wondering what I would do with Ella, whether I would have to drag her out with me, to which she would most certainly object, or risk leaving her here on her own.

Sam looked at me, strangely. 'What time?' he said.

And I thought of Ella, and of how late I dare leave her. 'Eleven?'

'Don't be stupid,' Sam wailed, the colour rushing into his face, 'I can't go home at eleven! Everyone would laugh at me!'

'Well . . . I can't really leave Ella,' I said.

'Then don't leave her. I'll stay at Max's,' Sam said, the fear of humiliation burning in his cheeks. 'That's what I always do. You just can't pick me up.'

Sam spent hours getting ready for that party. I did not know that boys could take so long. Eventually he came downstairs in a waft of cheap aftershave, every hair carefully preened into place.

'Lydia's going to be there,' Ella told me in a loud stage whisper, her big eyes gleefully round.

'Oh,' I mouthed back, and put a finger to my lips to hush her.

Sam had heard her anyway. His face, already flushed from the heat of the shower, turned pinker.

I dropped him off at Melanie's at about eight that evening, without going in myself. And I went back to collect him on Saturday morning, when Ella was at the stables.

But he wasn't there.

I knocked at Melanie's door, and she looked almost surprised to see me. We had not spoken for over a week. Looking back, I think she must have assumed I'd come with an apology for my sudden aloofness, or an explanation at least. She stood in the open doorway, waiting for me to speak.

'I've come for Sam,' I said, and now she really looked taken aback.

'Oh,' she said. 'I don't think he's here.'

'He stayed,' I said. 'After the party.'

It irritated me that Melanie didn't know that my son was sleeping in her house, but it didn't particularly surprise me. She walked into the living room and I followed, leaving the front door ajar. I didn't expect to be there for long.

'Max,' Melanie yelled up the stairs. 'Have you got Sam up there?'

We waited for a reply. I tried to think of some natural, chatty comment to make, to force myself to be friendly. I clutched at the start of sentences in my head: How are you . . . sorry I've been so busy . . . I love your top . . . How much easier things would be if I could bridge the gap somehow, if I could reach beyond what Max had done and keep hold of my friendship with Melanie. How much easier, in every way.

But I couldn't.

Melanie stood with her back to me, hostile.

'Max!' she shouted again, so loud the whole street would hear. Eventually Max stirred, and thudded his way down the stairs. I expected to hear a second set of footsteps in a moment: Sam's.

'What?' Max said, rubbing the sleep from his eyes.

Oh so sweetly, her sarcasm aimed wholly at me, Melanie said, 'Jane is under the impression that you have Sam hidden away upstairs.'

Max's eyes darted to mine and just as quickly darted away again. 'Well, I haven't,' he said.

'He hasn't,' said Melanie. She folded her arms across her chest and looked at me. 'OK now?'

'No,' I said. '*No*.' Panic flashed across my shoulders. 'He has to be here. He said he was staying here.' I looked from Max to Melanie and back to Max again. 'Then where is he?'

Melanie said, 'Perhaps he got lucky,' and Max smirked.

I wanted to wipe that smirk off his face. I wanted to slap him. I said again, half shouting now, 'Where is he?'

'I don't know,' Max muttered. 'I thought he went home.'

'But he didn't!'

Max shrugged, and avoided my eye.

'You want to calm down,' Melanie said to me. 'It's not up to Max to know where Sam is. Max isn't Sam's keeper, you know.'

I managed to get the address of the party off them. It was at the house at the end of Bath Rise with the caravan parked out front, Max grudgingly told me, though he had nothing so useful as a number.

'Where the hell is Bath Rise?' I said.

And Melanie, showing me to the door, pointed up the street. 'It's off Angel Street. The new estate.'

And she closed the door, leaving me to it.

Surely, *surely*, Sam knew always to phone me if he changed his plans. I tried ringing his phone but it was turned off; no doubt the battery had gone down. But he could have used someone else's phone, or the house phone. Anger with Sam competed with the panic in my heart and I clung to that anger – I did not dare consider that he might not still be at the house when I found it.

I drove erratically, looking for Bath Rise. It wasn't off Angel Street; it turned out to be off Winkfield Drive, which itself was off Angel Street, and so I drove straight past it at first, wasting precious time. I had to be back at the stables for Ella in less than half an hour. Sam better be there; he simply had to be there.

I realized I didn't even have the name of the person whose party it had been. 'Some boy in my year,' that's all Sam had told me, and I hadn't thought to ask Max. The new houses sprawled round, one road leading into another. I found the house; as well as the caravan parked out the front there were plenty of empty cans littering the drive, a smattering of broken glass and the partly burnt remains of an upholstered chair.

I rang the bell and a harassed-looking man answered.

'Oh no,' he said. 'No one stayed over. I got rid of the last of them in the early hours.'

I do not know how I managed to drive back to get Ella. All I could think was that I couldn't lose both my children; I had to get Ella back where she should be, safe, before I could even think what to do about Sam. I drove too slowly for fear of driving too fast and not getting there at all; people overtook me on the road, some of them blasting their horns as they did so. My hands were so numb I could barely feel the wheel. I could not see beyond a foot ahead; my world had shrunk in on itself, boxed in by fear.

Ella had made her way halfway down the lane and was standing there on the roadside, cross because I was late.

'Where were you?' she complained, getting into the car. 'I've been waiting for ages.' She slunk down on the back seat, smelling of fresh air and horses. I drove on, hunched over that steering wheel, straining my eyes to see.

'Where's Sam?' she asked when we were almost home, having noticed at last, that he wasn't there.

*

I would have to phone David. This thought came into my head as though written on a list and I wanted to cross it straight back off that list. I did not want to phone David. I did not want this situation at all. I had trusted Sam. How could he not be where he was supposed to be?

I pulled up in our drive.

I had half expected Sam to be sitting there on the doorstep, waiting for me. Max had said he thought Sam had gone home, and I wanted to believe that. I wanted for there to have been some mix-up, and for Sam, magically, to have been transported all those lonely dark miles across the fields. I wanted him to be sitting there, waiting for me, and for him to stand up now, tired, hungry, happy to be home.

My house greeted me, as bleak as I had left it.

'Put your stuff in the shed,' I said to Ella.

'What about Sam?' she said.

And stupidly, as if we still lived in London, as if there were buses coming by every ten minutes, all day, all night long, I said, 'He'll be home in a minute.'

I walked into the house. My heart, if I ever had one, was stuck somewhere close to my lungs, a squashed, misshapen obstruction of a thing. I could not even feel my feet. I slapped my way across the cold tiled floor. I had worried about Sam getting lost in London. I had worried about all manner of things. The social pressures; the wrong friends; the bad influences upon my dear sweet boy. I had watched him go off to school with my heart in my throat. I had ideals then. I had hopes.

I made it to the kitchen and stood at the sink. I really did not know what to do. There were no streets to go out searching, no friends on whose doors to knock. I was in the wrong place; we all were. And my Sam was lost.

'Mum! Mum!' Ella was running across the garden. I watched her, as though through a dream. She started hammering on the back door. I listened, unable to make myself move.

'Mum!' she called. 'Mum! Let me in. Sam's in the shed.'

TWENTY-SEVEN

He was just sitting there, down among the old boots and paint pots and the lawnmower, arms around his drawn-up legs, face hidden on his knees.

'Sam?' I said. 'What are you doing?'

'He won't talk, Mum,' Ella said. 'He won't say anything.'

'Sam?' I said louder this time, as if to make him hear. The panic that I had felt dissipated now with relief that he was safe, but the anger stayed. The anger that he had put me through this; that I'd had to go into Melanie's house and speak to Max; that whatever had happened, Sam hadn't phoned. 'I have just driven halfway across the county looking for you,' I said, exaggerating somewhat. 'How the hell do you think I felt when you weren't at Melanie's? Why weren't you at Melanie's and why didn't you phone me?'

Sam's arms unsnaked from around his legs, and wrapped themselves around his head instead. A beat of alarm kicked in my heart. Ella reached out a hand and patted him as if he was a cat and he flinched under her touch.

'Are you OK, Sam?' she asked tenderly.

'What happened, Sam?' I said, more gently now. 'And how did you get home?'

He didn't answer.

'You didn't walk, surely?' I said. 'It's miles away. You could have got lost. You could have ended up anywhere.' I could hear my voice, rising up again. Sam put his hands over his ears, shutting me out. He curled himself down into a tight, closed-up ball.

'Come on, Sam. Come into the house,' I said. 'You can't stay out here for ever. You'll freeze to death.'

'Good,' Sam muttered into his knees, and a butterfly of fear flapped its wings in my chest.

He did come in, eventually. We coaxed him between us, Ella and I. He hobbled into the house like an invalid, exhausted. I fussed around in the shelter of my kitchen, scrambling him some eggs, heating a can of soup. All the while I talked, rambling on in a way that I thought any mother would ramble on in such circumstances, trying to keep things normal. I peppered my sentences with comforting 'oohs' and scolding 'aahs', just like Peter Rabbit's mother in that dear old story, the story that Sam had loved so much as a child. But I was thinking on my feet, thinking ahead, covering myself. Because what if Max had said something to Sam?

He just couldn't have. He wouldn't dare.

'I take it you've fallen out with Max,' I said. 'It doesn't surprise me. That boy – I mean no disrespect – he isn't always truthful, Sam. He isn't an . . . easy character. I've thought it for a while. I know you've been friends for a long time, and I've been friends with Melanie, but, well, I don't know, sometimes people aren't what they seem, Sam. Sometimes it takes a while to realize that. Perhaps you'd do better to make other friends—'

Sam slammed down his spoon, splattering tomato soup everywhere. 'Stop going on about Max,' he shouted. 'I don't want to hear about fucking Max!'

He pushed back his chair so hard it fell over, smashing down on the tiles. And he went up to his room, and there he stayed for the rest of the day.

I had never heard Sam swear before, ever. That in itself was warning enough. I could not bring myself to think what Max might have said to him, but he had said something all right.

Later, Ella, who always loved a drama, said to me, 'Do you think Sam's upset because of Lydia? Do you think she doesn't love him?'

Oh how I wished things might be as simple as that.

'Maybe,' I said, and I tried to ignore the pulse of foreboding throbbing through my head.

Strangely, whatever was going on in our house was put on hold for the hours that David was here on Sunday. It was as if there was an unspoken agreement: none of us wanted to involve Dad. I should take comfort from that at least. I should see in that the faintest flicker of hope.

Sam was very quiet, but I hoped that David was too preoccupied to notice. He spent most of his time here up a ladder, unblocking a blocked gutter, then raking the acorns off the lawn and sweeping up all the millions of leaves. I watched him, realizing how strange it must be for him to come back and do these dull, domestic things. I saw the expression on his face and I rather think that he thought that too, and my sympathy for him vanished.

'The kids should be out here, doing this,' he complained when he'd swept those leaves into one enormous pile.

To which I said, 'Yes, but the kids aren't the ones who want to move.' Because it seemed to me that that was all it was about: keeping the place nice, keeping it tidy. Earlier in the week someone had put an offer on the house; too low, but an offer nevertheless. We were 'sitting on it' for now, hoping something better would come along. Though suddenly the idea of moving did not seem so bad; the idea of moving, of running far, far away.

Later, when David was soon to go, he came upstairs where I was hiding out of his way. I was lying down, half reading a magazine. He tapped on my door and then stood there awkwardly in that devil's space between door and bed. It was a long, long time since David had entered this room.

'What's wrong with Sam?' he said.

I kept hold of my magazine, and tried not to look at him. 'Nothing,' I said.

'Ella tells me he slept in the shed last night,' he said. 'Is that true?'

Damn Ella and her love of a show. I could so picture her, letting the secret out of the bag, clamping her hand over her mouth too late.

'He didn't sleep there,' I said. 'He came home early from where he had been sleeping.' Which wasn't so far from the truth.

David stood there. I could almost hear his mind working. And I could feel his sense of loss; that scary, weightless fear of not knowing where your children are when you are far away from them. Not knowing where they are, or how they are, or who they are with. The reins had slipped from his hands, and what did he have now to hold onto?

'Oh,' he said. And, after a moment, 'Do you think that's OK?'

'Well he's home, isn't he?' I said, trying to keep my voice casual, and my eyes fixed firmly on that magazine.

*

But on Monday morning Sam would not get out of bed.

'Sam!' I called from the chaos of downstairs. 'Sam, get up!'

Eventually I went up to his room and tapped on the door. His room was in darkness, and he lay on his bed with his face to the wall.

'Sam, come on,' I said and when still he did not move I went over to him and shook him. 'You'll be late for school.'

He kept his eyes squeezed shut. 'I'm not going.'

'Come on, you have to,' I said. I tugged at his duvet and he yanked it back, pushing me away at the same time.

'I'm not going,' he shouted.

I drove Ella to school on her own, my heart racing anxiously the whole way there and the whole way back again. I needed to know what had happened at the party, and why Sam hadn't stayed at Max's. I could not believe that Max would have told him about me – certainly not everything. But if he had told him even something I had to know.

Sam was still in bed when I got back, lying on his back and staring at the ceiling.

Bracing myself, I said, 'Do you want to talk about it?'

I sat down on the end of his bed, accidently brushing against his foot. Instantly that foot shot away from me. It was not so long ago that if Sam was sad or anxious about something he would curl up on my lap, burying his head into me. And how easy it was to comfort him then, how easy to just stroke and soothe him. Now his whole body tensed up, recoiling away from my nearness.

'What happened, Sam?' I said gently. 'Talk to me.'

He lay there with his mouth clamped shut.

'Please, Sam,' I said, and, as if to convince myself, 'It can't be that bad, surely.'

But he would not speak.

I swallowed, my throat dry.

'Look,' I said at last, in desperation, 'if you've fallen out with Max why don't you have some of your other friends round next weekend? How about Tommy and Will? Max doesn't have to come. You could call them later if you like, fix it up—'

'Oh you'd love that, wouldn't you?' he said and he leapt from the bed, in one sudden movement, so fast I had to duck. And then he stumbled past me and out into the bathroom, slamming the door.

'Sam and Max had a fight,' Ella told me from the back of the car on the way back from school.

'Yes, Ella, I think I'd worked that out,' I said.

'No, a proper fight, over a girl. Over Lydia.'

'How do you know?' I said.

'Abbie told me. I told her Sam slept in the shed, and she told Max and Max said Sam was a geek and that he threw a strop because Lydia liked him instead!'

I tried to follow this. 'Who threw a strop?' I said.

'Sam did of course. Because Lydia liked Max.'

Right then I felt this tremendous weight start to lift from me. I was almost light-headed with relief, with the unexpected hope that this was true. 'That's what this is about?' I said. 'It's about Lydia?'

I looked at her in the rear-view mirror, and she nodded, her eyes wide, teeth digging into her bottom lip. And for a brief, delirious moment I thought things might be OK.

Sam wasn't in his room when Ella and I got home; he wasn't in the house at all. We spotted him, eventually, sitting at the top of the hill, his small solitary shape silhouetted against the colourless sky. If this really was all about Lydia, Sam just needed some time alone, time to heal. That's what I told myself; that's what I let myself hope. He's just upset about Lydia. Please, please let it be true. My poor Sam; how sweet of him to hurt like this over a girl, and how typical for him to lose out to Max. Sam was a billion times the better person than Max, yet it had taken a cruel lesson for me to see it.

He was still up there when it was starting to get dark.

'I'll go and get him,' Ella said and I watched from the back garden as she first ran then crawled her way up the hill. At the top she stood with her hands on her hips, catching her breath. She crouched down to Sam, and put her hand on his arm, then she stood up again. I wished I could hear what they were saying. And I wished they would hurry up and come down; it would be properly dark soon.

I walked through the gate at the end of the garden and stood at the bottom of the hill. 'Come down,' I called, but the wind blew my words straight back at me. 'Come down,' I yelled louder. And I gestured with my hands.

Ella could see me; surely she could hear me too. She stuck out her arms in an exaggerated shrug, then started scrambling back down the hill towards me.

Sam stayed up there. I was getting really annoyed now, and anxious too. 'Sam!' I called. 'Come on!'

I started climbing up the hill, meeting Ella on the way.

'He won't come,' she said. 'I tried, I really did.'

'OK. Just go inside now.'

The hill was steep. I had only ever climbed it once before, just after we first moved here; we'd all climbed up then, the whole family, to see the amazing view. Now I puffed my way to the top, intermittently stopping, and calling, yet again, to Sam.

'For God's sake, Sam, I've been calling you. Why didn't you answer me?' I said when finally I reached him. He was sitting facing away from the house, with just more hills and more fields spread out before him, so grey, so bleak now, merging with the dark. It was cold up there with no shelter from the wind and I shivered, hugging my arms across my chest. Sam was wearing just his jeans and a shirt. 'Come on, Sam, this is silly,' I said. 'I'm freezing.'

'Then you go back down,' he said.

'Look, I know you're upset,' I said, 'but staying up here isn't going to help.' I crouched down beside him; I didn't want to sit because the ground was too cold and damp. And I tried to put my arm around him to warm him a little, to comfort him.

He slapped my arm away. 'Get off me,' he said.

'I'm trying to understand!' I said. 'I'm trying to be nice to you.'

'Well don't bother.'

'Look,' I said, 'if it's any consolation I can't think why Lydia would choose Max over you.'

He looked at me. 'What?'

Of course I wasn't supposed to know, so quickly I said, 'I'm just guessing, Sam. Call it mother's instinct.'

He stared at me in disbelief. Then, 'You don't know anything at all!' he yelled, right into my face. And he stood up and stomped away from me, heading back down the hill, because, let's face it, he had nowhere else to go.

'Sam!' I called. 'Sam!' I ran after him, tripping and sliding my way down, struggling to keep up. 'Sam, wait for me. And don't talk to me like that!'

But when we were back down on level ground, instead of going into the house, he headed for the shed. 'What are you doing?' I said, running along behind him.

He sat himself down, just as we'd found him on Saturday morning.

'Stop this, please,' I said. 'Just come inside.'

'No.'

'You need to eat. You need to get warm.'

'I'm not going in the house,' he said. 'I'm staying here.' And he made a circle with his arms on his knees, and hid his face.

'But this is stupid,' I said.

'I don't care,' he wailed, his voice muffled against his knees. 'I'm not going in to the house. Just *leave me alone*!'

I took him out blankets, and a sleeping bag. I cooked pasta in a tuna and tomato sauce; his favourite. I indulged him; I did not know what else I could do.

To Ella I said, 'He wants to sleep in the shed. Just let him.' I rolled my eyes and she rolled hers back, the words *Aren't boys strange?* unspoken between us.

And I loaded up a tray: pasta, drink, biscuits, and carried it to the shed. There I laid it down, and there he ignored it. 'This is ridiculous,' I said in desperation. 'I know you're upset about Lydia, but life's tough, Sam. I should know. And you can't react like this every time you get upset over a girl!'

But of course this wasn't just about Lydia. I was horribly aware of that.

TWENTY-EIGHT

I watched the shed all night. I didn't sleep a wink. I dragged the bedroom chair over and put it by the window, and looked down. I couldn't believe he would stay out there the whole night; he would be so cold, even with all those blankets, and so uncomfortable, down there on the dirty, hard floor. My Sam loves the comfort of his own bed; he was punishing himself as much as he was punishing me.

I tried to form a plan; some way of rescuing things. In my head, I ran through a multitude of possible explanations and reasons and lies, of course; I hoped I could get through all this with the help of lies.

Daylight dawned too slowly and it was still dark when I went out there the next morning. Sam was asleep, curled up in the most awkward position, the points of his elbows and knees jutting out from the tangled blankets like sticks. I crept into the shed, closing the door behind me, and sat down facing him in that very tight space.

He opened his eyes immediately.

'Tell me what happened,' I said.

He turned away from me, dragging a blanket up over his face.

'Go away!' he said, his voice muffled.

And I said, 'I'm not going anywhere till you talk to me.'

He pulled that blanket tighter over his head.

'I mean it, Sam!'

Still nothing.

'Damn it, Sam,' I said, 'if you won't tell me I'll have to ask Max.'

He threw that blanket off his face and sat up. 'What do you want to know?' he shouted at me. 'Max and I had a fight, OK?'

'About Lydia?'

He looked at me with the strangest expression on his face. 'Yes. About Lydia,' he said.

'Because Lydia preferred Max to you,' I said, still hoping, praying for it to be true.

'Yes.'

I knew he was lying.

'What really happened, Sam?'

He was sitting with his legs still tangled in a combination of sleeping bag and blankets. In a sudden, frustrated movement he tried and failed to free himself. He was breathing hard; I could almost hear him thinking. My poor boy; I'd got him trapped. He slumped his shoulders, defeated.

'Please, Sam,' I said, my heart thumping now, jacked up with fear. 'You have to tell me.'

He stared down at his hands. 'Lydia was drunk,' he said in a robotic monotone. 'Lydia went up to the bathroom. Max went up to the bathroom. Half an hour later Max comes down, then Lydia comes down crying.'

'What – do you think Max did something to Lydia?' I asked.

'Do I need to spell it out?' Sam said.

'You think he took advantage of her?' All over my skin goosebumps broke out, sharp as needles.

He said nothing. He'd clawed his hands and was now driving the nail of each finger into the soft skin behind the nails of his thumbs, stabbing at himself.

'So you and Max had a fight because you were upset at what he'd done to Lydia,' I said. 'Is that it?'

He made this awful choking sound then, half laugh, half cry. And he looked at me, and I will never, ever forget the expression in his eyes.

'No, Mum,' he said, 'that's not it.' He was trying so hard to stay in control but his bottom lip was wobbling away like anything, and his eyes were brimming with tears. 'I'll tell you why Max and I had a fight, shall I?' he said, his voice breaking up now. 'Max and I had a fight because he said . . . he said . . .' He swallowed hard, then slapped a sneer on his face, mimicking Max. 'He said, "What's the matter with you, Sam, are you upset because I fucked your girlfriend or your mother?" '

The blood in my veins stilled, and froze.

'There,' Sam said. 'Is that what you wanted to know?'

I felt like I'd been slapped. I forced myself to speak. 'It wasn't like that, Sam,' I said.

And he wailed, 'Oh my God, you're supposed to deny it.'

And so came the lies, kicking into place. 'Max . . . made a pass at me,' I said and oh how old-fashioned that phrase; how old-fashioned and safe and tame. 'One evening when he was here. He must have been drunk or something . . . I told him not to be so silly. I laughed it off.' I tried to laugh now, as if for example. It came out the most hideous trill. 'But Sam, some people, people like Max, don't like to be rebuked.'

Sam's hands stilled in his lap. He was listening; he wanted to believe me, I could tell.

'So . . . so what he said to you . . . that would be revenge, Sam. Sour grapes. I'm so sorry.'

Two big tears plopped down onto Sam's hands and he sniffed, hard. I shuffled round so that I was next to him, and this time when I went to put my arm around him he let me. I held him against me; I rocked him in my arms. 'I'm sorry, Sam. I'm so sorry,' I whispered into his hair. 'It must have been awful for you. That boy's so . . . cruel.'

After a while Sam pulled away from me, embarrassed now at being cuddled by his mum. He wiped his arm across his eyes.

'Shall we go inside?' I said and he nodded. 'Sam,' I said, oh so very carefully, 'you don't think Max might have forced himself on Lydia?'

'I don't know,' he said. 'She was drunk.'

Ella was up now, loitering in the kitchen in her pyjamas. She should have been ready for school by now; we should have been on our way.

'I didn't know where you were,' she wailed tearfully. 'I thought there was no one here.'

'Oh Ella,' I said, too tired, too drained to deal with her now. 'I was only outside.'

'But I didn't know that. And I'm late for school.' She looked at Sam, who brushed his way past her and staggered zombie-like up the stairs. 'I'm not going to school,' she said. 'If Sam's not going to school, why should I?'

And I really didn't care. I doubted I could have stayed awake to drive her there anyway.

*

I slept all morning, the black, dreamless sleep of oblivion; a brief reprieve. Sam slept too, and when he eventually got up he went straight downstairs to the den and turned on the computer.

I heard him screaming from the kitchen where I was making a coffee. Screaming: there is no other word for it.

I slammed down my cup and ran to the den. Ella was watching TV in the living room, still in her pyjamas; she stared as I passed her, too frightened to move. I slammed into the den and there was Sam, crouched down on the floor with his hands holding his head, no longer screaming but crying now, loudly; a deep, guttural moan.

I thought he was hurt.

'What is it? What happened?'

I bent down to him but he pushed me away, standing up now, still with his hands clutching his head.

'They all know,' he wailed in despair. 'Every single one.'

I looked at the computer, my heart pounding.

He had his Facebook page up, and there on his wall was message after message. Someone had taken a photo of Sam and Max fighting and posted it, with the caption 'Max and Samantha fighting!! Berry fights like a girl!!!'

Someone else had posted a picture of a topless model and written 'MILF Berry' underneath it. It took me a moment to work this out and when I did I felt the blood literally drain from my head.

'Oh my God,' I said.

Beside me Sam was sobbing uncontrollably.

'It's lies,' I said. 'It's nasty, nasty lies.'

But it made no difference now whether it was lies or not. It made no difference if Sam believed what I told him in the shed. It was out there; that was what mattered. The blood that had left my head flooded back suddenly in a prickling, fizzing rush. Spots flashed in front of my eyes.

'What's happened?' I heard Ella asking from the door.

'Nothing,' I snapped at her. 'Get out.'

But she didn't get out. She stood there, crying too. I yanked the computer plug from its socket, and lest she or Sam should ever see that poison again I took the scissors from the desk drawer and started hacking through the cable.

'Mum!' Ella cried. 'Stop!' And she started wailing now, loud enough to compete with Sam.

'Get out,' I yelled at her again, so fiercely that she did. I heard her howling her way up the stairs.

'Sam,' I said. 'He's not going to get away with it. He's not!'

'What are you going to do?' Sam shouted at me. 'You've done enough, haven't you, already? None of this would have happened if it wasn't for you! My life's over.'

'No it's *not*. For God's sake, Sam,' I said in desperation, 'you don't give in to bullies. You stand up to them.'

'You think that's all this is? Don't give in to bullies? You don't know anything at all!'

He pushed past me, out of the den. As soon as I could get my legs to move I followed him, up the stairs. He was already in his room, stuffing clothes into his kit bag.

'What are you doing?' I said.

'I'm leaving.'

'Don't be stupid, Sam, you can't.'

He grabbed a handful of T-shirts from his drawers, and shoved them into the bag.

'Sam, you can't,' I said again. 'You're only fifteen.'

'I'll go and stay with Dad.'

'Sam, you can't do that.'

'Why? Doesn't he want me either?' He looked up at me then, his face an open pit of pain.

'Sam, we both want you. You know that.'

'I know my life here is finished,' he said.

'Sam, it's late,' I said. 'It'll be dark soon. How will you get to London?'

'I'll walk if I have to.'

'Please . . . you're being stupid.'

He pressed down on the contents of that bag, squeezing them in. 'Well that's me,' he said. 'Stupid, stupid Sam.'

'Sam, you can't go to London. Please, just stop this.'

He zipped up his bag. 'No,' he said.

I stood in the doorway, blocking his way.

'Move,' he said.

And I said, 'No.'

'Move,' he said again, louder this time, but he didn't touch me. He didn't force me. My Sam is a kind and gentle boy, too good, far, far too good for this rotten world. His eyes filled with tears. 'Please,' he said. 'I don't want to be here any more.'

I put my hands on his arms. 'Let me call your dad, first, please? Let me call him, and if you want to go there, we can make arrangements, safely, properly. Please. I can't let you just go off like this. Please, Sam, for me.'

'OK,' he said at last, and he sat on his bed with his bag beside me while I went downstairs to phone David.

It was twenty past five. I registered that in the part of my brain that will always register such things, that will always observe the practicalities; I am, after all, a mother. David did not answer his direct line and I got put back to the receptionist.

'I need to speak to David Berry,' I said.

I waited while she tried the line that I had already tried myself. 'He isn't available,' she said. 'Can I take a message?'

'No,' I said. 'I need to speak to him. It's important.'

Within seconds he was on the line. 'What's wrong?' he said.

I said, 'You need to come home.'

'Why? What's the matter?'

'It's Sam,' I said and I started crying then, all those tears that had banked up inside me for so many miserable days.

'What is it?' he said, alarmed. 'Is he ill, hurt?'

'No,' I said, 'but something's . . . happened. He's . . . upset. He wants to go to London . . . now . . . says he's going to stay with you . . .'

'But he can't,' David said.

'I *know*, but I can't stop him. I said you'd come here . . . '

'But, Jane—'

'*Please*,' I said, my head, my throat too full of tears.

Seconds passed. At last he said, 'OK. Give me ten minutes here. I'll go back to the flat and get the car.'

Sam was still sitting on his bed when David arrived nearly four hours later, exhausted by the traffic and his own insular fears. Poor Sam, it was too long to wait for a lift; he knew we had conspired against him. 'I'm not staying here,' he said to us both with all the helpless terror of someone caged. 'I'll go on my own if I have to. I'll go anywhere.'

'OK, Sam,' David said. 'Let's talk about it.'

'I mean it,' Sam said.

David sat on the bed beside him. 'What happened?'

But Sam did not want to go through it all again. He did

not want to talk about it at all. 'Can't we just *go*,' he pleaded. 'I've got my bag. I'm ready.'

David looked at me, the frown deep between his brows, and I could see in his eyes the calculation, the realization, that he would not just be up and out at the crack of dawn tomorrow, back to London and work. Oh no, he might need to stay a little longer than that; a few hours more at least. How very inconvenient, how very unplanned.

He'd called me on his mobile from his place in the predictable, endless traffic jam, crawling its way out of London, wanting to know what this was all about.

'It's something to do with a girl,' I said evasively.

And he said, 'A girl? I'm rushing home because Sam's upset over a girl?'

'No,' I said. 'You're rushing home because you're Sam's father and he needs you.'

'Look, Sam,' he said now. 'It's a long drive back to London. And it's dark. Let me sleep here tonight. Let's all get some sleep. We'll talk about it tomorrow. We'll sort something out. I promise.'

And Sam stared at his knees, disappointment and despair etched pitifully on his face.

'Tell me,' David said, so concise, so economical with his words. We'd left Sam in his room and Ella in hers, each of them miserable behind their closed doors. It was late, and we were tired, too tired surely to talk tonight. I stood at the sink and filled a glass with water. I drank it down, and filled it again, playing for time. The darkness of the night pressed against the window, solid, black as the coat of a bear.

'I suppose you haven't eaten,' I said, though nor had we. 'Do you want a sandwich or something?'

'I'm fine,' he said. He pulled a chair out from the table to sit down, scraping it noisily on the tiles and my nerves rattled. 'Now tell me,' he said again, 'what's going on.'

I turned to face him but I could not bring myself to sit down. How much would I have to tell him? How much would he find out anyway, from Sam, from Ella, from someone, somewhere along the line? I thought of those pictures being bandied about on Facebook; I thought of Max hideously bragging. And oh how I wished this would all go away.

'Sam and Max had a fight over a girl,' I said.

'Is that all?'

'Pretty much.'

He sat there, frowning, considering me and my words.

'I cannot believe you got me up here tonight just because Sam had a fight over a girl,' David said.

'I got you here because Sam was going to leave and try and find his way down to you in London if I didn't,' I said thickly. 'I didn't know what else I could do. I do apologize if I have put you out.'

He winced, just slightly. 'I didn't mean it like that,' he said. 'You were right to call me. And I'll always be here for Sam and Ella. You know that.'

I could feel the tears prickling at the back of my eyes. I was too tired for all this talking. I wanted to just hide myself away, and sleep.

But David wanted to know more. 'Who's the girl?' he asked.

'She's called Lydia,' I said. 'You wouldn't know her.'

'But you do.'

'A bit. I've met her a couple of times.' And I could picture her with her wavy blonde hair and light-brown eyes. She'd seemed like such a sweet girl; quiet and smiley; certainly not the type that would just go upstairs with a boy like Max at a party. But perhaps I was wrong; you never can tell. And yet tiny fingertips of unease pressed their way up my spine.

'So when was this fight?' David asked.

'Last Friday,' I said. 'At a party.'

'Last Friday?' I could see him, working this out now. And the realization that we kept things from him clouded his face, as if it actually hurt him, but what did he expect? 'I knew something was wrong,' he said, more to himself than to me. Then, 'It's not like Sam to get into a fight, though.'

'Yes, well,' I said.

'Yes, well, what?'

I looked at him, sitting there like a detective, sifting through whatever information he could glean from me. Time was that I would have trusted him with anything. Time was that he would have been there for me, no matter what. But his betrayal had ruined all that. There was a barrier between us, impenetrable.

'Just I expect he had good reason,' I said. 'That's all.'

'Do you have to be so cryptic?' he said. And when I didn't reply he sighed.

'Look,' he said. 'I'll talk to Sam in the morning. I'm sure things will seem better then.'

And oh how I wished he might be right.

TWENTY-NINE

David went off to the den to pull out the sofa bed for the night, and I went upstairs to fetch him some bedding. When I came back down he was standing there, waiting for me. In his hand he held the partially severed lead to the computer, with the plug dangling from its end.

'What the hell happened here?' he said.

I stopped short, duvet and pillow bunched in my arms. I had forgotten about the computer. Not about those pictures on it, not about those oh-so-witty captions no doubt circling now among all of Sam's peers, but about what I had done with the scissors. Did I really think that by hacking at the lead I could make the damage disappear?

'There were pictures on Sam's Facebook page,' I said. 'I didn't want him to see them.'

He shook his head in disbelief. 'Couldn't you have just turned off the computer? Did you have to physically break it?'

'I didn't want anyone seeing them,' I said, my mouth dry, my heart beating all over the place, erratic, too fast.

'But why?' he said. 'What were these pictures?'

'They were just . . . horrible,' I said, my voice breaking on the word. I sat down on the sofa bed, still clasping that duvet, my legs too weak to hold me.

'But what were they of?'

'That party,' I said.

He stared at me, face like stone. Then he started scrabbling around in his overnight bag, and dug out his Blackberry.

'What are you doing?'

'I want to see these pictures,' he said.

'You can't.'

'What's Sam's password?'

'I don't know.'

He tried to log in anyway, swearing angrily when he failed. 'I'll ask Sam in the morning,' he said.

'No. You can't. Please.' I threw down that duvet and tried to snatch his Blackberry away from him. 'I don't want you to see them. I don't want anyone to see them.'

'Then tell me what the hell is going on,' he said, too loudly now, and automatically we both flinched, listening for sounds from upstairs. But the house was silent apart from us, trapped together in our private midnight hell. David closed the door, and sat down on the desk chair, facing me.

I felt like I was on trial.

'Sam and Max had a fight at that party,' I said.

'You told me that.'

I swallowed hard but my throat was raw. 'I think Max might have . . . forced himself on this girl Lydia.'

David's eyes narrowed. 'Is that what Sam said?'

'He said she was drunk. He said she went up to the bathroom and Max went up after her, and when she came down she was crying.'

'That doesn't necessarily mean anything,' David said.

…st wanted to go to the bathroom, perhaps …ng about something else.'

…at I could leave it there. That I could agree, say, 'Yes, …ure you're right.' But I knew he'd find out the rest even…ually, and how sordid would it seem then, second-hand? Besides, I had no reason to be ashamed.

'Yes, but . . . Sam seemed to think something had happened. I think Max was . . . boasting.'

'Jesus,' David said now. Then, 'Weren't there any parents at this party?'

I hugged my arms across my chest and said nothing. The truth is I didn't know. 'I got rid of the last of them in the early hours,' that man had said to me, but it didn't mean he'd been there all night.

'What was Sam even doing at a party like that?' David said and I stared at him, taken aback.

'What do you mean "at a party like that"? Do you expect him not to go out?'

'Not to parties where kids are drunk and having sex, no, I don't. Not when there are no parents there keeping an eye on things.'

'Look, I don't know if there were any parents there or not,' I said. 'But that's not the point.'

'Well it is the point,' he said. 'You let him go to this party and all this happens.' He spread his hands expansively. 'They shouldn't be out drinking at all at that age. He's fifteen, he's too young. I don't want him—'

Anger, white and sudden, flashed behind my eyes. 'You're not listening to me!' I jumped to my feet, my heart racing so fast I was shaking. 'The point is I think Max raped Lydia. I think he raped Lydia because he did the same to me.'

David recoiled as if I'd spat at him. Bizarrely, I was reminded of that long ago day when he came home from work to find me sitting at the table with my newly chopped-off hair. Then, too, he had recoiled, the shock stripping his handsome face bare.

'Max raped you?' he said, slowly, as if he could not process the words.

I wished I had not told him. I wished I had not told him because creeping into the shock on his face I could see the shadow of disgust now, though whether for me or what had been done to me I did not know. But I saw, and I felt it like a fist in my heart.

'He *raped* you?' he said again.

'Yes,' I said, through teeth clamped tight together.

He put his hand through his hair, a distancing, guarded move. 'When?' he said. 'How?'

'What do you mean, how?'

'I mean – ' still that hand was in his hair, his arm raised, a barrier between us '– where?'

He did not believe me. I do not know what he thought, but I saw his disbelief. I could see it in his eyes and I could hear it in his voice. Why else would he say when, how, where? What did he think; that I would make something like this up? I sat back down on that sofa bed, my whole body cold.

'Does it matter?' I said.

'Yes,' he said. 'Yes it does. My God, Jane.' He sat down beside me, as if to do so was to offer me empathy. As if he didn't know what else to do. His closeness both drew and repelled me. I'd wanted him to take me in his arms; I had. I'd wanted him to hold me tight and comfort me, but the only person to do that was Max.

And Max had violated me.

'He was staying here,' I said. 'He came up to my room.'

David stared at me, appalled. 'And?'

'He raped me.'

'But he can't have just . . . surely?' He shook his head in stunned disbelief. 'Didn't you stop him, didn't you . . . I mean, what was he doing even going up to your room?'

I know that he was hoping for me to take it all back; for this to be some low trick, a ploy of some sort. As if I would pull such a stunt. As if.

'I don't know, David,' I said, my heart so suddenly chilled. 'I think he was trying to cheer me up. I was upset, you see, because of you.'

'I cannot believe this,' he said, and there was the truth. He shook his head again as though to clear it. 'Max is just a kid.' Did I imagine it, or was there a needle of accusation in his voice?

'Max is not just a kid,' I said.

David rested his elbows on his knees, and cradled his face in his hands, thus removing himself from me. 'My God,' he muttered into his fingers. 'What the hell has been going on in this house?'

His words hit me like a slap in the face; the sting, so unexpected, the ensuing numbness flooding in. I began to feel strangely, floatingly detached. 'In this house . . . let me think. Ah yes, my husband ran off with someone else,' I said. 'My children's father decided he'd rather live elsewhere. As a result we are having to sell our home. My kids are miserable. I am miserable. It's been quite a barrel of laughs lately in this house.'

'For God's sake, not that again, please.' He looked up, irritation now added to the many other emotions gathered upon his face. 'I know things have been tough. They have been tough for me too. But that is no excuse for . . . ' He stalled.

The heat burned in my face, electric.

'For what, David?'

'I don't know, Jane. I truly don't know. But I come here and I don't recognize this place. I see empty cans and bottles lying around and teenage boys just coming and going—'

'I'm sorry? Are you saying this is my fault in some way? Are you saying I actually encouraged him?'

'No. No I'm not. Of course not.'

'You think I'd be interested in a 15-year-old boy? You think that?'

'No,' he said. 'But . . . maybe with everything else going on in this house . . . maybe he thought . . . Oh, I don't know, but where are the boundaries, Jane?'

I stared at him, too stunned to speak.

At some point, we each retired to our separate beds, though I doubt if either of us slept. Certainly I didn't. I lay on my back, eyes wide open, staring at the dark. My whole body was rigid, my heart thumping hard and fast.

This was worse than what had actually happened, this . . . aftermath. This questioning, and doubt; here was the true abuse. One quick fuck; that's all it was for Max. So easily done, with a little taking off guard.

Did he rape me?

Max didn't think so. I saw it in his eyes when he removed himself from me. He'd done what he wanted to, that's all. Whether I wanted it or not wasn't much of an issue; after all, what's a little coyness, a little playing hard to get?

He'd barely had to use any force.

I am not so innocent that I have not encountered sex with a teenage boy before. Of course I have; when I was a teenager. The drunken fumble at a party; the way they get you in a room, the way it's done before you know it. So quick, with teenage boys. You can almost forget it ever happened.

But that he could do that to me, a grown woman. I had let him into my home, let him into my family. That is the grossest betrayal of trust. I clawed my fingers, digging them into my stomach. I squeezed my eyes tightly shut. Inside my chest there was a solid, seething mass.

Max didn't think he'd raped me. And David wasn't entirely convinced either. David clearly thought there was room for doubt.

And now I questioned myself. I should have fought him off; I should have screamed. I should have seen it coming; my antennae should have been aware: watch out, there's a jumped-up kid with designs on you. I should have sensed the badness in that boy the minute I met him; I should have seen it in his mother even before I met him. I should have steered well clear, and kept myself alone here, in this new and friendless place. I should have been content on my own in my isolated house, baking cakes, and I should have carried on just baking those cakes after my husband had left me. I should have been a super-woman, immune to any weakness. Immune to loneliness. My children and I should have lived in splendid, virtuous isolation, never slipping up at all.

Max raped me.

There were no excuses, no other words.

THIRTY

In the morning, David was in the kitchen, waiting for me.

'Does Sam know?' he said straight away, in an almost farcical stage-whisper, glancing over his shoulder lest anyone should hear.

'Of course not,' I said. 'I told him Max tried it on, that's all.'

He closed his eyes in relief. 'Thank God for that,' he said. Then, as if that really was all that mattered, 'Poor Sam.'

Oh yes. Poor Sam.

Me, I was just flotsam and jetsam in all this, a little cast-away rubbish, tangling underneath. It was I who had muddied the waters around here.

David made a little thing about putting the kettle on, and hunting to see if there was any bread going spare for toast. He adopted an air of not exactly ease – that would be going too far – but of camaraderie in this time of crisis.

'I did not encourage Max,' I said. 'I do not know how you could even think such a thing.'

David stopped what he was doing. Carefully he placed the knife he was holding down on top of his half-buttered toast, and turned to face me.

'I'm sorry if I seemed . . . unsympathetic last night,' he

said. 'I do not blame you. What happened . . . it must have been awful.'

'Yes,' I thought, 'it was,' though I said nothing.

'Look, I know you didn't want it to happen,' he said, his eyebrows peaking so that they met in the middle, a triangle of concern. He was a teenage boy once, my handsome, upright, estranged and unfaithful husband. 'I know that. Things haven't been easy lately, for you especially. I do know that, believe me.' He paused. 'But to use the term rape, Jane. Are you sure?'

Did he think I would take it back? Did he really think I would say 'Oh well actually, now you come to mention it . . .'

'Of course I'm sure,' I snapped.

David blinked a couple of times, shuttering the solidness of me from his vision. He folded his arms across his chest; I could see that he was trembling, just slightly, inside his shirt. 'Jane, he's fifteen,' he said. 'He's a minor.'

'I know.'

'He was here in your house, in your care.'

'Yes, he was here in my house,' I said, spitting the words back at him.

I stared at him and our eyes locked. I knew exactly what he was thinking. It was written all over his face.

'It would be your word against his,' he said.

'Yes,' I said, the tears burning in my eyes now. 'And who's going to believe me when you so clearly don't?'

Sam's bag stayed packed beside the front door. He'd put it there as soon as he got up, making it clear he still intended to leave. He was in his room now, arguing with David. I could hear them, from my room; David's voice so appeasing, calling for calm, Sam's just so utterly wretched, veering from rage to tearful despair.

'You have to go to school,' David was saying. 'It's the law. You know that.'

'I'll go to school in London,' Sam pleaded. 'I'll go to a school near you.'

'I don't have any room,' David said. 'It's not my flat.'

'That's just excuses. You don't want me. You don't care.'

'I do care.'

'No you don't. You just care about yourself. You don't care what happens to me.'

And on, and on.

I stood in front of the mirror above my dressing table, and listened to them. And I stared at my reflection. I looked every one of my 44 years right then. My hair was a neglected, badly bleached mess; I was too thin. Stress and lack of sleep had taken all the colour from my face except for around my eyes; there it was painted purple. You could never say I dressed to please; you could never say I courted attention. I didn't primp and groom and flirt; by nature, I am the opposite of that. But so what if I wasn't. So what if I wore a faceful of make-up and the shortest skirts ever; had we not moved beyond that?

It was her fault m'lud, she was asking for it.

It was her fault m'lud, she gave me a beer; she made me feel too at home.

She was a lonely old woman; I was doing her a favour.

I'm just a kid, m'lud. I'm not yet sixteen.

I closed my eyes. I saw myself at that campsite in Dorset, so desperate to be free. I saw myself drunk, and stoned, and laughing; the shame of throwing up. And here in this house, again and again; come on in boys, let me bring you a beer. What did I do but try too hard?

David made Sam show him those pictures on Facebook. I heard him go downstairs, to fetch his Blackberry, then come back. I knew what he was doing, and I came out of my room, and followed him back in to Sam's. I did not want David looking at those pictures; more than that, I did not want to be hidden away in my room when he did look at them, as though in shame.

Could Sam be any more cornered? He was sitting on his bed, shaking, his eyes swollen from crying. He looked up at me when I walked in, his face raw with pain.

Yet miraculously the pictures had gone. All of them: removed.

Those boys were not stupid. They knew not to leave them there for long. Besides there was no need; the damage had already been done.

David could not take the next day off work too. He had an important meeting with clients, a pitch he felt his job depended on.

'I'll get up early and drive in,' he said. 'I'll be back tomorrow evening – as soon as I can.' He paused. 'If that's all right with you.'

'Do what you like,' I said.

It was late and we were in the kitchen. David was sitting at the table, his shoulders hunched. I found a half-empty bottle of wine in the fridge and poured him a glass; he certainly looked like he needed it. For hours he had been up there with Sam, though Sam wouldn't talk to him at all now. Nor would he come out of his room. He would not forgive David for not taking him back to London.

'Jane, I feel bad about having to leave you at all,' he said.

Those words: on what level did he mean them? Wasn't it a little too late now for regret?

Coolly, I said, 'I'm sure we'll be fine.'

He put his head in his hands, spreading his fingers into his hair. 'This is just such a mess,' he said.

I heard him leave the house at just gone four. It was pitch dark; night-time still, and raining, a steady pitter-patter hitting the roof and the trees. I heard David moving around downstairs; the running of water through the pipes. The click of his shoes on the tiled floor of the hall; the careful opening and closing of doors.

No sound escaped me any more.

The front door clicked shut behind him. I listened to his feet crunch across the gravel, and the slow, depressing start of the car. I listened as he drove away down our lane, the tyres swishing on the wet ground, and faded into the world beyond.

I buried my head into my pillow, wrapping it around my head, pressing it against my ears.

Sam would not go to school.

'I'm never going there again,' he said. 'Never. I don't care what you try and do.'

'Come on, Sam,' I said, so tired, so weary from all this. 'You have to go to school. It's the law. You know what your father said.'

Sam glared at me in disgust. 'You think I care what he says?' he shouted at me. 'What has he got to do with anything?

He doesn't even live here any more.' He jabbed his finger at me, my sad little boy. 'He is just a liar. You both are. And if you try and make me go to that school I will run away and I will never come back. I mean it.'

Ella started crying. 'I don't want to go either,' she wailed. 'I hate it there now too.'

'For God's sake,' I said to her. 'This has got nothing to do with you.'

'Yes it has!' she cried. 'I hate school and I hate it here. All anyone ever does is argue. If Sam's running away so am I.'

'Sam's not running away,' I said.

Still in my nightdress, I went outside to start the car. It was pouring with rain and the morning was pitch black, yet those few seconds alone in my car were blissful. For those few seconds, I could cry. I turned the ignition over; it spluttered, and failed. I waited the count of ten seconds and tried again; our daily damp-weather ritual. A good ten minutes it took to get the car started, a good ten minutes in which to consider the unrelenting meanness of the morning darkness. Nothing was on my side here, nothing at all.

After the car finally rumbled into life I stomped back to the house; in that short distance my nightdress was soaked. I grabbed Ella by the arm.

'We're going to school,' I said.

'No,' she yelled, letting her legs give out from under her.

I yanked her arm hard before I let it go, and then she sat there on the cold floor, rubbing at it, as if I'd hurt her. And she cried. No one cries like an 11-year-old girl; the pitch of it split through my head.

I slammed my hands into my hair. 'What do you want from me?' I screamed at her, at Sam too. 'If you don't go to school you'll be taken in to care. Is that what you want? Is it?'

'Yes,' Ella sobbed. 'If it means we don't have to live here any more.'

At three o'clock I was still in my nightdress, locked in my house by the hammering rain, having my kids' misery rammed down my throat. I felt like I would explode. Already it was getting dark. There was no escape. Ella had not stopped crying all day, as if she was crying on behalf of all of us.

What now? I could see no end.

This was Max's fault, all of it. I wanted that boy to pay.

They'd be coming out of school in half an hour. I grabbed an old jacket off the pegs by the door and flung it on over my nightie; I stuck my bare feet into wellington boots. And I went out to my car, swearing to God I would commit murder if it didn't start first time. It did, for the first time ever, and I drove along those lanes like I have never driven before. I didn't even care about the rain bucketing on to the windscreen, nor the slackness of the brakes on those wet, dark roads. Oh yes, I courted fate, right then; what else had I got to lose? I covered a twenty-minute journey in ten, only slowing when I hit the traffic into town.

I pulled up outside the school gates at 3.25. Right outside, bumping my tyres up onto the pavement.

I was looking for Lydia.

I'd only met her a couple of times; really, I couldn't even be sure if I would recognize her now. How would I pick her out from all these other girls that looked so much the same with their long hair and their princess faces?

The rain flooded across the windscreen and I kept the engine running and the wipers going full pelt; still the glass kept on steaming up and I had to rub it and rub it again with the sleeve of my jacket.

The kids started streaming out, some huddled under umbrellas, most of them just running, heads down into the rain. How would I see her? How would I stop her in time? I wound down the window and leaned out, and the rain came beating in. That could be her, or that girl, there.

'Lydia!' I called out. Faces turned, looked at me in curiosity, looked at me as though I was mad.

'Lydia!'

A couple of girls slowed down and sniggered. No matter, at least she'd hear me when she did appear. I saw several faces from Sam's year; kids who'd been in my house. I hoped to God I saw Lydia before Max came along – and then there she was.

'Lydia!'

She turned and looked towards the car, squinting into the rain. She frowned and carried on walking but I called her again; I started rolling the car along the pavement after her, still leaning out the window.

'Lydia! I'm Jane Berry – Sam's mum,' I called, in case she didn't remember me.

'What do you want?' she hissed at me, still walking, hugging her bag to her chest.

'I want to talk to you,' I shouted after her, the rain catching in my mouth. There was an audience gathering now; they had to jump to get out the way of my car.

'Why?' She stopped and turned to me, her face scarlet.

'Get in,' I said.

'No,' she said, 'I can't.' So I turned off the engine, started getting out the car. And they laughed at me, those kids gathered around; laughed at me in my nightdress and wellies. How I hated them. How I hated Lydia, too, for breaking my Sam's heart.

'OK,' she said, and she scurried round to the passenger door, opened it and threw herself into the seat, hunching down low to try and hide herself from her friends. She held her bag on her lap and she looked at me, and I could see her fear.

I realized I was breathing noisily and I tried to quieten myself. I wiped my hand across my wet face, pushing back my hair. The windows had steamed up totally, locking us into a cave.

'I want to know what happened at that party,' I said.

Poor Lydia. She looked terrified.

'With Max,' I said.

'Nothing,' she said. And she turned as if to get back out of the car. I leant across her, holding her down.

She stared at me in alarm.

'Did he rape you?'

'No.' Her eyes were as frightened as a rabbit's. 'Please, just let me go.'

But I wouldn't. I held my arm across her. And then I realized what I was doing; I loosened that arm, I softened my hand. I patted the bag on her lap; a friendly gesture, I hoped.

'Did he, Lydia? Did he force you to have sex with him? You must tell me.'

Her eyes filled with tears. 'No,' she said again. 'I was drunk,' she said. 'I don't want my parents to know. They'd kill me.'

'You're lying.'

'I'm not! Please don't tell my parents. Please. I just want to forget it.'

She was crying. I had to let her go. She scrambled out of the car, banging the door behind her. For a while I sat there in my steamed-up car, my heart pounding, my breath coming hard and fast.

She had to be lying.

I whacked the fan on full speed to try to clear the windscreen, wiping it at the same time with my arm. Most of the kids had dispersed now. Max would have come out the gates at some point; he'd probably seen my car. And now he'd be sauntering along on his smug way home. I couldn't let him get away with it.

My car was facing the wrong way; I had to bump my way off the pavement into the incoming traffic and do a U-turn. Several cars blasted their horns at me; I nearly hit a couple of boys dashing across the road in the rain.

Max was almost at his house when I spotted him. I slammed the car to a halt in the middle of the road alongside him and opened the door. 'Max!' I yelled, leaning right out, but he ignored me, and carried on walking. A car came up behind and beeped me to move. So I drove on, winding my window down. 'Max!' I yelled again, and he started walking faster, breaking into a run as he got near to his house. He scuttled up to his front door, closing it quickly behind him.

Rage burned inside me.

I had to find somewhere to park but there was nowhere. I ended up leaving the car right down past the petrol station and then had to run all the way back to Melanie's house; I was drenched when I got there, my bare legs raw from the cold. I hammered on Melanie's front door, pounding it with my fist.

Abbie answered. She opened it just a crack, peering round with wide eyes.

'I want to see Max,' I said.

She opened the door a little wider, and from somewhere inside Melanie called, 'Who is it, Abs?'

'It's Jane,' Abbie shouted back, and she smiled at me, a familiar habit of a response.

I pushed my way inside and stood dripping on their carpet. Melanie came out of the downstairs bathroom, wiping her hands on her jeans.

'Oh,' she said. 'Hello.'

'I want to see Max,' I said.

She looked me up and down and folded her arms across her chest. 'I don't know if he's in,' she said.

'He is in,' I said, and I turned my head to the stairs and yelled, 'Max!' at the top of my voice.

Abbie ran to her mum, startled.

'Now just you hang on a minute—' Melanie said but I yelled again.

'Max!'

'Jane!' Melanie said. 'What's this about?'

'I want to speak to Max,' I said.

And she said, 'You'll speak to me first.'

I stared at her. 'OK,' I said, but then we heard Max's footsteps, creeping down the stairs. Into the room he came, as if everything in the world was normal, an easy smile upon his face.

'Hi, Jane,' he said, and I wanted to slap him.

'I want to talk to you,' I said.

'What's this about?' Melanie said.

I stared at Max. 'Do you want to tell her or shall I?'

'It's nothing,' he said. 'Just some stupid misunderstanding.'

'I don't agree with you, Max,' I said.

'Max,' Melanie said. 'What's going on?'

'Maybe I should speak to Jane on her own,' Max said, the ease flickering from his eyes now.

'You'll do no such thing,' Melanie said. She turned from

Max to me. 'You don't just come barging into my house talking to my son like this.'

'Please, Mum, just leave it,' Max pleaded.

'I think Abbie might like to go upstairs,' I said.

Melanie narrowed her eyes at me then she gave Abbie a quick shove. 'Go on,' she said, 'upstairs.'

Abbie complained for just a second; of course I didn't think at the time that she would hear it all anyway, listening from the stairs. Hear it all, and then tell it all to my Ella, at school. Oh no, I didn't think of that, right then.

'Well?' Melanie demanded, hands on hips. 'What the hell is going on?'

I looked at Max. My heart was slamming inside my chest. 'Shall we tell her what you've done?' I said.

He was really squirming now, like a rat in oil.

'Look,' he said. 'This has all got out of hand.'

'Indeed it has,' I said.

'I'll apologize if that's what you want,' Max said. 'I'm sorry, OK?'

But I wanted more than a surly apology. I wanted an admission. I wanted Max to acknowledge what he had done.

I jabbed my finger at the air in front of his face. 'Sorry for what, though, Max? For what you did to me? For what you did to Lydia? For what you said to Sam?'

'What the hell are you talking about?' Melanie pushed herself between us, slapping my hand away from Max's face. Automatically, Max slunk behind her. How close they were, this family; how tight.

I leaned around Melanie so that I could still see Max. 'There is a word for what you did to me. You know what that word is, don't you, Max? That word is rape.'

The colour drained from Max's face. 'I never raped anyone,' he said.

Melanie stared at me, as stunned as if I'd slapped her. 'How dare you?' she said. And then, as she realized the greater implication of my words. 'You? You and my son – that's absolutely disgusting.'

'Yes it is,' I said. 'He came up to my room when he was staying in my house and he forced himself on me.'

'It wasn't like that,' Max said, half sobbing now.

'Oh yes it was,' I said. 'You completely abused my trust.'

'He's only fifteen for God's sake!' Melanie yelled. 'You come round here crying rape – you want to be locked up!

'You know what you did to me!' I said to Max. 'You know and I know.'

'Get out of my house,' Melanie spat. She slammed her hands square into my chest, shoving me back towards the door. 'You fucking ... *pervert*. I'll have the police on you. I'll have them do you for child abuse.'

'Just try it,' I said. 'And I'll do him for rape.'

'No one will believe you.'

'Try me,' I said.

She literally pushed me out of her house, and slammed the door. I staggered backwards into the street, lost my balance and fell, smashing my knee down on the wet pavement. Pain seared through me. For a moment I could not move. I crouched on all fours, the rain hammering on my back.

Slowly I turned and sat down. I'd scraped the skin right off my knee and the blood was running down my leg in rivulets, made more fluid by the rain. I could not stop shaking, my teeth clattering together like old bones. No one was out walking in that weather now that the kids had all gone home but there were still cars going by; their lights flashing into my eyes made me dizzy. Someone slowed up, and called out, 'You all right, love?'

I nodded a vague OK, and started forcing myself to my feet. The blood roared into my head, throbbing in my ears. I started walking back to my car in small, limping steps. God knows what I looked like, with the rain running off my head and my nightie clinging to my thighs. And people would see me, even if I couldn't see them. From windows, from cars. They'd see me, they'd talk, they'd know.

What had I hoped to achieve by having it out with Max in front of Melanie like that? I'd wanted his humiliation, but all I'd got was my own.

Melanie wouldn't take it any further; she was too smart, too protective. She'd never risk it, just in case I really did stand there in court pointing my finger, screaming rape. She'd never put a child of hers through that.

And I wouldn't take it any further either. How could I put my own family through that? I'd done my worst. If there was a pit of judgement I was right at the bottom of it, sliding in the mud.

It took me a long time to drive home.

I struggled to see, beyond the hell inside my head, beyond the rain. The windscreen wipers whacked and whacked back and forth, but outside was just endless, flickering blackness, and it wasn't much after five. I gripped that steering wheel so tight that my fingers locked stiff, and I drove at a crawl, sliding the car through rivers of surface water. You could die on these roads, I thought. You could die, and for hours no one would know.

I never wanted to drive this route again. I never wanted

to go into that town, to see any of those people. I didn't want them looking, talking. I didn't want to have to hold my head high.

I felt the cloak of the hermit, closing me in.

Ella was waiting for me,

'Where were you?' she said. 'I was frightened.'

Frightened of what? The rain, the dark, the unbearable isolation? We could all die in this house and no one would know.

'I thought you'd gone too,' she said. 'I thought you'd gone, like Daddy.'

I sat on the sofa, still in my wet nightie, and she clung to me. 'I don't like it here any more,' she said. 'I want to go back to our old house.'

We did not move from the sofa, Ella and me, for the rest of the day. Soon Sam joined us, curling up on my other side. None of us had dressed. None of us saw fit, now, to pretend. At some point somebody fetched biscuits from the kitchen for us to eat for our supper, but other than that we did not move. We watched TV in our pyjamas, the three of us; we stayed close.

Only when David returned at gone eleven that night would they leave me. Only then would they go to bed.

My nightie had dried by then, but so too had the blood and dirt on my leg. My knee had gone stiff; I didn't want to move it.

I didn't want to move at all.

'My God,' David said as soon as we were alone, 'what happened to you?' He crouched down in front of me, looking from my knee to my face in horror.

I could not seem to find my voice. My mind, my whole being, had slowed right down.

'Jane,' he said. 'What happened?'

I forced myself to speak. 'I went to see Max,' I whispered.

In an instant he was on his feet, the sudden movement jolting me out of my numbness. 'Max did this?' he said. 'I'm going round there. I'm going round there right now.'

'No,' I said. 'I fell.'

He stared at me, mouth clamped tight, breathing hard.

'I went to talk to him,' I said. 'And I fell over.'

'God, Jane,' he said. 'I'm still going round there. I'm sorting this out.'

'You don't need to,' I said. 'I already have.'

Our eyes locked. I could feel my heartbeat thumping against my ribs.

'He's not getting away with this,' David said.

'Please, David,' I said. 'You'll make things worse. Leave it now. It's done.'

He made me sit there while he hunted through the house for plasters, antiseptic, anything else useful he could find. He brought warm water in a kitchen bowl, cotton wool, and a clean towel. He turned me sideways, and lifted my leg, laying it on the towel. First he cleaned off the mud with wet lumps of cotton wool, dropping them down on the fireplace when he'd done. Then he dabbed at the graze itself, so carefully, so patiently, his hand shaking slightly with the effort. It must have hurt, though I don't remember.

I just remember the tenderness of his touch, and the pain on his own face when he looked up at me.

'I'm so sorry,' he said. 'Believe me, Jane. I am so, so sorry.'

THIRTY-ONE

We stayed around the house all weekend, regrouping ourselves, simply trying to cope.

Together, we talked to Sam. We said all the right things, crowding out his bedroom with both our presence and our words. 'This will pass,' we said. 'Rise above it, and Max will soon tire. Don't give him the pleasure of seeing that you care.'

This will pass.

He didn't believe us.

To Ella, who didn't really understand what was going on, we said 'Just keep away from Max. Don't believe what he says. He's been spreading lies.'

'And don't listen to Abbie if she tries to tell you otherwise,' I said, unable to stop myself. 'In fact, keep away from both of them.'

'But they're our *friends*,' Ella cried.

On Monday David frog-marched us all in to school.

The kids were dragged from their beds, forced into the car, shoved into the playground. He and I went in the front entrance for an impromptu appointment with the headmaster. We had to wait in the foyer while the secretary went to see if he was free. I could feel everyone staring at me. I was that woman Max Wilkins had fucked. I was that woman who'd come up to school in her nightdress, shouting for Lydia. Oh yes, I was worth a stare and a laugh.

'The headmaster can see you very briefly now,' the secretary said when she reappeared, 'or this afternoon if you'd prefer a longer appointment.'

'Now, thank you,' David said.

I had scrubbed up today. I was as clean as could be, in a skirt that covered the gash on my knee, a neat shirt, and boots. I sat in the headmaster's office with my ankles together. Did he cruise on Facebook, I wondered. Did he keep in touch, check up on his pupils?

The headmaster's name was Mr Saunders. We knew that, though he did not know ours. We introduced ourselves. 'We are Sam Berry's parents; Sam Berry from Year 10.'

He listened to our concerns. An incident of internet bullying, David called it, though I had not thought of it like that. I had thought of that Facebook business as a sort of by-product, an undesirable result of a more undesirable occurrence. But David had worked out his angle; it is his forte after all. Not once did he mention the real issue, that his son's friend had uninvitedly fucked his son's mother. Oh no. That would be too much, for all concerned.

It made no odds. I saw the blankness in the headmaster's eyes as soon as we mentioned our son's name; I saw him trying and failing to place him in this small school of his. David saw it too, as I could tell by the persistent pitch of his voice.

'I should have been here,' David said. He sat on the sofa with his head in his hands and his elbows on his knees; he had been crying, for quite some time. I sat beside him, trying to find some feeling in the ice plane of my heart.

Earlier, he had collected the children from school on his own; I could not bear to go back there with him. He had had their misery to himself all the way home; he had seen it in the raw. His family was the subject of gossip and speculation; even Ella was suddenly friendless, cold-shouldered now by Abbie and therefore by the rest of Abbie's gang. She ran in to the house when they got back, teeth chattering she was crying so hard.

'Abbie said she hates me,' she howled. 'She said her and Max and their mum hate all of us. She said we were poison.' She threw herself on her bed, inconsolable. She was still up there now; her sobs pumped through the house like the beat of a bleeding heart.

What do you do when you are ostracized in a place like this? There is no other place to go. You cannot just turn the other cheek and carry on.

'This is all my fault,' David said now. 'None of this would have happened if I'd been here. You're my family.' He lowered his hands from his face and looked at me, his eyes red-rimmed in his pale, drawn face. 'You're my wife,' he whispered. 'I should have protected you.'

Tentatively I reached out a hand to touch his arm. I watched my fingers move as if they did not belong to me; clumsily, I patted his sleeve. How strange that it should be for me to have to offer him comfort now; for me to try and find comfort to offer at all when I had had none given to me. He let out his breath on a shuddering sob, and grabbed my hand in both of his. He put it to his forehead, then to his lips.

'I'm so sorry,' he said. 'So very, very sorry.'

I let him hold me. He clutched me to him awkwardly, crushing my ribs. His breath came laboured against my neck whilst I could barely breathe at all. The familiar feel of him and the scent of him made me want to close my eyes and die, at that moment, in that fleetingly safe place. He loosened his grip and started moving his hands on my back, sort of pressing me with his palms, as if to remember.

'Oh, Jane, Jane,' he said over and over. 'I'm so sorry.'

I did not speak. I couldn't. I had slipped inside myself where all was dark, all was quiet. I had no forgiveness to offer, and none to ask. I took the comfort of his body against mine, and let him take comfort from me. Comfort, that was all.

He held me for a very long time.

That night David slept beside me, on this bed that used to be ours. He lay there in his T-shirt and boxers, and I lay there in my nightie – a clean one, all modesty preserved. His arm was beneath my neck, and I rested my head uncomfortably on his shoulder. In times gone by we would have started the night like this, then one of us – usually me – would have moved away to sleep. This night we stayed as we were; a continuation of our embrace downstairs. And oh what a fragile embrace. Our lower halves did not touch. We could not part, yet nor could we move any closer than this.

He slept, still with that arm beneath me. If I moved, his hand around my shoulder tightened; he did not want to let me go. He was beside me for his benefit as much as mine. I surely did not need protecting now. It was a little too late for all of that.

I lay awake, trying to locate proper feeling. I listened to him breathing; such a familiar, forgotten sound. How much warmer it was in the bedroom with him there. I thought of all the empty drawers, cleared of his stuff. I thought of my body, naked beneath my nightie, and what had been done to it. I thought of his naked body; I pictured him with Diana. I thought of him loving someone else.

Did any of it matter? Did anything matter now but what we had been through, and the easing of pain?

THIRTY-TWO

The summer we first moved here I planted a fig tree. I had always dreamed of having a fig tree one day; I pictured the large, drooping leaves shadowing branches bowed under the weight of such luscious, purple fruit. What could be more beautiful, more representative of nature at its most generous and bountiful and of the start of our new lives here? I had the perfect spot for that tree, against the outside wall of the den, where the L shape of the extension created a courtyard; a sun trap on bright, summer days, and in the winter sheltered from the cold northern winds.

That first year my tree did not grow fruit, nor did it last summer really, apart from a few tiny green bullets, the promise of a harvest to come. Next summer will be its year. Next summer, someone will pick the first fruit, and open it, and eat its sweet flesh. That that someone will not be me is an irony too sour, too cruel to bear.

David did not return to the London flat, other than to collect his stuff. He moved his clothes back into our bedroom, folding them away into the empty spaces in the drawers, hanging his suits back up in the wardrobe. He could not stay sleeping on the sofa bed. Step by step, he moved back into my room.

Once again I was listening to him starting so early for the station in the morning, and waiting for him to come home again at night. I kept his supper ready for him; I asked him about his day. We moved around each other so carefully, each of us treading on glass.

But where could we go from here? We could not go back; that was done for us.

Sometimes, I took the children to school, and collected them again, though their silence in the car broke my heart. Other times, I had not the heart to take them at all, and I phoned the school instead with excuses about them being sick. Occasionally I had to go into town for the shops, out of absolute necessity. I kept my eyes down and spoke to no one. I learnt to blinker out the world. We three, Sam, Ella and I, we were not part of this place any more.

'We have to carry on as normal,' David said in desperation. 'You cannot just give up and hide away.'

But there could be no normal for us, here, now, however much we tried.

David brought home with him the print-outs from various estate agents. Details of properties in places like Walton-on-Thames and Weybridge. Small towns, but not too small. And not so very far from London, though still far enough away from here.

'There are schools nearby,' he said. 'There are trains to London; regular, frequent trains.'

Eagerly, he showed me pictures of the houses he had earmarked in his quick-sought, quick-found suburban idyll. Houses with yellow window-frames; houses with ivy creeping up the walls. Small houses, in streets crammed with other small houses. In towns where no one knew us; where we could start again.

I tried to imagine myself living in those houses, walking along those streets. Putting out the bins, going to the supermarket; knowing people. I pictured my children making friends, going to the park; and David marching briskly back from the station at the end of another ordinary day. It seemed like a different world.

Living any normal life, now, seemed like a different world.

'We won't get so much for our money, of course,' he said, apologetically, as if I even cared about such things. 'But these are nice areas. We'll have shops nearby; the schools. I'll have the train.'

We had come full circle. Here was the parallel hoop. I felt myself slip out of my life and into it again.

'If we take that offer on our house we can move straight away,' he said. 'We've got to do it, Jane. We've got to try. It can be a new beginning, for all of us.' He put his hand on mine, so keen to take care of me now. It had taken a terrible thing to bring David back to us, yet none of this would have happened at all if perhaps I had taken a little more care of him.

Sam was at the top of the hill, a matchstick shadow of a boy. David was up there with him. Sam was sitting on the ground, hunched over his crossed knees. David stood in front of him, one hand on his hip, the other moving about in the air as he emphasized whatever it was that he was saying. From this distance they looked like two little plastic toy soldiers, grey, anonymous, achingly small.

A cold front had driven in from the west, drying the rain

out of the air. How bleak things could look out here, unrelenting, like the end of the world.

In the comparative warmth of the kitchen Ella sidled around me. We were making spaghetti bolognese for supper. I chopped up an onion, clumsily.

'Daddy will stay with us if we move, won't he?' she asked so hopefully, tears springing into her voice. 'I don't care where we live so long as we always live with Daddy.'

I slammed the knife up and down, nearly hacking off my fingers. Did it matter where we lived? How I had cared about such things once; how I had dreamed. But what difference did a bit of scenery make, the presence or absence of an aeroplane or two overhead? Wherever we went, we'd take ourselves with us. There was no escaping that. You paint yourself differently, that's all. You're still the same inside.

Up on that hill, Sam slowly rose to his feet. David stuck out his hand and Sam took it, and kept hold of it. I cannot tell you how it struck my heart at that moment; that tender reaching out, and taking, of the hand. I watched them walking down from that hill together, my husband, my son, my eyes smarting with tears.

'Of course we'll live with Daddy,' I said, my voice thick in my throat.

And I drew down the blinds, shutting out the night.

THE SAFEST PLACE

Book club discussion points

1. Do you agree with Jane's decision to uproot her family and what do you think the primary driving forces behind this were?

2. Discuss Jane and David's relationship. What are the key factors in their marital breakdown?

3. Compare Sam and Max's friendship with Jane and Melanie's friendship.

4. How do Jane and Melanie's approaches to parenting differ?

5. How important is the notion of belonging in this book, particularly in relation to moving to a new community?

6. Overall, which character in the book did you feel most sympathetic towards and why?

7. Discuss the decisions made at the end of the book. How do you think these would impact upon the Berry family's future?

8. Discuss the author's writing style. Which passage of the story stood out for you the most?

9. If you could ask the author a question about the novel, what would it be?

10. Have you read the author's previous novels, *This Perfect World* and *The Child Inside*? If so, how do the themes of *The Safest Place* compare?